DISCARD

RUSH FOR THE GOLD

ALSO BY JOHN FEINSTEIN

JOHN FEINSTEIN

RUSH FOR THE GOLD

MYSTERY AT THE OLYMPICS

Alfred A. Knopf
New York

THIS IS A BORZOI BOOK PUBLISHED BY ALFRED A. KNOPF

Visit us on the Web! randomhouse.com/kids

Educators and librarians, for a variety of teaching tools, visit us at randomhouse.com/teachers

Library of Congress Cataloging-in-Publication Data
Feinstein, John
Rush for the gold : mystery at the Olympics / John Feinstein. — 1st ed.
p.   cm.
Summary: Two teenaged aspiring journalists who are dating solve a mystery at the 2012 Olympic Games, while one simultaneously competes for a gold medal in swimming.
ISBN 978-0-375-86963-1 (trade) — ISBN 978-0-375-96963-8 (lib. bdg.) —
ISBN 978-0-375-98455-6 (ebook) — ISBN 978-0-375-87168-9 (pbk.)
[1. Swimming—Fiction. 2. Dating (Social customs)—Fiction. 3. Journalists—Fiction.
4. Olympic Games (30th : 2012 : London, England)—Fiction. 5. Mystery and detective stories.] I. Title.
PZ7.F3343Ru 2012
[Fic]—dc23
2011045215

The text of this book is set in 12-point Goudy.

Printed in the United States of America
May 2012
10 9 8 7 6 5 4 3 2 1

First Edition

This is for all the Ancient Mariners but most notably my fellow FWRH's: Clay F. Britt, Wally Dicks, Mike Fell, Jeff Roddin, Jason Crist, and Mark Pugliese.

1: THE MAKING OF A CHAMPION

From somewhere off in the distance, Susan Carol Anderson thought she heard her father's voice, which wasn't possible because her head was underwater and she was searching for one last spark of energy to close the ten-meter gap between her and the wall. And yet, even though she knew she couldn't possibly hear his voice this clearly, there it was again.

"Susan Carol, sweetheart; are you listening?"

She was in lane six in a swimming pool in Shanghai, China, and yet she kept hearing her dad's voice, almost as if they were back home in Goldsboro, North Carolina, sitting in their living room.

"Susan Carol, snap out of it."

That's when it hit her. She *was* sitting in her living room in Goldsboro. Shanghai was thousands of miles away and nine months in her past. She had drifted off into her own safe little world in the pool while her dad was talking to the three people seated across from her.

And now her father was looking at her expectantly, which was a problem since she had no idea what he was expecting. Finally, the man seated directly across from her, whose name she remembered was Jeffrey Paul Scott—"call me J.P.," he had said, walking in the door—gave her a clue.

"You don't have to decide anything now, Susan Carol," he was saying in a soothing voice. "We just want you and your dad to have an idea of where this could all go. We aren't in the business of trying to pitch fantasies; we try to tell people what to expect realistically. In your case, the sky's the limit, but even if you don't hit the sky, the bar is pretty high."

Susan Carol nodded because that felt like it was the right thing to do. She looked back at the coffee table and all the brightly colored folders that J.P. and his two partners—William Arnold (she was to call him Bill) and Susie McArthur—had laid out in front of them. One was labeled SWIMMING SPONSORS, another said BEAUTY SPONSORS, a third said TEEN SPONSORS, and a fourth said modestly HOW LIGHTNING FAST WILL MAKE SUSAN CAROL ANDERSON A STAR.

Maybe it was that one that had sent her spinning back in time to that amazing week in Shanghai last summer. She had gone to China hoping to swim the meet of her life. She never dreamed that succeeding would completely *change* her life.

Her father was talking again. "Susan Carol, I think

J.P., Bill, and Susie understand that this is a lot for a fifteen-year-old to digest in one evening," he said. "Actually, it's a lot for a forty-six-year-old to digest in one evening."

As if on cue, J.P., Bill, and Susie laughed as though her father was David Letterman and Jimmy Kimmel rolled into one.

"Your dad's right," Susie said. "All we really want to know is if any of this makes sense to you, and if not, what *would* make sense to you. Our job is to make sure you're comfortable with all this."

In that case, Susan Carol thought, *please take your folders, and let me go back to being a fifteen-year-old girl who loves to swim and loves to be a sportswriter.* She thought of something one of her heroes, Duke basketball coach Mike Krzyzewski, had said: "When you're growing up, you train to be an athlete. Then you train to be a coach. But you never train to be a celebrity."

She hadn't trained to be a celebrity and, having had brushes with it in the past, had no real interest in it. But the dollar figures that the Lightning Fast trio had been throwing around were stunning. Even her father, who had some experience in the world of professional athletes, had been wide-eyed. Speedo was willing to guarantee $1 million for the first year, including a $500,000 signing bonus, with another four years open to negotiation depending on how she did in London. That didn't include any of the performance bonuses written into the contract. Nike was interested and so was Dove. Not to mention Under Armour, the Disney Channel, and—this one she knew would make Stevie Thomas, her closest friend, gag—*Seventeen* magazine.

The Andersons weren't poor by any means. Susan Carol's dad made a solid living as a minister at the local Episcopal church, and her mother made decent money teaching freshman English at Goldsboro High School. But being the second of four children, all of whom were absolutely going to college if their parents had their way, Susan Carol knew that every added dollar helped. Now the Lightning Fast people were sitting in front of them saying that she could sign her name to a piece of paper and take care of all four kids' college tuitions—and perhaps a lot more.

"I'm a little overwhelmed," she finally said when it felt as if everyone in the room had been staring at her for hours. "I mean, this is incredible, what you're talking about. It just sounds too good to be true."

"But it *is* true," J.P. said. "This is what these companies think about you and your potential. These are just starting points we're talking about right now because we don't want to get ahead of ourselves. If London goes well, that's when that sky-high scenario kicks in."

London, Susan Carol thought. *My God, the London Olympics are less than five months away. The trials are less than*—she almost gasped out loud at the thought—*fifteen weeks away!* How could all of this be happening so fast? A year ago the idea of making a national team was a fantasy. Now all this. The grown-ups were talking again—bonuses, roll-over deals, options. Her mind retreated to the pool; no, actually she was back a bit further in time. . . .

It had been at a Grand Prix meet in Charlotte that she had gone from being a solid age-group swimmer to a national contender.

She had expected to swim well in Charlotte. In fact, she had been fairly certain she was going to blow past her previous best times. Between the ages of fourteen and fifteen she had filled out and put a good deal more muscle on her body, going from a lean five-eleven and 135 pounds to a rock-solid six feet and 150. She was grateful that she'd only grown another inch but even happier knowing she now had the strength she needed to finish off a 200-meter butterfly.

Even so, she had been stunned when she realized on the final length that she was not only ahead of her longtime nemesis, Becky Ausmus, but was pulling away from her. And she wasn't dying. Even in her best 200-fly races in the past, her arms felt as if there were weights inside them as she got close to the flags. This time was different. Ten meters out, even though she could feel the pain of her effort from head to toe, she knew she wasn't going to die, that the proverbial piano was landing on someone else's back, not hers.

When she hit the wall, she could hear shrieks coming from her teammates. Pushing her goggles up, she glanced at the electronic timing board and gasped in disbelief. The time next to her lane said 2:08.55. She looked around to see if it was possible that anyone else had somehow beaten her and their time had been recorded for her lane. No, that wasn't it.

She had never gone faster than 2:19.05 for a 200 in her life. She had been hoping with her new size and strength to break 2:15—which would have been huge. This was impossible—a drop of more than ten seconds?

Still gasping, she looked up at her coach, Ed Brennan, who had the widest smile she had ever seen.

"The time?" she managed to say.

Ed held up his stopwatch. "It's right," he said. "You beat Ausmus by almost five seconds. You might be going to the Worlds after that swim."

It turned out he was right. Only one American swimmer, Teresa Crippen, had produced a time faster than hers in the past twelve months. Each country was allowed two swimmers per event in the Worlds, and Susan Carol's swim in Charlotte qualified her as the second American in the 200 fly. Her 100-fly time in Charlotte, which had dropped almost four seconds from her previous best, didn't earn a spot at the Worlds but did cause Ed to say something that stopped her cold.

"If you keep going like this, there's no reason you can't make the Olympic team in both the 100 and the 200," he said. "You're good enough if you really want to do it."

Prior to Charlotte, Susan Carol's goal had been to make the Olympic *Trials*. A trials swim would guarantee she'd be recruited by colleges. And her number one swimming goal had always been to get a college scholarship. Now she'd be going to the Olympic Trials *and* the World Championships.

The trip to China had been a blur. Susan Carol knew almost nothing about Shanghai and was stunned when she Googled it and found it was almost twice the size of New York City, with a population of 14 million. The pool was an indoor facility—which was good because the temperature was close to ninety almost every day they were there.

Frank Busch, who was coaching the American women, told her she had to conserve her strength in the heats and the semifinals. "You'll only need to go about 2:12 or 2:13 in the heats," he said. "Anything under 2:10 should be enough in the semis. You're going to have to swim the 200 fly three times in three days. I'm guessing you've never done that before."

She'd done it twice in two days on occasion but never three times. Still, she knew she was in the best shape of her life. Ed had made her do a set of *five* 200s on three minutes' rest in practice before she'd left. It had hurt—*really* hurt—but she had felt okay, even after the last one. And sure enough, she cruised through the heats and the semifinals, qualifying fourth with a time of 2:09.12. She was amazed how easy that swim felt. Easy!

Liu Zige, the Chinese world record holder, had gone the fastest time in the semifinals: 2:05.99—well off her world record time of 2:01.81. She was in lane four. Teresa Crippen, the other American, had qualified second and was in lane five. And Susan Carol was next to her in lane six. Susan Carol planned to let Crippen pace her for the first

100 meters so she wouldn't go out too fast. Crippen was too experienced to make that mistake.

Susan Carol followed that plan for fifty meters. But coming off the first wall, she could see she was already half a body length ahead of Crippen, and she had almost been holding back. She decided to just swim smoothly and not look around at all. She went into the routine she used in practice to try to keep her stroke steady: *Nice and easy*, she kept repeating with each two-stroke sequence. *Nice . . . and easy . . .*

At the halfway point, she felt as if she was just starting the race and could go 200 more meters if need be. Crippen was nowhere in sight, but as Susan Carol turned, she glanced over two lanes and saw that she was dead even with Liu. A little bit of fear crept through her. Was her mind fooling her body? Had she gone out too fast?

She could hear the building getting very loud as she and Liu churned through the third length. That wasn't surprising: Liu was a national hero in China. Sometimes, though, a swimmer can actually hear a tone to the crowd. There is a difference between cheering and pleading. Susan Carol thought the crowd's tone sounded as if someone was threatening Liu. She knew she wouldn't see Liu on her last turn because she would turn her head away from her not toward her. *That's not important*, she told herself. *Holding your stroke and kicking hard for the last fifty is what's important.*

When she came off that final wall, though, she got a shock: As she pulled out of the turn and started to take her first stroke, she saw Crippen go by her heading *toward* the wall. That meant Susan Carol was at least ten meters ahead of her. Was something wrong with Crippen? Or was it possible that something was incredibly right with *her*?

Halfway home, she felt her arms start to tighten, but she still had energy left and she picked up her kick. She could now see the flags in front of her and the noise had become impossibly loud. Could she actually be in medal contention? Suddenly she was under the flags that marked five meters to go. She took one last breath, put her head down, and reached for the wall with her last bit of strength, *just* getting her fingertips on the timing pad without having to add an extra kick.

She surfaced in time to see that Liu was on the wall but others were just touching. *Did I finish second?* she wondered. *Could that be possible?* She heard shrieks from where the American team was sitting, and she pulled her goggles up and glanced over to see people jumping up and down and waving their arms. Becky Ausmus, who had made the team as a freestyle relay swimmer, was pointing at the scoreboard.

Susan Carol finally looked: She had gone 2:03.44. Liu had gone 2:03.46.

Crippen had actually rallied in the final length to finish third, way back at 2:05.85. Susan Carol couldn't believe it.

She had WON the World Championship. The World Championship. Won. It.

Later she would find out that she had put up the second-fastest time any woman had *ever* gone in the history of US swimming.

Teresa Crippen had called it right then. She was leaning on the lane line, reaching to give Susan Carol a hug. "Do you realize what you've just done?" she said. "You've just become a star—a *big* star."

Nine months later, sitting in her living room, Susan Carol could still hear Crippen's voice. The question now was a little more complex: Just how big a star did she *want* to be?

2: A DIFFERENT STORY

Stevie Thomas had watched the Shanghai race live on his computer. He had set his alarm for 7 a.m. because the race was scheduled to start at 9:15 p.m. and Philadelphia was fourteen hours behind Shanghai. He had felt a little chill run through him when he heard Dan Hicks introduce Susan Carol as "the fifteen-year-old American who has come from nowhere to be the fourth-seeded swimmer in this final."

When Susan Carol was almost dead even with Liu at the 100-meter mark, Stevie felt more nervous than excited, worrying that she had gone out too fast. He hardly qualified as a swimming expert, but in the two and a half years he'd known Susan Carol, he'd learned enough to know that the 200 fly was a dangerous race. It was the only one in which even world-class swimmers might not finish if their arms went dead on the final few strokes.

"This is a surprise, isn't it, Rowdy, to see young Anderson out there with Liu at the 100-meter mark?" Hicks had said.

"It is, Dan," answered Rowdy Gaines, NBC's swimming analyst. "You hope she hasn't pushed herself too hard. Don't forget Teresa Crippen, though; she's probably the best closer in the pool."

When Susan Carol and Liu were still dead even coming off the 150 wall, Stevie almost couldn't watch. They had left the rest of the swimmers in their wake. And then they were down to the final strokes, and Hicks was screaming.

"It is STILL Anderson and Liu, stroke for stroke to the wall!" he shouted. "CAN ANDERSON PULL OFF A STUNNING UPSET?! YES, YES, SHE DID IT! SHE OUT-TOUCHED HER! SUSAN CAROL ANDERSON HAS PULLED OFF THE UPSET OF THE WORLD SWIMMING CHAMPIONSHIPS!"

"Unreal!" Gaines added. "She just beat her best time by five seconds! *Five seconds!* That's impossible!"

Stevie was on his feet, dancing around his room, screaming at least as loudly as Hicks and Gaines. "SHE DID IT! SHE DID IT!"

His father popped open the door. He was already dressed for work at his law office downtown.

"What happened?" he demanded.

"Susan Carol WON, Dad, she won!" Stevie said.

His dad broke into a wide smile. "She WON? Are you kidding me? She won? She beat the Chinese girl?"

"Touched her out—two-hundredths of a second. Beat her own best time by *five* seconds."

His dad shook his head. "Wow," he said.

"Isn't it amazing!?"

"Incredible! You know . . . I think your girlfriend is about to become famous. I mean *really* famous, not like a couple years ago on TV."

Stevie hadn't thought about that. He had been focused on Susan Carol's stunning rise in the swimming world. He'd been writing about her success for the *Washington Herald*. In one story, he had quoted Bob Bowman, best known as Michael Phelps's coach, as saying, "For a teenage girl to see a sudden drop in times isn't that unusual. They can mature and get a lot stronger in a short period of time. This is another level, though. I'm not sure I've ever seen anything quite this dramatic."

Still . . . "She was a pretty big star when we were doing the TV show, Dad," he said. "I remember what it was like that year at the Super Bowl. . . ."

Bill Thomas was shaking his head. "Back then she had one little cable channel promoting her. Now she'll have a bunch of big-time sponsors lining up.

"Think about it, Stevie. The Olympics are coming, she's a great story, and she's a very pretty girl—as I think you've noticed."

His dad was right—Stevie knew it then and the next few months had proved it. Susan Carol sent him texts and emails updating him: *Three Speedo guys at the house tonight. They want me in a commercial with Phelps. . . .* And: *Nike offering ridiculous money . . .* Not to mention: *Here's my new cell and email. Had to change both. Agents won't go away for five minutes. Same with my dad.*

So far, Don Anderson had turned them all away, not wanting his daughter to become a professional swimmer, which would mean—among other things—that she could no longer compete for her high school team or when she got to college. Of course, the money being offered would more than pay for Susan Carol's college. . . .

Stevie didn't know what to think. But he'd started scheming ways to get to cover the Olympics in London. He had made enough money working as a freelancer for the *Herald* that he could pay his own way there if the newspaper would get him credentialed. Bobby Kelleher, his friend and mentor at the paper, was convinced Matt Rennie, the *Herald*'s sports editor, would go for it. "Getting an extra reporter there, someone good, without paying expenses?" he said. "Book your flights now."

That was back in March, when Stevie had spent most of his spring break covering the first and second rounds of the NCAA basketball tournament. It had been at the Final Four two years earlier that he and Susan Carol had met as winners of a writing contest. They had been skeptical about each other at the start. He was north; she was south. She loved Duke; he loved the Big Five; she was tall, he was . . . not. But they had discovered that they liked each other a lot when they stumbled onto a plot to throw the National Championship and had to work together.

Now they were unofficially boyfriend and girlfriend. Unofficial because it was tough to see much of each other when boy lived in Philadelphia and girl lived in Goldsboro, North Carolina. They came together fairly often to cover big sporting events—he for the *Herald,* and she for the *Washington Post.* Technically that made them competitors, but somehow they always ended up working together on big stories.

Stevie had been thinking the Olympics would mean spending three weeks in London covering the games with Susan Carol. But if Susan Carol was there as an athlete, he wasn't likely to see much of her.

And yet, how could he not be thrilled for her? He had known almost from their first meeting how important swimming was to her. He still remembered the first time he had actually seen her in the water. He had been awestruck then—and he still was.

Stevie knew that part of the reason Susan Carol was being offered so much money wasn't really about her ability as an athlete: It had to do with her looks. Apparently attractive teenage girls were a marketer's dream. A little research had clarified things further. Jennifer Capriati, a tennis player who had been ranked in the top ten in the world at the age of fourteen, had been a multimillionaire the day she turned pro. Michelle Wie, a golfer who turned pro at sixteen, was also an instant millionaire. Figure skating was *full* of teenage wonders who sold everything from automobiles to watches.

And teenage swimming phenoms were certainly nothing new. Amanda Beard had become a star at the Atlanta Olympics, where she carried a teddy bear with her to the blocks for good luck. By the time the next Olympics rolled around, she was a big-time model. Natalie Coughlin had won her first Olympic gold medal in Athens in 2004, and she'd also become a star. She had been hired by MS-NBC as a Winter Olympics co-host in 2010 and had been on the ultimate look-at-me TV show, *Dancing with the Stars*.

You didn't have to be biased about Susan Carol to know she had the looks marketers would love. People always thought she was older than she actually was because she was tall. She was at least six feet (Stevie was convinced she was an inch taller but wouldn't admit it). Stevie was still hoping to catch up with her, but at five-nine, he hadn't gotten there yet. Kindly, she never wore heels when they were together.

Susan Carol had long dark hair, a smile that could light up a dungeon (Stevie called it The Smile) and was—obviously—in great shape. She was smart and sharp and yet full of southern charm. Stevie was sure she could charm a Red Sox fan into rooting for the Yankees if she really put her mind to it.

For a long time after they first began "dating," Stevie had wondered what someone like Susan Carol saw in him. He guessed he was good-looking enough—although not in her class. But he was no athlete, though he loved sports and worked hard at it. He was maybe the fifth-best player on his basketball team—the junior varsity team. He was a reasonably good golfer but had never made the finals in the junior club championships.

No, he had found his best success as a sports reporter. He knew and loved sports and had, as the old saying went, a nose for news. That much he and Susan Carol had in common. And working together brought out the best in both of them. They spurred each other on and could spend many hours talking sports. Plus, she seemed to think he was funny. "Never underestimate the importance of being funny," his dad had once told him. "I never would have had a second date with your mother if she didn't think I was funny."

Stevie and his father shared the same acerbic sense of humor. But Stevie had never been sure why that had impressed his mother. She was, without doubt, the serious one in the family.

Still, for whatever unlikely combination of reasons, Susan Carol had chosen him. And Stevie had chosen her right back.

Now, on a Friday afternoon in April, as he sat watching the second round of the Masters golf tournament, his mom came into the living room, holding out the telephone.

Most of the time Stevie and Susan Carol communicated by video-chatting or texting when Stevie was at home, since his cell phone signal in the house stunk.

"You aren't online," she said as soon as he said hello.

"I'm downstairs watching the Masters," he said. "Did you have your meeting with Lightning Fast?"

"Just ended," she said.

"And?"

"We signed."

She hardly sounded jubilant.

"How do you feel about that?"

"Good," she said. "There's a lot of guaranteed money involved, although not as much as they implied when they first approached us."

Stevie could tell she was feeling stressed because her southern accent was in full gear—she was talking fast and the word *implied* came out *implaahed*.

"What do you mean?" he asked.

"All the contracts have some up-front money and some guaranteed money—and it's a lot; enough to pay for college, probably for all of us. But most of the money is keyed to how I do in the Olympics. Which means first I have to *make* the Olympic team, which is no lock. And then I have to win a medal, of course, and for the big money to kick in, I have to win a *gold* medal, and then, well . . ."

"You're rich."

There was a pause on the other end. "Pretty much," she finally said.

"What happens if you don't make it to London?" he asked.

"We still keep the up-front money, which is good, but then it pretty much becomes a trickle rather than a waterfall," she said. "On the one hand, it's more than I ever dreamed of, but on the other hand, I also dreamed of swimming in college."

"And you won't be able to swim in college now because you're a professional."

"Right. But not making this Olympics doesn't mean my career is over. I'll only be nineteen for the 2016 Games in Rio, and they say if I keep swimming well, they can renegotiate my deals then."

"Lot of ifs in there," Stevie said, then felt bad because he was probably making her feel worse.

"I know," she said. "In the end, Dad and I decided the guaranteed money was enough to make the ifs worth it. I hope we were right."

"I'm sure you were," he said, trying to be more positive. "For one thing, you're *going* to make the team and you're *going* to swim well in London. Look at how much you've improved in the last year. And you're *still* improving. The timing for London is perfect."

"I know," she answered. "That's what Ed said too. He thinks I can improve more because I can train harder now that I'm older. But you know how the trials are. You have to finish first or second to make the team. And it's the 200 fly—if you miscalculate your swim at all . . ."

"You'll be fine," he said. "Plus, you're ranked third in the country in the 100 fly, so you have a chance there too."

She sighed. "Stevie, honestly, I don't know what I'd do without you."

That made him smile. "Well, Scarlett," he said, using

the nickname he had put on her the first time he'd seen her turn on her southern charm, "the good news is, you don't have to do without me. I'm right here whenever you need me."

"Thank you," she said quietly. Then, "Who's leading the Masters?"

"Someone you like," Stevie said.

"Rickie Fowler?"

"Yup."

"He is *so* cute."

"What's that, Scarlett? The line's breaking up. . . . I can't hear you."

They were both laughing by the time they hung up the phone. Stevie felt better. He hoped Susan Carol did too.

3: RETURN TO CHARLOTTE

In May, Susan Carol returned to Charlotte—to the meet that had first put her on the swimming map a year earlier.

A lot had happened since she had signed the contract with Lightning Fast. During her spring break, she and her father had flown to New York for a day of "appearances." She had started her morning on the *Today* show (since NBC had the Olympic TV rights, the network was happy to promote a potential swimming star), where she stood outside in a steady drizzle while Ann Curry gushed about how cute her dress was and how she wished she could learn to swim butterfly. Susan Carol, who had done enough TV in the past to know how the game was played, offered to give her lessons.

The most surprising part of her morning was discovering how short Matt Lauer was. Even in flat shoes, Susan Carol was several inches taller than the co-host.

From there, they went upstairs to the Carousel Room in 30 Rockefeller Plaza for breakfast and a press conference—where Speedo announced that Susan Carol would join Michael Phelps, Ryan Lochte, and Natalie Coughlin as their main spokespeople leading up to the Games in London. Speedo and Lightning Fast had proposed that Susan Carol walk into the press conference in a Speedo bathing suit, but her father had nixed that idea. When J. P. Scott tried to argue for a moment, her father fixed him with a look.

"You and I had an agreement, J.P.," he said firmly. "We're promoting her as an *athlete*."

Scott backpedaled quickly after that, and a Speedo sweat suit was agreed on as the outfit for the press conference.

The only question from the media that made Susan Carol a little uncomfortable was one she had been prepped for.

"How do you feel about being part of such a major marketing campaign when you've never even been on an Olympic team?"

"Lucky," she said, flashing The Smile. "And as I recall, Michael Phelps hadn't won an Olympic medal when he signed with Speedo before the 2004 Olympics."

"But he was a world-record holder."

"Yes. And I'm a world champion."

That seemed to take care of that. The rest of the day was photo shoots, another press conference to announce deals with New Balance, Nikon, and Neutrogena—the three Ns, J. P. Scott called them. What wasn't announced was that all of Susan Carol's deals would be worth about

$1 million total if she didn't win an Olympic medal. A medal—silver or bronze—would double that. A gold medal would up their value closer to $20 million.

Just the thought of it staggered Susan Carol. She couldn't begin to think of how to spend that much money. The guaranteed $1 million was more fathomable—college for her and her siblings would put a big dent in that. And the security of it comforted her because she was having a hard time accepting that she would never be a college swimmer. All the things she'd imagined for her life were suddenly changing—it was hard to keep up.

One thing was clear from the long New York day, though. She would earn every penny. Being a show pony for corporations was hard work.

Even her life at school had changed. Suddenly everyone wanted to be her new best friend. Some teachers wanted her autograph for their children. Fortunately, her dad and Ed Brennan kept her in line. Especially Ed, since he had her in the pool for four hours a day, not to mention another hour in the weight room three days a week.

Their approach to the Charlotte meet was entirely different this year. Last year, it had been a full taper meet, meaning she cut back on her yardage and changed her workouts a solid three weeks before the meet so she would be as fresh and strong as possible when she stepped on the blocks. This time, with the Olympic trials only seven weeks away, she would swim through the meet—meaning she wouldn't slacken her workouts at all. She would begin her taper two weeks before the trials, which began June 25 in

Omaha, Nebraska. Then, if she made the team, there was only a four-week break before the Olympics began.

Even though Charlotte was now just a warm-up meet, it was going to be a zoo. Michael Phelps had decided to make it *his* last warm-up meet before the trials, along with several other past Olympians. Phelps's presence alone would create a media circus. But Susan Carol, especially in her home state, had become a pretty big deal in her own right.

After consulting with the Lightning Fast people and Ed Brennan, it was decided that Susan Carol would drive to Charlotte early Thursday morning, even though the meet didn't start until Friday. She would work out in the pool that morning and hold a press conference right afterward. Everything seemed set, but then Susie McArthur, who was taking care of all her interviews, called a few nights before the meet.

"We're going to have to change your schedule," she said. "Phelps wants to hold a press conference on Thursday too so he doesn't have people bugging him before he swims on Friday."

"So, what's the problem?" Susan Carol asked. "I'm supposed to talk at two o'clock, right? If we have to move it up an hour or back an hour, that's no big deal."

"You don't understand," Susie said. "You have to move it up a *day*. You have to do it Wednesday."

"Wednesday? Why? I'm already missing two days of school. No way my dad and mom will agree to three days."

"I'll talk to your parents. But we need to do this."

"Why?"

"Because if we have a press conference the same day as Phelps, you're the second story, not the first. As popular as you are, Susan Carol, we're talking Michael Phelps. We can't compete with the greatest swimmer ever for publicity."

Well, that was certainly true. Still . . .

"You're going to have to talk to my dad about me missing another day of school," she said.

She heard Susie sigh on the other end of the phone. "I will. But last I looked, you're making straight A's. And you aren't being *paid* to go to school."

Susan Carol wasn't thrilled with her tone, but she let it go. Not long after that, her dad walked in to say he had talked to Susie. "I told her we'd do it," he said. "J.P. and Susie will drive you down on Wednesday, Ed will be there Thursday, and I'll join you Friday. And I want you to ask your teachers to give you your assignments for the rest of the week before you leave."

In truth, Susan Carol's teachers had always been accommodating about letting her miss some class time when she was covering major sporting events since she was such a good student. But somehow this felt different to her.

"Dad, is this going to get out of hand?"

"Not if I can help it," he said, which was about the least confident answer she'd ever heard from him. He walked out. She picked up *Of Mice and Men* and resumed reading. She had a lot of studying to do.

Stevie was also missing school the week of the Charlotte meet—but just one day, and even that hadn't been easy. As usual, his mom was concerned about him getting behind, and his English teacher, Ms. Granato, had called to say that Stevie was in danger of getting a C for second semester and that certainly wouldn't help him get into college. As usual, his dad argued that his experiences as a reporter were just as important as an A in English. And so he was going.

Stevie would actually be covering the meet for the *Herald*. Bobby Kelleher was going down to write columns, but the *Herald* wasn't sending a staffer, so that meant Stevie would get to write the leads. Susan Carol had told Stevie that the *Post* had wanted her to write a daily journal on her experiences at the meet, but the Lightning Fast people had nixed it.

They said we don't give away anything, she told Stevie in an email. *Anything I do outside a press conference, they want to get something in return.*

Does this mean you can't talk to me? Stevie had emailed back.

I hope not, she answered, without a hint of humor.

Stevie watched Susan Carol's Wednesday press conference live on ESPN News. Apparently the Lightning Fast people had told ESPN they would change Susan Carol's pre-meet press conference to Wednesday if it would be covered live. And ESPN had agreed.

Susan Carol walked into the press conference looking like a human billboard. She had on her Speedo sweats with a different corporate logo on each arm. She was wearing a Kellogg's baseball cap. When a photographer asked if she could take off her cap, she shook her head. "Can't," she said. "The Kellogg's people want y'all to see their logo."

Stevie groaned. His girlfriend looked like a cross between a NASCAR driver and a PGA Tour golfer. Getting the logos airtime was their key to success in life.

But apart from that, Susan Carol handled the press conference with ease. When someone asked her about missing three days of school, she laughed. "Oh, I brought my books with me," she said. "And my teachers are being nice about letting me make up the work. My whole school's been so supportive. One of my teachers asked if she could come with me." The southern accent was turned on full power and so was The Smile. Stevie figured her sponsors would be very happy.

On Thursday afternoon, he watched the Phelps press conference. Michael Phelps was clearly an old pro at this, but he didn't have Susan Carol's spark or charm. Then again, he didn't need to sell himself: He'd already made his millions, and the 2012 Olympics would be the last swim meet of his career.

After watching that press conference, Stevie headed for the airport, and by nine o'clock he was in Charlotte too. He took a taxi from the airport to the downtown Marriott, where a lot of the swimmers—including Susan Carol— were staying. Bobby Kelleher had somehow secured a suite so that Stevie could share it with him and his wife, fellow newspaper columnist Tamara Mearns.

"A buddy of mine named Terry Hanson is a big-shot radio guy here," he had explained. "He was able to get us the upgrade." Most of Kelleher's stories on how he got things done began with the words "a buddy of mine."

Stevie called Susan Carol from the cab, hoping they could see each other as soon as he got to the hotel.

"Why don't you come to my room when you get here," she said. "You can order some room service because *I know* you're hungry and we can talk a little before I have to go to bed. My first swim is at 8:30 in the morning, so I have to be up by 6:30 to get over to the pool and warm up."

"Sounds great," Stevie said, liking the idea of some quiet time, even if it would be limited by her need to get a good night's sleep. "You've got 100 fly first, right?"

"Right. Trials in the morning, finals at night."

"I'll see you in a few minutes."

When the cab pulled up to the hotel, Stevie stopped at the front desk, where Kelleher had left him a key, and then he went straight to Susan Carol's room. He knocked on the door and felt himself grinning in anticipation as he heard Susan Carol's footsteps. He dropped his bags to prepare for a hug.

The door opened and he put out his arms.

"Can I help you?" Some guy in a pressed shirt and tie with perfect hair was standing in the doorway looking at him as if he had just landed from Mars. Stevie put his arms down.

"I'm Stevie Thomas," he said, forgetting that he introduced himself to strangers as Steve.

"Oh yeah," the guy said. "Come on in. You can stay for

a few minutes. We told her this one time it was okay. The rest of the weekend, though, you'll have to come to the press conferences like everyone else in the media."

O-kay. Not exactly the greeting he'd been hoping for.

"Stevie?" he heard Susan Carol say. "Is that you?"

Stevie raised an eyebrow at the guy and walked around him into what turned out to be the living room of a suite. Susan Carol jumped from an armchair to run across the room and hug him.

"About time you got here," she said, giving him a firm kiss on the lips, which he happily returned. Now *that* was more like it.

As usual, Susan Carol looked great. She was wearing a blue-and-gold Goldsboro High School Swimming T-shirt, shorts with a Speedo logo on them, and flip-flops.

"Is Goldsboro High one of your sponsors now?" he said, smiling.

"No," someone behind her said. "If we were out in public, they wouldn't let her wear it, believe me."

Stevie recognized Ed Brennan, Susan Carol's coach, who he had met when he had gone to Goldsboro to visit for a few days—before Susan Carol became a star.

Coach Brennan walked over to shake Stevie's hand. He was the only one in the room other than Susan Carol who appeared glad to see him.

"Stevie, I guess you already met Bill at the door," Susan Carol said, clearly unaware of their exchange. "This is J. P. Scott and Susie McArthur—they're from Lightning Fast, like Bill. And this"—she was pointing at someone standing by the window—"is Billy McMullen. He's from Speedo."

"And for the record, the flip-flops have our logo on them too," Billy McMullen said, shaking hands with him and smiling, unlike the Lightning Fast people, who barely managed to nod in his direction.

"What do you want to eat?" Susan Carol said, picking up a phone.

Before Stevie could answer, J.P. was shaking his head. "Susan Carol, I think it's too late to order any food for your friend. We really need to finish talking and get you off to sleep."

Susan Carol looked at her watch. "J.P., it's 9:30. I can stay up another hour and get eight solid hours of sleep. I'm fine."

"You need to wind down," J.P. said.

"Talking with my friend *is* my way of winding down," Susan Carol said, and hit a button on the phone to dial room service.

"Stevie?" she said.

"Burger, fries, Coke," he said—his normal room-service order.

"Anyone else?" she asked.

"I'll do the same thing," Coach Brennan said, instantly winning Stevie's loyalty for life.

"Coach, don't you think she needs her rest?" Susie said as Susan Carol was ordering.

"I think hanging out with Stevie is exactly what she

needs after her long day," Ed Brennan said. "I think she could use a little space."

Susan Carol hung up. The Lightning Fast trio were now glaring at Ed Brennan.

"We're not done yet, Ed," J.P. said.

"I'm sure whatever you've got can wait till the morning." Ed glared right back.

"Well, I've got to get going," Billy, the Speedo guy, said. "Good luck tomorrow, Susan Carol. I'll see you at the pool."

That diffused the situation a bit and the Lightning Fast people all said their good-nights, some with less grace than others.

As soon as the door closed, Stevie looked at Susan Carol and smiled.

"Nice representation you've got there," he said. "Super-friendly."

"You saw them on a good night," Coach Brennan said.

Susan Carol collapsed into one of the chairs. "I can't wait to get into the pool in the morning and just *swim*."

4: ON THE BLOCKS

The moment Susan Carol had been waiting for came at 7:32 a.m. the next morning. That was the moment she found an opening among the swimmers warming up for the morning session of the 27th annual Charlotte UltraSwim and slipped into the water.

Being in the water *was* therapeutic for her. It always had been, ever since she had started to swim competitively at age twelve. No matter what else was going on in her life, the pool was a place she could escape. Focusing on her workout cleared her head in a way nothing else could.

The scene in her room the night before with her various agents and sponsors had upset her. Having three or four people around her all the time, all seeming to want something from her, was exhausting. The more time she spent with them, the more she longed to escape. And then seeing how they treated Stevie, and hearing his take on them . . . In the reporting she and Stevie had done, especially on some of the really big stories, the agents they had encountered had been—almost without fail—people you couldn't trust. That had even proved true of her own uncle on one story.

And now every time J.P. began talking about how rich she was going to be, she remembered something Bobby Kelleher had said to her and Stevie early on: "You know how you can tell when an agent is lying? His lips are moving."

She knew the Lightning Fast people were good at what they did and that it was in their best interests for her to succeed. And yet she couldn't shake the tension that built up whenever she talked to them. Even more, it worried her to see how friendly her dad had become with all three of the Lightning Fast people. It was strange that he seemed to trust people her instincts said shouldn't be trusted.

She had glided through the first 100 of her warm-up knowing she had to shake all those disturbing thoughts out of her head. As she went into her second flip turn and began to stretch out her stroke a little bit, she tried to focus on feeling her muscles loosening up as the cool water and her body meshed. She picked up her pace a little more, and by the time she popped her head out of the water at the end of her first 400, she felt far more relaxed. She took a long, deep breath and was about to push off when she heard Ed Brennan's voice.

"Remember, don't over-sprint this morning," he said. "We aren't trying to go that fast until tonight. Don't do more than about 1,200 or 1,300, then get on the blocks a couple of times and get out."

He was standing on the deck right above her, and she moved over to the lane line so she wouldn't be in the way of other swimmers who were turning.

"Got it on the sprints," she said. "You sure that's enough yardage?"

"Plenty. You're going to warm up again tonight, and you've got to swim the 200 fly twice tomorrow. You need rest right now more than yardage."

She nodded. Ed was the other person besides Stevie she trusted without question. A lot of coaches, especially small-town high school coaches, might have seen her sudden stardom as their way to a bigger, more lucrative job. Ed was happy coaching where he was—he just wanted what was best for her. She followed his instructions, finished her warm-ups, and was heading into the locker room to shower and change into a dry suit when she saw J.P. coming toward her dressed in a Speedo warm-up suit.

"You ready, kid?" he asked.

"J.P., how did you get down here?" she asked. "It's supposed to be just swimmers and coaches on deck."

He smiled and pointed at the credential dangling around his neck, which said COMPETITOR SUPPORT. "They'll give Phelps's people pretty much anything they want," he said. "These badges are for close friends."

"But you don't represent Michael Phelps."

"The people running the meet don't know that. Now look, are you ready to go? There's media all over the place this morning. Phelps doesn't swim until late, so you can knock their socks off early."

"I don't want to knock anyone's socks off in the morning, J.P. I just want to have a decent swim and be ready for the final tonight."

He frowned. "But it's just the 100. You can swim it hard twice, right? It'd get great coverage."

She looked at him and shook her head. "I'll take my swimming instructions from Ed, if you don't mind. That's what I need to be thinking about right now—swimming."

She slipped her feet into her flip-flops and headed for the locker room. It was 8:25 in the morning and she was already feeling stressed. The sooner she could get back in the water, the better.

Stevie barely got to the pool in time to see Susan Carol swim. For once, Bobby Kelleher hadn't planned ahead when it came to parking. When they got to the pool shortly after eight o'clock, there was a security guard blocking the entrance to the parking lot.

"Completely full," he said as Kelleher rolled down the window.

Kelleher displayed his media credential. "I was told there was a section of the lot for media," he said.

The guard nodded. "There is. It's full too."

Kelleher smiled. "You mind if I go take a look? Sometimes there's a space that's opened up or you can't see."

The guard shrugged. "Be my guest," he said. "But you aren't going to find anything."

He was right. There were only eight spots designated media and no one to stop someone who *wasn't* media from parking in them. Kelleher sighed. "This is the problem when you're dealing with people who aren't used to a lot of media showing up for their event."

"But they've had Phelps here before . . ."

"Not in an Olympic year. And not with a budding star from in-state also swimming."

They circled back to the guard. Kelleher asked him if he had any ideas where they might park.

"There's a lot about two blocks down on your right," he said. "But they're gouging today. I think they're charging fifteen dollars for the day. If I were you, I'd go on over to the McDonald's and just park there. They won't mess with you."

Kelleher thanked him and laughed as they drove away. "I guess *gouging* is a relative term," he said. "In Washington, fifteen dollars a day to park is a good deal, and in New York you would figure something was wrong with the lot if they only asked for fifteen bucks."

They found a spot near the back of the McDonald's lot and then Kelleher insisted on going inside for coffee.

"Two reasons," he said. "One, I could use another cup; two, I'll have a receipt showing I was a customer in case there's some problem."

Stevie was practically jogging—worried that they might miss Susan Carol's swim—but Kelleher wasn't nervous at all. "This isn't the Olympics," he said. "I've never been to a meet like this where they stuck to the timeline."

Kelleher had picked up both their credentials the day before, so they got right in and found what looked like the last two empty seats in the media seating section, which, thankfully, was a good deal larger than the parking area.

Stevie saw that the swimmers climbing on the blocks were male and they were swimming the 200 freestyle. That was the event before the women's 100 fly. He paged through the heat sheets they'd been handed and saw they were on heat eight of ten. There were eight heats in the women's 100 fly, and Susan Carol was in the sixth. Christine Magnuson, who had the fastest American time in the event in the last year, was in heat eight. Taylor Ames, who swam for University of Tennessee Aquatics, had the second-fastest entered time and was in the seventh heat.

Stevie could see how the system worked: The three fastest-seeded swimmers were in lane four of the last three heats with seeds four through six next to them in lane five. The sixth seed in the 100 fly was Becky Ausmus, Susan Carol's high school rival. She was the only other pre-college swimmer seeded in the top twelve from what Stevie could see.

The pool started to get loud. Stevie glanced up from his study of the heat sheets to see what was going on.

"Lochte," Kelleher said, pointing to where Ryan Lochte was climbing onto the blocks in lane four for the last heat of the 200 free. Lochte was considered the biggest threat to possibly outshine Phelps in London. He had beaten him the previous summer in Shanghai in both the 200 individual medley and the 200 freestyle. Phelps wasn't swimming the 200 free because the order of the finals that night was men's 200 free, women's 100 fly, women's 200 free, and men's 200 fly. That would mean he'd have to swim in the 200-fly final about fifteen minutes after the 200 free, which wasn't enough time to recover. Phelps had opted to swim the fly.

Lochte blitzed the field in his heat, touching in 1:48.55—winning the heat by almost five seconds. "I'll bet he's under 1:45 tonight," Kelleher said. "He'll only be a couple seconds off the world record. The guy looks like he's ready for London already."

"How much swimming have you covered?" Stevie asked.

"A fair amount," Kelleher said. "I've done several Olympics and trials, but Washington is also a huge swimming area."

Stevie was always amazed at the depth of Kelleher's knowledge. He'd thought swimming might be one sport where Bobby had to do some studying. But the fact that he knew the world record in the 200 free off the top of his head told Stevie he was wrong.

An announcement came into the media section: "Ryan Lochte will be available in thirty minutes in the interview room, which is at the diving-board end of the pool. Thirty minutes."

Stevie judged Susan Carol would be swimming in about fifteen minutes since the first heat of the 100 fly was being called to the blocks. He should have time to talk to Lochte after. Maybe he could ask him about Susan Carol—what did he know about her? Did he have a chance to watch her swim?

As was often the case, Kelleher read Stevie's mind. "Might be worth talking to Lochte, you know, ask him if the old swimmers notice the new ones," he said.

"I'm on it, boss," Stevie said.

Kelleher smiled. "I'm not your boss, I'm your colleague."

"You're my CIC," Stevie said. "Colleague in charge."

"I like that," Kelleher said. He pointed at the pool as heat one was finishing. "Four heats to go."

Susan Carol had spotted Stevie and Kelleher when they walked in. She was toward the back of the deck, sitting in her chair, wearing headphones—not to listen to music but in the hope that no one would talk to her. The only person who knew she didn't have any music clanging in her ears was Ed Brennan.

J.P.—thankfully—wasn't around. As heat two hit the water, Susan Carol stood up, took off her headphones, and began walking to the block area. She saw Ed heading that way too—he knew she liked to arrive three heats before she swam. With two heats to go, she would take off her sweats and stretch. With one heat to go, she'd put on her bathing cap. When the heat before hers came off the last wall, she would put on her goggles and try to flush everyone and everything from her mind. She wanted to step onto the block thinking she was in an empty pool, swimming a time trial that only she—and perhaps Ed—would ever know about.

"Remember," he said. "You just swim a smooth race,

especially the first 50. It should almost feel like you're taking out a 200."

"What if I go out too slow?" she said. "I do have to make the top eight."

"You'll make the top eight," he said. "You could swim ten of these on two minutes and make the top eight with your time from the tenth one."

He always knew what to say. He batted her on the back of the head gently as he always did before a race, and she walked the length of the pool to reach the blocks. She could hear a few "Go get 'em, Susan Carol"s from the stands, but she was already in her zone. No one on deck said anything to her. Swimmers know that when a swimmer is headed for the blocks, they aren't usually in the mood to talk.

She sat on the bench that ran along the wall behind lane four and stretched as the third heat went off. When she heard the whistle ordering heat six onto the blocks, she and Becky Ausmus glanced at each other and nodded.

"Good luck," Becky mouthed.

"You too," Susan Carol mouthed back.

She heard, "Take your mark," and she slowly moved into the starting position, knowing the starter would wait until everyone was frozen. She heard the familiar *beep* of the starter's horn and a moment later she was in the water. As she took her first two strokes before coming up to breathe, she felt completely calm.

Stay smooth, she told herself as she stretched her arms forward and felt the water rolling back as she made her way down the pool. She heard nothing except the sound of her own arms entering the water with each stroke.

What was silence for Susan Carol was a complete din for Stevie. It seemed like the entire crowd—the place seated about 3,000 and was packed—had gotten to its feet when Susan Carol was introduced just before the heat began.

Now, as Susan Carol left everyone in her heat behind her—including Becky Ausmus—the noise grew louder. Kelleher said something as Susan Carol came off the wall at the fifty, but Stevie couldn't hear him. Susan Carol was pulling away from the other swimmers. Stevie thought *fly* was just the right word for her race. As she went under the flags, her head went down and she charged into the wall.

As soon as her hands hit the electronic timing pad, Stevie heard a roar go up. Her time on the scoreboard read 58.29. Stevie had done a little research prior to the meet, and he knew that Christine Magnuson had recorded the fastest time by an American all year at 57.32. He also knew Susan Carol had never broken fifty-nine seconds before.

Susan Carol had pulled her goggles off and was staring at the scoreboard. No fist pump, no excited or satisfied slap of the water. She just stared. After Ausmus hit the pad in 59.88, she leaned across the lane line to congratulate Susan Carol. The crowd was going nuts, knowing just how fast the time was—especially for the morning heats.

"She doesn't look too excited," Stevie said to Kelleher, who was scribbling notes.

"Maybe she's worried she went too fast for a qualifying

heat," Kelleher said. Like everyone else in the building, he was standing. As Susan Carol pulled herself from the pool, waves of applause broke out. Magnuson, who was standing at the blocks waiting to swim in the final heat, gave her a hug. Ed Brennan was talking intently to her as they walked away.

"Maybe you're right," Stevie said, pointing to Brennan, who didn't appear nearly as excited as everyone else.

"Well, there's only one way to find out how she's feeling right now," Kelleher said. "Let's go talk to her."

5: MAKING A SPLASH

"That's a great time," Ed Brennan said to Susan Carol as they walked away from all the glad-handing people who wanted to congratulate her. "But tell me how it felt."

They were heading in the direction of the diving well, which had been set up as a warm-up/warm-down pool. Susan Carol was still a little bit out of breath, but she understood the point of the question.

"Honestly, I didn't feel anything but . . ." She paused for a breath. "Smooth. The only time I pushed at all was when I put my head down at the flags for the last three strokes. Until then it was . . ." Another pause. "Easy."

Ed nodded. "I've seen this coming in your speed workouts the last couple of months. Right now you've got Magnuson and all the other Americans shaking in their Speedos."

"What about Sarah Sjöström?" she said, unable to resist

a smile at the thought of the world-record holder feeling threatened by her.

Ed laughed. "We aren't quite *there* yet. Go warm down."

Susan Carol slipped into the diving well and pushed off right away, the better to avoid anyone starting a conversation. She wanted to get moving so her muscles didn't tighten up after her swim.

But she was smiling underwater thinking about Sarah Sjöström. If there was anyone Susan Carol wanted to be like in swimming, it was Sarah. Sjöström had broken the world record in the 100 fly two years ago, just before her sixteenth birthday. Susan Carol would turn sixteen six weeks after the Olympics. Sjöström was proof that you could be the best in the world at a very young age.

Sjöström didn't look fifteen when she broke the world record, and she didn't look eighteen now. Although she was officially listed in her bio as being almost the same size as Susan Carol—six feet and 150 pounds—there was little doubt that she was bigger than that. Susan Carol was in great shape, but she didn't have Sjöström's shoulders— swimming shoulders, most people in the sport called them. Susan Carol relied more on her long arms and the strength of her legs to propel herself through the water. Sjöström swam on sheer power. Seeing her standing on the blocks— Susan Carol had seen her on TV but never in person—it occurred to her that Sjöström could probably bench-press her with ease. She was, if nothing else, intimidating to look at—even on a TV screen.

Sjöström's record was 56.06. In swimming, the difference

between 56.06 and Susan Carol's best time of 58.29 in a 100-meter race was huge. But the race just now had felt *so* easy. Susan Carol was sure she could go faster—the question was how much faster.

She was starting to flip, having gone 200 yards, when she heard someone call her name. She looked up and saw J. P. Scott standing at the end of the lane.

"Great swim, Susan Carol! That's just the splash I was talking about. They want you in the interview room in twenty minutes," he said.

"Okay," she said. "I'll swim another 200, take my shower, and be there."

"Good girl. And be sure to leave your hair down," he said.

"But I always tie my hair back when it's wet," she said, a bit baffled.

"Just trust me," he said. "Don't tie it back."

She decided an argument was pointless, so she put her head back into the water and pushed off. She was a little irked that he thought she'd put up a fast time because he'd wanted her to. She knew that was unreasonable—should she have gone slower to spite him?—she just didn't like there to be even a suggestion that some marketing deal affected what she did in the pool.

In her old life, she would have taken a lot more time to warm down because it would have involved stopping several times to chat on the wall with other swimmers. Then would come a long, hot shower and a trip to McDonald's. She didn't have to swim again for at least nine hours, so a Big Mac and fries would hit the spot. Now she pulled herself out of the pool as soon as she finished and took a speed shower—just enough to wash the chlorine out of her hair. She put on a clean T-shirt and sweats, left her hair down (sigh), and found no fewer than four people wearing buttons that said USA SWIMMING waiting for her outside the locker room door.

One was a familiar face: Mike Unger, who did most of the PR for USA Swimming. She remembered him from Shanghai as someone who seemed to stay calm when all those around him were losing their heads.

He reintroduced himself and then introduced the others. Susan Carol instantly blurred on the names although two of them were locals from Charlotte who were just *thrilled* by her swim.

"Interview room is right down the hall," Mike Unger said. "We aren't keeping anyone long since you all have to swim again tonight."

"It's no problem," Susan Carol said. "I'm a reporter too, you know. I understand most of them have to file for the Internet as soon as possible."

"That's right," Unger said. "You do understand. You make my job a lot easier."

They headed down the long hallway. As they passed the men's locker room, they saw a swarm of people heading in their direction.

"Phelps," she heard one of the Charlotte people say.

Sure enough, walking down the hall, swim bag over his shoulder, was the greatest swimmer in history. In spite of herself, she gave a little gasp when she recognized him. He'd been in Shanghai at the Worlds, of course, but because she'd only been in one event, she'd never actually crossed paths with him.

The entourage Phelps had trailing in his wake made Susan Carol's little group look like they were invisible. There were two rent-a-cops, walking just behind Phelps, and right behind them Susan Carol recognized Bob Bowman, Phelps's longtime coach. There was a TV camera crew half running alongside Phelps, with yet another security person clearing a path so no one got in their way as they filmed Phelps—gasp!—walking down a hallway.

A man and a woman both wearing suits walked with Bowman. Susan Carol guessed the guy had to be Peter Carlisle—who else but an agent would wear a suit to a swim meet? Behind them was a coterie of still more USA Swimming officials and then, just for good measure, two more rent-a-cops.

When Phelps saw Susan Carol heading toward him, he came to a complete stop, which nearly caused a twelve-person pileup.

"Susan Carol Anderson!" he said. "I was really hoping to meet you here." He put out his hand. "I'm Michael Phelps."

Susan Carol was completely paralyzed. A small part of her wondered what Stevie would say at that moment. It would no doubt be something along the lines of "Really, you're Michael Phelps? I'd never have guessed."

She managed to hold out her hand and squeak,

"Naahs to meet y'all," slipping into a nerves-induced drawl. Thank God Stevie wasn't there. She'd never hear the end of it.

Phelps was smiling down at her. He was at least six-four and his arms seemed to go on forever. His hand completely enveloped hers when they shook.

"What a fantastic swim," Phelps said. "You made it look so easy. Just once I'd like to swim a race and look that smooth."

She almost started laughing. Michael Phelps broke world records in the 200 fly routinely and looked like he was warming up during the swim.

"That's very nice (oh God, it came out "naahs" again) of you (at least she said "you" and not "y'all") to say, but, Michael, my goodness (yes, she said "ma"), if anyone makes swimming look easy, it's you. I've been watching you do it as long as I can remember."

Phelps laughed. "Sadly, that's true. If you saw me swim in Sydney, you'd have been three at the time. Getting old sucks."

That caused everyone in the Phelps entourage to laugh like they were some sit-com laugh track.

"You're only twenty-six," Susan Carol said. "That's hardly old."

"Be twenty-seven soon," Phelps said. "Call me if you're still swimming at twenty-seven and tell me if you don't feel old."

Mike Unger jumped in. "Hey, guys, we need to get Susan Carol to the interview room and, Michael, I know you have to warm up."

"True enough, Mike," Phelps said. He turned back to Susan Carol. "I really look forward to seeing you swim tonight. We need new stars like you in swimming." He laughed. "Even if you *do* want to be a reporter when you grow up."

Wow, she thought, he really *did* know her.

"Maybe someday I'll write a book on you," she said, finding a little bit of her bearings.

"Nah," Phelps said. "Write a book on *you.* That one, I'd read."

He shook her hand again, and as he walked off, Susan Carol noticed that the TV crew had recorded every second of their chat. She wondered if that was why he was so nice to her. Then again, he *had* watched her swim and he knew she wanted to be a reporter. Case closed, she decided. Michael Phelps was a genuine good guy.

Stevie and Bobby decided to stand in the back of the interview room to await Susan Carol's arrival. The door was in the back and they'd get a chance to see her when she came in and, Stevie hoped, find out what she was planning to do that afternoon.

Stevie wasn't prepared to see his friend ushered in like a head of state. She was completely surrounded.

"Susan Carol," he called out as they were whisking her to the front of the room.

Hearing his voice, she stopped, and Stevie saw The

Smile break out on her face. She made a quick right before anyone could object and walked over to Stevie and Bobby.

"About time you showed up," she said, giving Kelleher a hug. "Where's Tamara?"

"Slept in this morning," Kelleher said. "You'll see her tonight. You are amazing."

She gave Stevie a hug too.

"What are you doing after this?" he asked.

"Going to lunch with you guys, I hope," she said. "Let me get this done and we'll talk."

Stevie was relieved. Susan Carol was still Susan Carol.

She handled the press conference just as Stevie expected: perfectly. Her answers were honest and stayed away from the usual sports clichés the two of them always rolled their eyes at. She never once said she was going to give 110 percent. Or that she hoped to "step up" for the final. And she certainly didn't thank God—which, coming from a minister's daughter, was no small thing in Stevie's mind. He wasn't surprised, though: Susan Carol's religion was important to her, but private.

When she finished, Mike Unger asked that people not stop her for follow-ups since she had to swim again that night. "Tonight, after finals, all the swimmers will have more time," he said.

Susan Carol made her way back to Stevie and Bobby, and they all stepped outside.

"Where do you guys want to go eat?" she asked.

"Whoa," a voice said behind her. "We're going to get

you food, Susan Carol. But first you've got to talk to Bob Costas, and then the Speedo people want you to come by their hospitality room." J.P. had materialized from nowhere.

Susan Carol was clearly as upset to hear this news as Stevie was.

"No one told me about this," she said. "I thought the NBC show wasn't until Sunday."

"No, it airs on Sunday, but Costas is in town today. He's interviewing you, Phelps, and Lochte."

Stevie's heart sank. He knew that NBC was taping highlights of the meet for a one-hour show on Sunday. This would lead up to its blowout coverage of both the Olympic Trials and the Olympics. Phelps had made swimming into a TV sport, at least in an Olympic year.

Kelleher, no doubt seeing the look on Stevie's face, jumped in.

"Susan Carol, it's cool. Stevie and I will wander over there with you and wait until you're done. There's no rush; it's early."

Ed Brennan had now appeared behind them as well.

"Costas is fine, J.P., but I want her to go sit down and eat after that. I'm sure the Speedo people will understand that she needs to be off her feet this afternoon."

J.P. did *not* look happy with either Coach Brennan or Kelleher.

"Look, these are important people in Susan Carol's life. . . ."

Brennan raised a hand. "And she'll be important to them as long as she wins, right? So let's make that her priority. She can schmooze after she wins her races."

"Okay, fine, but I don't think the NBC people are going to want anyone hanging around while Costas does the interview."

"I don't think it'll be a problem," Kelleher said. "Bob and I are old friends."

"Okay, okay," J.P. said, trying to regain some control of the situation. "Let's get going. Once Phelps swims he'll be right in there, so we have to get this done."

"Phelps doesn't swim for another half hour, J.P.," Susan Carol said. "And then he'll warm down before he goes anywhere else. Stop making everything a problem."

Another voice came from out of nowhere at that moment.

"Susan Carol, watch your tone. You're speaking to an adult."

Susan Carol's tone suddenly softened. "Yes, Dad," she said. "Sorry."

6: IN DEEP WATER

They had to walk outside the Aquatics Center to find Costas and his crew. The temperature had warmed considerably since they had arrived, and Stevie wished he had thought to wear shorts.

NBC had created a small set in the back of the building, complete with an anchor desk and two comfortable armchairs next to it and lots of NBC logos. Bob Costas was sitting in one of the chairs when the group—which included Susan Carol, Ed Brennan, J. P. Scott, Susie McArthur (who seemed to have magically appeared as they walked out the door), two USA Swimming people, Don Anderson, Stevie, and Kelleher—arrived.

Costas smiled when he saw them all coming and said, "Well, I know this can't be Phelps because there aren't quite enough people." He apologized for not getting up to greet people since he was already miked and was wearing an earpiece, which Stevie knew from his own TV experience allowed him to hear what a producer off the set was saying to him.

Susie introduced Susan Carol, and as Costas was shaking her hand, he spotted Kelleher.

"Bobby Kelleher covering swimming?" he said. "Ladies and gentlemen, with all due respect to Ms. Anderson, we have a much bigger story on our hands here than anything in the pool. I suggest we contact the news department right away."

Kelleher pulled Stevie along with him onto the set. "Knowing the names of three swimmers hardly makes you an expert either," he said, shaking Costas's offered hand. "Bob, meet Steve Thomas."

Costas's eyes lit up. "Aha! The other half of the dynamic duo of Anderson and Thomas. Now I *really* feel badly about not being able to stand up."

Stevie had always been a Costas fan. He came across smarter and smoother than almost anyone else doing sports on television and was—in Stevie's mind—the best TV interviewer going. If he hadn't already felt that way, he probably would have as soon as Costas referred to him and Susan Carol as "the dynamic duo."

"Mr. Costas, I can't tell you what a thrill this is," Stevie said, taking a couple of steps forward to accept Costas's offered hand. "I've been a fan of yours for as long as I can remember."

Oh my God, I sound like Susan Carol meeting Andy Roddick! he thought. He glanced at Susan Carol, who was being miked by a soundman, and was convinced he saw her smirking.

"Well, since I started in the business before you were born, I guess that makes sense," Costas said with a smile.

"Oh yes, Steve has looked up to you for as long as I've known him," Susan Carol said.

She *had* been smirking. He was searching for a clever response when Costas said, "Well, Steve, almost *no one* looks up to me, so I'm flattered."

Costas was famous for making jokes about his height— or lack of it. Now—happily—it was Susan Carol who was flustered.

"I didn't mean it that way, Mr. Costas," she said. "I was just . . ."

Costas waved a hand. "I know you didn't. And call me Bob—both of you."

"We need to clear the set," someone wearing a headset said, waving his arms to indicate that Stevie and Kelleher should get out of the way. A makeup woman was brushing powder on Susan Carol's face.

"Diane, if I've ever seen anyone who didn't need makeup, this would be the girl," Costas said.

"You are *so* right," Diane said. "I'm just taking a little bit of the shine off, that's all."

Diane had a bigger southern accent than Susan Carol did, even at her breathless Scarlett O'Hara best. What she actually had said was, "Aahm jus takin' a little bit of the shaan off."

She backed off the set, and Stevie heard Costas say—no

doubt to some producer out of sight—"Let's just go for a while here and then we can figure out how long we have later."

Costas nodded in confirmation of whatever was said into his earpiece and turned to Susan Carol. "Remember, this isn't airing until Sunday, okay, Susan Carol? Try not to say 'today' or make any specific time reference and, obviously, my questions will be more about what's coming up than about this weekend."

"Sure, that's fine," Susan Carol said. If she was nervous, she didn't show it. Then again, she didn't get nervous very often.

The guy wearing the headset was asking for quiet.

"Hang on one second, sorry," Stevie heard a voice say behind him.

It was J.P., the increasingly annoying agent. He charged onto the set and put a baseball cap with a Kellogg's logo on Susan Carol's head. J.P. looked at Costas apologetically. "My fault for forgetting," he said. "It's in her contract to wear this during all television interviews."

Susan Carol looked confused. Costas looked angry.

"Look, fella . . . ," he said.

"It's J.P., J. P. Scott," J.P. said, putting his hand out to Costas, who shook it with clear reluctance. "I'm Susan Carol's agent."

"I would never have guessed," Costas said dryly. "Look, P.J., we don't like the athletes to wear caps during these sit-downs. For one thing, they look a lot better without them on. Phelps never wears a cap when we talk to him."

"It's in our contract," J.P. said.

"It's not in ours," Costas answered. "Why don't you take the cap off her and let us get started."

Susan Carol took the cap off and was about to hand it to J.P. when Stevie heard yet another voice behind him.

"With respect, Mr. Costas, it's our call what she wears."

Costas was peering past the lights to identify where the voice was coming from. "Who's that, another agent?" he said.

"No," Don Anderson said, stepping forward. "I'm Susan Carol's father."

Stevie wasn't quite sure who was more stunned—Costas or Susan Carol. Both stared for a second, saying nothing. Before Costas could answer, Susan Carol, clearly embarrassed, said, "Daddy, really, it's okay."

"No, I don't think it is," Don Anderson said. He walked up to Costas, who must have been feeling as if he was on a receiving line at this point.

"Mr. Costas, I'm sure you must have dealt with athletes who have this sort of obligation before. When NBC interviews golfers, they're always wearing their caps. We're not trying to be difficult but, as J.P. said, it's written in her contract, and I take that seriously. I hope you understand."

Stevie realized he was right about the golfers. He couldn't remember ever seeing a golfer interviewed who wasn't wearing a cap with a logo on it.

It was clear now that Costas was pretty much done with Team Susan Carol Anderson. "Reverend Anderson"— apparently he'd done his homework on Susan Carol's family—"if it is important to you, then we'll do it that way," he said. "I think your daughter looks great without the cap on, but if that's your choice, fine. But we need to get started because my producer is screaming in my ear." In less than five minutes, Costas had gone from smiling and joking to stone-faced.

"Thanks very much," Don Anderson said, nodding to Susan Carol, who put the cap back on her head. "I'll get out of the way now and let you work."

"That would be a real blessing," Costas said—not without a hint of sarcasm in his voice. Reverend Anderson looked at him for a moment, clearly considering a reply, then turned and walked off the set.

"This is *not* going well," Kelleher whispered in Stevie's ear.

Once again quiet was asked for on the set and—finally— the interview began with Costas asking a very simple first question: "Susan Carol Anderson, where in the world did you come from?"

"Goldsboro, North Carolina," Susan Carol answered, giving Costas The Smile, which appeared to break the ice that had formed. Then she answered the question seriously, talking about Ed Brennan and gaining strength as she got older and her breakthrough race a year ago in this same meet. From there, it all went well.

By the time they finished, Mike Unger from USA Swimming had joined the group that was watching.

"Bob, Phelps will be here in about fifteen minutes," he said as soon as the guy in the headset who Stevie had learned was the floor director called, "Clear."

"Good," Costas said. "I can stretch my legs."

Someone rushed to help him get untangled from his earpiece and microphone while someone else was doing the same for Susan Carol. Costas stood at the same time Susan Carol did. Even in flip-flops, she towered over him.

"Now you see why I do all interviews sitting down." Costas laughed. "It was very nice to meet *you*."

Stevie wondered if Susan Carol noticed the extra emphasis on the word *you*. If there was any doubt that he was making a point, it went away when Costas turned and walked off the back of the set without saying goodbye to anyone else.

"That's as close to totally pissed off as you'll ever see Bob," Kelleher said to Stevie as J.P. and crew surrounded Susan Carol. "That was a bad scene right there."

"She did well in the interview, though, right?" Stevie said.

"She did great. But at this level, people don't remember that she was charming. They remember that she was charming, but the people with her were a pain in the butt. Trust me, when he called J.P. by the wrong name, he was making a point."

"As in, 'you're a nobody, what are you doing on my set?'"

"Bingo," Kelleher said.

Susan Carol, having received hugs from her team, came over to them.

"What'd you think?" she asked.

"You were fantastic," Stevie said.

She narrowed her eyes and looked at him suspiciously.

Stevie was convinced she could read his mind. J.P. and Reverend Anderson were talking to Mike Unger. Susan Carol looked at Kelleher.

"Tell me what you really think," she said.

"I *really* think we should go get something to eat," Kelleher said. "Without your entourage."

Even standing a few yards away, Stevie could clearly see that Susan Carol's plan to eat with him and Bobby wasn't greeted enthusiastically. When she walked back over to them, she said quietly, "Let's go before my dad changes his mind. J.P. was *not* happy."

"What a shock," Stevie said.

As they made their way across the parking lot, they passed Michael Phelps and company headed the other way. Phelps saw Susan Carol and gave her a friendly wave, which she returned.

"When did you meet him?" Stevie said, trying not to sound jealous and failing.

"Oh, Stevie, stop," she said. "I met him a little while ago in the hallway, and he was very nice."

Susan Carol went into the locker room briefly to get her swim bag and then the three of them walked to Kelleher's car. Susan Carol was happy to wear the cap now, pulling it low on her head so she wouldn't be recognized, but there were still quite a few people congratulating her on her swim. Once they were in the car, Kelleher asked where they wanted to go.

"Right here," said Susan Carol, pointing at the McDonald's. "Right now."

"You want breakfast?" Kelleher said.

"It's 10:45," Susan Carol said. "They start serving Big Macs at 10:30."

"And this will be okay with Ed?" Kelleher said.

"You bet. I don't swim again for nine hours."

So they went through the drive-through, ordering enough food for at least six people. Stevie and Susan Carol both dug into their French fries on the short ride back to the hotel. The lobby was almost deserted, and they decided to go to Stevie and Kelleher's room because it was less likely that any of Susan Carol's minders would show up there. Tamara had left a note saying she had gone to meet Lochte and his coach for lunch.

As soon as they were sitting down, with food spread out around them at a table by the window, Kelleher came right to the point.

"What's up with your father?"

Susan Carol made a face that Stevie couldn't quite read. Then she sighed, which Stevie *could* read.

"I'm honestly not sure," she said. "I'm just guessing because we haven't talked about it. But I think he really believes J.P. and his people have my best interests at heart and that we should listen to their advice. Plus, he's always been a believer that if you hire someone to do a job you should let them do the job, and not tell them how to do it."

Kelleher was giving Stevie a look that he knew meant he should shut up, but he couldn't help himself.

"Didn't he learn anything after what happened with your uncle Brendan?" he said. "I mean, he was an agent who was part of your *family* and you couldn't trust him. How can he be so trusting of these guys?"

Almost two years earlier, Stevie and Susan Carol had gotten caught up in what turned out to be the fake kidnapping of a glamorous Russian tennis player and had been shocked to find out that Susan Carol's uncle, who was a tennis agent, was involved in the deception.

Susan Carol was nodding. "I understand what you're saying, Stevie. But there *is* a difference here because my best interests really are their best interests—or at least my financial interests. I don't think Dad trusts them because he thinks they're good people. He trusts that they know what they're doing."

Kelleher took a long sip of the coffee he'd gotten with his hamburger. "There's truth in that, but it isn't quite that simple," he said. "They see you as a commodity, and one that needs to be exploited quickly because the Olympics window opens and closes quickly. They have absolutely no interest in you as a person or in your future long-term. Your dad should understand that."

Now Susan Carol looked a little miffed. "Bobby, you just hate all agents—"

"No, I don't."

"I know, I know, your pal Tom Ross, the tennis guy. But that's the list, isn't it? You don't know these guys at all. . . ."

"You're right that I don't like many agents, but I will say a lot of them are very smart. What J.P. did with the cap and what your dad did in backing him up—that wasn't smart. If you tell Kellogg's, 'NBC said no to the cap and Phelps isn't wearing one either,' they'll understand. No harm, no foul. But J.P. and your dad just pissed off Bob Costas—which means they pissed off NBC. Strictly in a business sense, that's a bad idea. Kellogg's doesn't want to piss off NBC."

Susan Carol took a deep breath.

"I guess, deep down, I know you're right," she said. "I'm not crazy about J.P. or any of the others. But my dad is a different story. He's my dad."

"I know," Kelleher said. "I get it. And I get that you're being hit with a lot here."

"I thought I knew what athletes' lives were like from all of our reporting. But it's so overwhelming being on the other side of the story. . . ."

Stevie slid closer and put his arm around her. It was a little unnerving to see the unflappable Susan Carol struggling with something.

"Listen," Bobby said, "this is all new and things may settle down as your family gets used to how things have changed. Ideally your dad would be looking out for you. But it's *your* instincts I trust. You may need to have a heart-to-heart with him at some point—just to remind him how this is all affecting you. And that you need to stay in control of how things go."

"Me, in control?" She sighed again. "Life just isn't that simple anymore."

7: RACING AROUND

The alarm startled Susan Carol. After leaving Bobby and Stevie's room, she had decided to try to take a nap. Usually when she had time to kill between trials and finals, she read a book or trolled the Internet to find out what was going on in the world.

But the morning had sapped her—not so much her swim, which had felt great, but everything else. She knew Bobby and Stevie were right about J. P. Scott and his people. It was hardly news that agents weren't to be trusted completely; she knew that. What was confusing was that her dad didn't seem to know it. At least not yet.

She had set the alarm for four o'clock. Warm-ups started at five, and her father would drive her back to the pool at 4:30. She hoped that none of the Lightning Fast people—especially J.P.—would be in the car.

The alarm surprised her. She had only set it as backup,

not expecting to sleep for almost three hours. Now, hearing the buzzer, she needed a moment to re-orient herself: Where was she? Charlotte. What time was it? Time to swim.

She decided she needed a wake-up shower even though she'd already showered twice that day.

"I'm becoming Kramer," she said aloud as she stretched and walked toward the bathroom. She and her father watched reruns of *Seinfeld* together all the time. Swimmers shower a lot—the hot shower at the end of a workout is often the carrot that gets them through the last thirty minutes when everything seems to hurt. So Susan Carol had especially enjoyed the episode when Kramer had decided to simply *stay* in the shower all the time because that was where he was most happy.

By the time she had dressed in what Stevie called "the teenage girl's summer uniform" of T-shirt, shorts, and flip-flops, she felt a lot better. Her dad had said he'd pick her up out front, and he was as good as his word. Walking out the front door of the hotel, she was very glad the meet was being held indoors since the temperature had to be close to ninety. She loved swimming outdoors, especially during practice, but for a big meet she preferred a controlled air and water temperature.

"You ready to go?" her dad asked as they eased out of the hotel driveway.

"Hope so," she said. "I took a nap."

"Good. I was afraid Stevie and Bobby might talk your ear off and keep you from resting."

She'd been trying to decide whether to bring up the

events of the morning and had been leaning against it—especially with an important swim only a couple of hours away. But her father's comment made her change her mind.

"Dad, Stevie and Bobby would never do anything to keep me from preparing for an important race," she said.

Her father turned away from the road for an instant and looked at her. They were in fairly heavy late-afternoon downtown traffic.

"What?" he said. "I didn't mean that."

"Then what *did* you mean?"

"I guess that they aren't your father or your coach or your agents, so . . ."

"So you think J.P. and Bill and Susie care more about me than Stevie and Bobby do? Come on, Dad."

He was waving his hand in the air as if to say "wrong."

"Hang on, honey. I know how much you like them and I like them too. Same with Tamara. But you have a once-in-a-lifetime opportunity here—"

"To make the Olympic team, Dad, *not* to get rich. If I swim my best and do well, we'll make all the money we need and more whether I wear a stupid Kellogg's cap during an interview or not."

"Is that what this is about?"

"That and when you yelled at me for telling J.P. to cool it with all of his 'do this, do that' stuff."

"I simply reminded you that the tone you were using when talking to a grown-up—*any* grown-up—wasn't acceptable. Which it wasn't."

He might have a point about her tone, and he had always been consistent about that. "Okay, maybe you're right about that one, though you didn't hear the beginning of the conversation, so you missed the context," she said. "But getting Mr. Costas upset—"

"I don't think he was upset."

"Really? I do. And so did Stevie and Bobby."

Her father laughed. "I think Bobby might be a bit biased on the subject. We both know how he feels about agents."

"That's true. But he also knows Mr. Costas, and he can tell when he's ticked off."

Her father didn't answer. The rest of the trip to the pool passed in silence.

Stevie and Bobby didn't need to be back at the pool as early as Susan Carol. They pulled up about a half hour before the evening session was scheduled to begin at six. This time, Kelleher circled to the back lot, where they had gone for the NBC interview. Sure enough, the lot was only half full.

"Good call," Stevie said as they climbed out of the car. Both were carrying computers since the plan was to write from the small media room in the Aquatics Center.

They walked past the NBC set—which was deserted—to the back door they had used that morning.

There'd been a security guard at the door in the morning, but this time he stopped them.

"Sorry," he said. "Media entrance is around front."

Kelleher looked confused. "We came through here this morning and there wasn't a problem. And the media room is right down this hallway."

The security guy was nodding. "I know, sir, I'm sorry. But someone from USA Swimming came by about an hour ago and put that up." He pointed to a handwritten sign that said COMPETITORS ENTRANCE. SWIMMERS, COACHES, AND SWIMMER-SUPPORT BADGES ONLY.

It looked as if someone had literally drawn up the sign on the spur of the moment.

"Who put that up?" Kelleher said. "It looks like something a sixth grader made."

The security guy laughed. "I hear you," he said. "But he was definitely with USA Swimming."

"Right, all those USA Swimming guys wear big badges with their names on them, like they're afraid they might forget who they are," he said. "Did you happen to see his name?"

The guard thought for a moment. Then he snapped his fingers. "Last name was James. I noticed because that's my first name."

"That's helpful, James, thanks. Now, since no one's around, can you do us a favor and let us go through rather than walk all the way around this enormous building in the heat?"

James looked around. "Look, I know who you are, Mr. Kelleher. I've seen you on TV. And I'm not trying to give you a hard time. But you walk down that hall now and someone sees you, I'm the one who gets fired."

Kelleher nodded. "I hear you. Thanks for your help."

They turned to leave. "I'm really sorry about this," James said.

"Not your fault, James. Don't worry, I'll take care of it."

By the time they circled the building to the front entrance, Kelleher and Stevie were both steaming—literally and figuratively. Soaked in sweat, they walked in and Stevie could see through the windows behind the lobby that the pool was filled with swimmers warming up for the evening's finals. Each event would have a consolation final for swimmers who had finished ninth to sixteenth in the morning and then the championship final. The women's 100 fly was the second event. The men's 200 fly, which Phelps would swim, was the fifth. Then there were two relays after that to finish off the program.

They headed for the media room, which appeared to be a fitness room where desks had been set up for the weekend meet. They found a couple of empty spots for their computers. Kelleher looked at his watch. It was 5:50. He picked up the program that had the heat sheets in it and opened to the first page.

"Here it is," he said. "USA Swimming staff."

It didn't take him long to find what he was looking for. "Trevor James," he said. "Assistant executive director."

"Do you know him?"

"Never heard of him. Let's start with Mike Unger and see what we can find out."

"Is it that big a deal?" Stevie asked.

"No," Kelleher said. "But it's stupid. And I hate stupid.

And there's two more days to this meet—might as well complain early."

Mike Unger was in the interview room, apparently trying to figure out where to put all the TV cameras for the post-race interviews.

"Hey, Bobby, Steve, what's up?" he said with a friendly smile when they walked in. "You might want to get to your seats pretty soon. We're going to be packed by the time the 200 free starts."

"Yeah, I'll bet," Kelleher said. "Mike, did you know they made the back door over by the locker room hallway off-limits to the media?"

Unger frowned. "First I've heard of it," he said. "I know they get a little jumpy when Phelps is coming and going, but I didn't think it was a big deal. Most people don't even know that back door exists."

"That's what I would think," Kelleher said. "Who is Trevor James?"

"Chuck Wielgus's new number two. Hired him at the beginning of the year to help with rules and sponsorships mostly."

"Where was he before?"

"Octagon. He helped make a lot of Phelps's deals for them, apparently. But he's also an international swimming official. He's one of the US reps at all the big meets. That was one reason Chuck wanted him: gives us a little more influence with FINA."

FINA was the Fédération Internationale de Natation. That was French for International Swimming Federation. A lot of international sports organizations used French for their official name. French was the official language of the Olympics because it had been Baron Pierre de Coubertin—a Frenchman—who had started the modern Olympics in 1896.

"So Chuck hired an agent?" Kelleher asked.

"Not exactly," Unger said. "Trevor James didn't represent specific athletes. He mostly worked the other side of the street, bringing corporations to the agents for deals."

"Right, I know the type," Kelleher said.

"He shouldn't have anything to do with media access, though," Unger said. "He steers clear of you guys, best I can tell."

Stevie started to say something, but Kelleher gave him a look that told him to keep quiet.

"I'm sure you're right," Kelleher said. "Come on, Stevie. We better go find a seat."

They left Unger to finish his work and made their way upstairs to the media seating area. Unger hadn't been kidding about getting there early. Since there was no assigned seating, it was first come, first served, and there were exactly three seats left when Stevie and Kelleher arrived—two of which Tamara Mearns had been saving for them.

"Wow, it looks like a lot of people didn't bother to come this morning," Stevie said as they squeezed in.

"Makes sense," Kelleher said. "Except for Susan Carol, no one really swam fast this morning. They want to save their best for the finals."

"You think she went *too* fast this morning?"

Kelleher shrugged. "We'll find out soon."

Unlike the morning session, where swimmers simply reported to the blocks when their heat was up, the swimmers for each race stayed together in a holding area underneath the stands until it was their time to swim. Stevie knew from watching the Olympics that at big meets the swimmers had to sit in a "ready" room until they walked onto the deck to be introduced. Since this meet was a warm-up for the Olympic Trials, they were doing their best to follow that setup to give the swimmers a chance to get accustomed to it.

As the swimmers in the women's 100-fly final marched onto the deck, they were already lined up so that the swimmer in lane one came out first and the swimmer in lane eight came out last. Susan Carol was smack in the middle since she had qualified first and was in lane four.

Christine Magnuson, who would be in lane five, was directly behind her, and a Chinese swimmer named Li Lin-Yu, who had qualified third, was right in front of her. Becky Ausmus would be in lane seven after qualifying sixth. Even from a distance Stevie could see that all the swimmers were tall and most of them had broader shoulders than Susan Carol.

As soon as they reached their lanes, they began peeling off their sweats and putting on bathing caps and goggles.

Each swimmer was introduced with a good deal of fanfare. The loudest roar from the crowd, not surprisingly, was for Susan Carol.

"Swimming in lane four with a qualifying time of 58.29 seconds, from Goldsboro, North Carolina, Susan Carol Anderson!"

The cheering might not have been as loud as at a basketball game with Susan Carol's beloved Duke Blue Devils, but it was close.

"North Carolina's favorite daughter," Tamara said with a smile.

Susan Carol waved quickly when she heard her name, then put on her cap and began adjusting her goggles. A moment later, the swimmers were called to the blocks. Stevie heard the starter say, "Take your mark . . . ," and then *boom*, the horn sounded and the swimmers were in midair for a second before knifing into the water. Since the race would be decided in under a minute, the crowd was shrieking before anyone had even come up for a breath.

Christine Magnuson had clearly watched Susan Carol closely in the morning. She'd seen her pull clear in the first twenty-five meters and wasn't going to let her do it again. She came up off the dive with a slight lead and began extending it as they closed in on the fifty-meter wall.

Susan Carol and Li were almost a body length behind as they reached the wall, and out in lane seven Becky Ausmus, the other North Carolinian in the race, was actually ahead of both of them. Stevie glanced at the electronic timing board as they all pushed off the wall. Magnuson had gone out in 27.01, which Stevie knew was lightning fast—as opposed to Lightning Fast. Ausmus was second in 27.34 and Li was third in 27.52, trailed by Susan Carol in 27.55.

"She's got some work to do," Kelleher shouted in Stevie's ear.

Stevie was nervous, but not that nervous. He and Susan Carol had talked about the fact that she didn't mind being behind in the 100 because her training for the 200 almost always made her second 50 better than her first. He started to tell Kelleher but realized it was pointless. By the time he explained, the race would be over.

Halfway back, both Ausmus and Li began to fade. Susan Carol had pulled into second place, but Magnuson was still looking strong. Both swimmers breathed every second stroke, and Stevie could see they were both staying as low as possible when they came up to breathe, saving energy by not climbing too high out of the water.

"She's gonna get second," Kelleher yelled as they approached the flags that were five meters from the wall.

But just then, Stevie saw Magnuson breathe on her second consecutive stroke. She was cracking! He couldn't find his voice, so he just pointed in her direction, which told Bobby and Tamara absolutely nothing.

As soon as Magnuson took the extra breath, you could see Susan Carol close the gap. Magnuson was now breathing every stroke. The piano might not have hit her, but she was clearly hurting. As they went under the flags, Stevie could see Susan Carol stretching her long arms in front of her and he knew she was going to win. Magnuson was bobbing up and down; Susan Carol was plunging forward. Magnuson stole one last breath and it cost her the race.

The building exploded as Susan Carol touched in 57.88. Magnuson plowed in at 58.01. They had dusted the rest of the field. Lucy Griffin, way out in lane one, actually came on to take third in 59.69. Li faded to fifth; Ausmus, after trying to go out as hard as she could, finished seventh.

"How about *that!*" Kelleher yelled.

"I knew it," Stevie said. "I knew she had her when Magnuson started breathing every stroke."

Kelleher gave him a look. "You noticed that Magnuson was breathing every stroke?"

"Well, yeah. Susan Carol told me that's how you can tell when a butterflyer is getting tired."

"Okay, that makes it official: You are the Susan Carol Anderson beat writer for the *Washington Herald*."

Stevie laughed. "When did Susan Carol get her own beat writer?"

Kelleher looked down at the deck. Susan Carol had just climbed out of the water and was waving to the crowd, which was still on its feet.

"About sixty seconds ago," he said.

8: WINNING?

Tamara stayed behind to watch Phelps swim so Stevie and Bobby could go downstairs to the interview room to see Susan Carol. When they made their way into the jam-packed room, they spotted Mike Unger in the back. Kelleher and Stevie worked their way through the crowd to talk to him.

"Great race, huh?" Unger said. "Hey, you were asking about Trevor James before?" He pointed to the podium. "That's him. He's taking care of this press conference because I have to go out and get Phelps organized once he swims."

A short man wearing a USA Swimming tracksuit was standing at the microphone and calling for quiet. He had closely cropped graying blond hair and the look of someone who had once been an agent, though Stevie wasn't quite sure he could articulate what that meant.

The room quieted enough for James to tell everyone why he wanted quiet. "I want to be sure all of you understand our guidelines. Susan Carol Anderson and Christine Magnuson will be here in five minutes. You'll have a maximum of fifteen minutes with them because Michael Phelps will be in soon after that and we know you all want to talk to him.

"So, let's keep the aisles clear as the swimmers come in and out."

"Where can we talk to the swimmers after they finish in here?" someone up front asked. James was shaking his head before the questioner had even finished.

"No, no, no. You'll get plenty in here. The swimmers all have races early tomorrow, so—"

"Susan Carol doesn't," Stevie heard himself say, before he remembered he was in a jam-packed room. Everyone turned to look at him. "Um, she's got the 200-fly heats at noon and then the final isn't until Sunday morning."

James was glaring at him. "Young man, are you credentialed to be here?" he said in the sort of condescending tone Stevie truly hated. He was about to take his press pass from around his neck and wave it in the air when he heard Kelleher's voice.

"He's got a credential," Kelleher said. "The real question is, when did you take over PR for USA Swimming, and how do you know what reporters need and don't need? Normally we have access to the swimmers outside of this room."

Several voices backed Kelleher up. Now James looked *really* annoyed.

"This is a USA Swimming event, Mr. . . ."

"Kelleher," Bobby said. *"Washington Herald."*

"Mr. Kelleher, this is our event and you play by our rules. If you don't like them, you're free to leave."

Kelleher looked about as angry as Stevie had ever seen him. He didn't say another word to James. Instead, he turned to Mike Unger, who looked pretty horrified by the exchange himself. "Where's Chuck Wielgus?" Kelleher said.

"Probably on deck somewhere waiting for Phelps to swim—"

Kelleher didn't wait for him to finish; he just headed out the door. Stevie figured somebody from the *Herald* better stick around. Plus, he wanted to see Susan Carol. And a moment later, she walked in the back door with Christine Magnuson. Susan Carol was clearly searching the room for him because the minute she spotted Stevie, she veered away from the path that had been cleared in the middle of the room for the swimmers and darted over to him.

She hugged him and, before he could congratulate her, said, "Where are Bobby and Tamara?"

"Long story," Stevie said. "I'll tell you when you're done . . . if I'm allowed to talk to you."

She gave him a look, but Trevor James was calling her name. "Ms. Anderson. We need you up here," he said.

"Walk with me on the way out," she said, and headed up the aisle to join Magnuson on the podium.

Most of the questions were for Susan Carol: How surprised was she by the time; did she think she could catch Magnuson those last few meters; how surprised was she by her improvement in the last twelve months? When someone finally asked Magnuson a question, it was about Susan Carol.

"How amazed are you by the way she has come out of nowhere to be such a threat in the upcoming Olympics?"

Magnuson looked frustrated. "Look, she's a terrific swimmer," she said. "But teenage phenoms are nothing new in our sport. Almost every year someone new comes along, especially among the women.

"She put up a really good time for this early in the season, but we're all going to have to go a lot faster than that to win anything in London. And if I hadn't been swimming through the meet, I wouldn't have died the way I did."

Stevie knew that "swimming through" the meet meant she hadn't cut back on her training to be less tired for the real races. He also knew Susan Carol had done the same thing. He looked at her to see if she would make that point. She didn't.

Someone who had apparently not picked up on Magnuson's simmering frustration asked a follow-up. "Don't you think this is kind of special, though? Especially swimming like this practically in her hometown . . ."

Magnuson looked at Susan Carol and said, "Didn't you tell me you live, like, three hours away from here?"

Susan Carol nodded.

"Hardly her hometown," Magnuson said. "And trust

me, there won't be a hometown crowd when we get to Omaha and, I hope for both of us, to London. Look, she's a damn good swimmer and, from the little time I've spent around her, she seems like a real nice person. But let's be honest here: What makes her special as opposed to other promising young swimmers is the way she looks. That's why she's got all these agents and sponsors and, frankly, you-all, trailing in her wake."

Stevie was studying Susan Carol as Magnuson talked. He thought he saw an eyebrow twitch, but other than that she seemed composed. After a moment of silence, a reporter asked Susan Carol if she had any response to what Magnuson had just said. Susan Carol smiled. It wasn't The Smile, but Stevie suspected it was the best she could do.

"Well," she said, "I think Christine is a great swimmer who has earned my respect by her consistently strong races. I hope to be around long enough to earn hers, and yours, with my swimming as well."

After that there were a couple more mundane questions before James said the fifteen minutes were up. When the swimmers made their way off the podium, there was a security guard leading them and one following as they walked up the aisle. Susan Carol waved Stevie over as they got close to the door, but when he walked in her direction, one of the security people put a hand out.

"Sorry, no media," he said.

"It's okay, he's with me," Susan Carol said.

The security guy looked confused but held firm. Stevie

checked around for Mike Unger, but he had disappeared, no doubt to round up Phelps after his race. There was a lot of noise coming from the pool deck, so he figured Phelps was in the water.

Magnuson jumped in. "Hey, fellas, cool it," she said. "This is her boyfriend—right, Susan Carol? The other kid reporter you told me about? It's fine for him to walk with us."

"No, it's not," said a voice from behind them.

It was—of course—Trevor James.

"Rules are rules. He's in here on a media badge, he abides by the same rules as anyone else."

Now Susan Carol looked frustrated. "Don't you make these rules to protect the athletes? So we aren't harassed? This is my boyfriend. I promise you, he's not harassing me."

"We make these rules for the safety and security of everyone. There are no exceptions, even for swimmers' boyfriends," said James.

"For goodness' sake, this is a swim meet, not the White House," Susan Carol responded.

"What would you know about the White House?" James said in a sneering tone.

"I've been there!" Susan Carol said, clearly trying to remain calm—though the "I've" came out as "Aahve." "I interviewed the president. So did he"—she pointed at Stevie—"and we were treated a lot more politely there than here!"

"I really like this kid," Magnuson said. She turned to Trevor James. "You want to pick a fight right here with your next glamour girl? Or you want to walk away and cut your losses?"

Stevie decided he really liked Christine Magnuson.

James seemed torn but said, "Fine. We'll discuss this further in the morning."

He stormed off, forgetting, it seemed, that he needed to keep the rest of the media in line. The world's best swimmer would be arriving in a few minutes.

When they got to the end of the hallway near the locker rooms, Kelleher was standing there with a tall, middle-aged man who was also wearing the USA Swimming uniform.

"Susan Carol, I'm sure you've met Chuck Wielgus," Kelleher said. "Stevie, Chuck is the executive director of USA Swimming."

"Then he needs to do something about Trevor James," Stevie said, still angry.

Wielgus frowned. "Was there more trouble after Bobby left to come find me?"

"Oh yes," Susan Carol said. "It was outrageous."

Stevie loved both the fact that she said "outrageous" and the *way* she said "outrageous."

"I'm truly sorry," Wielgus said. "Trevor's new at all this. Mike always handles the media, but I guess he needed some help because of the throngs around Michael Phelps. I told Bobby I would find out what happened as soon as we wrap things up tonight."

"How did Michael's race go?" Susan Carol asked.

"He won pretty easily," Wielgus said. "Slow time: 1:56

plus, but he looked pretty smooth and easy." He smiled. "It was *not* as impressive as what you did."

Susan Carol gave him The Smile. "I got a little bit lucky," she said. "I'm not sure Christine knew I was closing in on her. She'll be watching for me next time."

Wielgus laughed. "Still, 57.88 is 57.88, and your coach told me you didn't taper at all.

"Look, my apologies for all the confusion tonight. I'll take care of it. The back door and the locker room hallway are open again, and everyone will get all the time they need with the swimmers after their swims tomorrow and Sunday."

"That's great," Stevie said. "And I think you might want to talk to Mr. James about his attitude toward the media."

Wielgus nodded. "Actually, Steve, I think I need to talk to him about a lot of things."

Susan Carol headed to the locker room to shower while Stevie went to the media room to write. Bobby walked with him on his way back to the interview room to listen to Phelps. Stevie was going to write about the Anderson-Magnuson race. Kelleher planned to write about Phelps, and Tamara was working on a Phelps-Lochte rivalry column.

Stevie filled Bobby in on what Magnuson had said in the interview room. "Do I need to include that?" he asked Kelleher.

Kelleher laughed. "What, do you think not writing it will keep it a secret?"

"No. I know it's kind of a juicy story, but I don't want to be one more writer talking about Susan Carol's looks rather than her swimming."

Seeing the look on Stevie's face, Kelleher put a hand on his shoulder. "Look, I know how you feel about Susan Carol. But when you're writing about her, you have to think like a reporter, not like a boyfriend."

"How do I do that?"

"Pretend you're writing the same story, only it's about Phelps instead of Susan Carol," he said. "Would you include the exchange then?"

Stevie tried, but failed, to imagine someone saying reporters only liked Phelps because he was so attractive.

"We'll talk more about it later," Kelleher said. He pointed down the hall. "Meantime, here comes the entourage. I have to get in there."

Stevie saw Phelps and company coming down the hallway. The crowd was so big he stood back against the wall to make room, but Phelps stopped when he got to him.

"Hey, I know you," Phelps said. "I remember seeing you do that show—what was it called, *Kid Sports*?—with Susan Carol Anderson a couple of years ago. You were good."

"Um, thanks," Stevie said, trying to refocus his brain. "I'm Steve Thomas."

"Michael Phelps," he said, offering his hand.

"Yeah, I know," Stevie said, then wished he could snatch the words back.

Phelps was smiling, clearly unbothered by Stevie's lack of imagination.

"Susan Carol had some swim," Phelps said. "I was watching it in the locker room."

"Yeah, it was amazing," Stevie said. "I don't think *she* even knew she could go that fast."

Phelps nodded. "I remember that feeling—I'd look up at the clock after a race, see my time, and think it must have been someone else who had gone that fast." He sighed just a little. "Nowadays it might very well be someone else."

Stevie was amazed by how relaxed Phelps seemed to be. He could feel the posse getting antsy. One of the guys in a suit was tapping Phelps on the shoulder to indicate he needed to get going.

"I think you're doing just fine," Stevie said as Phelps held out his hand again to let the nervous people around him know he understood he needed to get going.

"I guess," Phelps said. "But I'm not the one dating America's newest sweetheart. That must be a great feeling."

Phelps gave him a friendly wave and moved down the hall, his various minions following as if attached by some magnetic force.

Phelps was clearly a good guy, even after all the fame and money that had come his way. But he was wrong about one thing: Dating America's newest sweetheart was *not* a good feeling at all. In fact, it made Stevie feel a little bit sick to his stomach.

He walked into the media room. It was time to write. Or at least *try* to write.

9: *USA Today*

Susan Carol was relieved when the meet finally ended. After all the hoopla and hassles of the first day, the weekend felt like a cakewalk.

Her only swim on Saturday was in the heats of the 200 butterfly. Ed Brennan told her to swim it as if it was the first one in a set of five: smooth and steady. She did as instructed and qualified second—behind Becky Ausmus. None of the big guns from around the country or the world had entered the 200 fly. Ed had even talked about having Susan Carol skip it too on the grounds that a swimmer only had so many good 200-fly swims in them.

Susan Carol wanted to swim—she still thought of it as her best event. "Phelps is swimming it," she argued.

"I'll tell you what," Ed said. "When you win fourteen Olympic gold medals, you can swim anything you want to and not listen to me. The Olympic Trials are what matter. I think you should rest."

She had finally talked him into it by making the point that it would be good for her to get the feel of swimming it in a fifty-meter pool again at least once before the trials.

So, after following Ed's instructions to the letter on Saturday afternoon and having a very nice dinner alone with Stevie at a great steak place called Del Frisco's, she climbed on the blocks Sunday morning hearing Ed's final words of encouragement.

"If you break 2:10, I'll kill you."

Susan Carol had gone 2:03.44 in Shanghai, but that was tapered and swimming the race of her life. What's more, she knew the only swimmer in the pool who could go any-where close to 2:10 was Becky Ausmus. She knew what Ed was thinking: Don't put too much into a swim you can win easily and, ultimately, means nothing. Standing on the block, she thought maybe she should negative-split.

Or at least try to.

To negative-split meant to swim the second half of the race—in this case the second 100—faster than you swim the first half of the race. It was a tactic used most often by distance swimmers, who would patiently build their speed as the race wore on. It was unheard of in the 200 fly because even if you held back the first 100, you were going to be tired in the second 100. But the best way to not break 2:10, Susan Carol thought, was to come as close to negative-splitting as she possibly could.

When the horn went, Susan Carol glided into the pool and almost went into a daze during the first 100. When she hit the wall, she could see that she had a body length on Ausmus, surprising since she knew she hadn't gone out fast at all and Becky almost always did—even in the 200.

On the third length, she began to pick up speed and she could hear the crowd getting into it. Coming off the third wall, she could see that Ausmus had dropped back and no one was close to her. The last length felt like a victory lap. She barely felt any pain in her arms—no doubt Ed's insistence on doing that brutal 5 × 200 fly series four days a week had something to do with that—and so, almost for yuks, she picked up her kick the last fifteen meters.

She glided into the wall and heard the cheers. She turned to see Ausmus just getting to the flags. Before she could look at the clock, she heard Ed's voice: "I warned you," he said. "I'm gonna kill you."

Confused, she looked at the clock and started to laugh. She'd gone 2:06.22.

"Ed, I swear I took it out as slowly as I could," she said. "I was trying to negative-split."

"You *did* negative-split, you nutcase," Ed said, using a term he only used when he was happy with her. "You were out in 1:03.5 and back in 1:02.7. You're insane!"

Ausmus finished second in 2:12.79. No one else in the pool was close to 2:15.

After she had gone through what had now become the ritual post-swim interviews, Susan Carol barely got to say goodbye to Stevie, Tamara, and Bobby before she had to hit the road—she had school in the morning.

She had grown accustomed to the extra attention she had gotten in school after Shanghai. In fact, that hadn't been nearly as difficult an adjustment as a couple of years earlier, when she and Stevie had co-hosted a TV show for a few months and she actually had kids stopping her in the hallway to ask for autographs. Now that sort of thing felt almost like old hat to her.

But she wasn't prepared when she got to school on Monday and several of her friends, without saying a word about her swims over the weekend, started going on about "the USA Today story." She had no idea what they were talking about.

She wasn't sure she *wanted* to know, given their comments, but she sneaked down to Ed Brennan's office during second period—when she was supposed to be in study hall. When she walked in, she knew instantly he had read the story. "Those agents of yours have to be reined in," he said, clearly upset. "And your father is going to have to be the one to do it."

She could see USA Today on his desk.

"I haven't seen it yet," she said. "Is it that bad?"

"You be the judge."

He handed her the newspaper, and she sat down on the couch next to his desk to look. When she unfolded the sports section, she gasped. In the middle of the page, running almost from the top to the bottom, was a photo of her, clearly taken shortly after she had gotten out of the pool after winning the 100 fly. She had taken off her cap and was shaking out her hair and beaming—Stevie called it The Smile.

The headline read TEEN WONDER GIRL BRINGS NEW "HEAT" TO AMERICAN SWIMMING.

"Oh, God," she said under her breath.

The story confirmed her worst fears. It had almost nothing to do with her win over Magnuson or her easy win in the 200 fly. It was all about the "marketing frenzy surrounding the long-legged teenager with the incandescent smile who has people talking as much about how she looks in her bathing suit as about how fast she swims in it."

"Jesus," she said, reading that sentence, then looked around instinctively because if her mother had been in the room, she would have barked her name in disapproval.

The story was full of quotes from J.P. and Bill on all the companies who wanted her to represent their products. There were quotes from various sponsor-reps on why her looks were every bit as important as her ability.

One quote from J.P. really made her cringe.

"Look, this is a fifteen-year-old girl. She's a minister's daughter. The girl next door, the girl every boy in the school dreams about going out with. So we're not marketing Britney Spears here. But Amanda Beard has made a lot of money selling sex appeal. There's nothing wrong with that."

Oh yes, there is, Susan Carol thought. Amanda Beard had posed in the *Sports Illustrated* swimsuit issue and in

Playboy. She had also been in her mid-twenties and had made a conscious decision that her future was at least as much in modeling as in swimming. Susan Carol had no desire to be a model—now or ever. And she and her father had made that very clear to the people at Lightning Fast. They agreed that she would be seen as an athlete and only an athlete.

She finished the story and looked at Ed.

"Do you think my father has seen this yet?" she said.

"I would think so, unless he moved to Siberia this morning."

"Should I call him or wait until I get home?"

"Wait," he said. "You should have this conversation face to face."

She stared at the photo again. Then she thought of Stevie reading the story and didn't know whether to laugh or cry. He would absolutely want to kill J.P. and Bill and anyone who had ever worked for Lightning Fast. She kind of liked that idea.

Stevie was standing at his locker putting books into his backpack when he first heard about the story.

"Wow, Thomas, your girlfriend really *is* hot," Andy Hague said as he pulled open his locker a few feet away from Stevie's.

This was nothing new. Stevie was often asked if he was *really* going out with Susan Carol Anderson or if that was just big talk on his part. Actually, he didn't talk about it that much. Others did.

"You saw her swim yesterday?" Stevie said, knowing the taped highlights of the meet had been on NBC while he was flying home from Charlotte.

"Nah, I don't watch swimming," Hague said. "I saw *USA Today*. Whoa! Good luck hanging on to her."

He banged his locker shut and walked off, leaving Stevie desperate to find a copy of *USA Today*. There was a 7-Eleven two blocks from school. He wondered if he had time to run there to get the paper before first period started. Then he heard the bell signaling that first period was starting in three minutes. He would have to wait until lunch.

The morning crawled along, not helped by several other guys making comments similar to Hague's. Lonnie Levine, the captain of the basketball team Stevie had once dreamed of playing for, poked him in the chest walking out of Spanish. "You better not ever bring her around here. She'll drop you for Buzz in a heartbeat," he said, talking about himself in the third person.

Levine's nickname was Buzz for reasons Stevie didn't know and didn't really care to know.

When lunch finally came, Stevie ignored his usual midday hunger pangs and sprinted the two blocks to 7-Eleven. There was one copy of *USA Today* left. He forked over a dollar for the paper—which seemed like a lot since he only wanted to read one story—walked outside, opened to the sports section, and almost choked at the headline and the photo. He got angrier and angrier as he read all the quotes from the agents about how they planned to market Susan Carol as America's newest sweetheart/sex symbol.

He was just reading the last quote from the soon-to-be-dead-if-he-came-anywhere-near-Stevie J. P. Scott when his cell phone buzzed. It was unusual for someone to call him during school, so he pulled the phone out of his pocket. It was Bobby Kelleher.

"I assume you've seen USA Today by now" was Kelleher's opening gambit.

"I'm just finishing the story," he said. He read J.P.'s last quote aloud just to see if it sounded as slimy as he thought it did: "She wins gold in London and she'll make people forget Michael Phelps in the advertising world. I mean, look at her. Who wouldn't buy anything she was selling?"

When Stevie finished, Kelleher was laughing. "There's steam coming through the phone," he said. "If it makes you feel any better, Tamara says she prefers Phelps."

Stevie recovered his sense of humor for a minute. "Well, that should at least make you feel good," he said.

"Yeah, my wife is going to run off with Michael Phelps. Makes me feel great. Listen, I talked to Matt Rennie and we agree you should write about this."

"Write what about this?" Stevie said, horrified at the thought.

"A first-person piece about how tough it is to watch your friend—you don't have to say 'girlfriend,' but you can if you want to—become a celebrity. How it's not all wonderful and how it can bring out the worst in those around her."

"Can I write that I want J. P. Scott dead?" Stevie asked.

"Sure. The lawyers may cut it, but go ahead and write it."

Stevie felt better just imagining it. Writing about something always seemed to make him feel better.

"I'll write it when I get home from school," he said.

"Do your homework first. I don't want your mom mad at me."

"Deal," Stevie said.

He shut the phone. He knew he couldn't kill J. P. Scott, but he might be able to shame him a little. It would have to do.

10: SETTING BOUNDARIES

Stevie and Susan Carol talked for quite a while that evening. He wanted to be sure she was okay with the idea of his writing about the USA Today article. And she wanted to prepare herself for a serious talk with her dad.

In her family a "come to Jesus" meeting had special meaning. This would be one of those. And it would not be easy. She had always been her daddy's girl. Because of their shared love of sports, they had a special bond that was completely different from her relationship with her mother.

She knew Stevie's dad always backed him up when he wanted to miss school to cover a big-time sports event. Stevie had told her it was a "father-and-son thing." He was wrong. It was more a "jock-and-jock" thing. In her family, she was the jock, not her brothers.

But for the first time she wasn't sure what her father would say. And that was as upsetting as the problem itself.

She went into her father's study and found him at the computer. "Just answering a few emails," he said when she walked in. "Something up?"

She sat down in the chair across from his desk and nodded. "Have you read the *USA Today* story yet?" she asked.

"Read it at work."

"What did you think of it?"

"Well, it was very complimentary and—"

"Dad, stop. You know what that story was saying about me. You read the quotes from J.P. and Bill."

"They're doing a job, sweetie."

"Is their job to make me into some kind of fifteen-year-old sex symbol?"

Now—finally—Susan Carol saw concern on her father's face. "Do you think I would ever allow something like that to happen?"

"Daddy, it's happening already! Look at the picture! Look at the headline!"

"Susan Carol, calm down. You're a great swimmer *and* a pretty girl, and right now both of those things are assets. I've talked to J.P. and Bill about it, and I trust them to know where to draw the line."

Susan Carol took a deep breath and tried to be calm as she said, "No, *I* need to be able to draw the line. I'm trying to tell you that I'm uncomfortable with this *now*. J.P. is comparing me to Amanda Beard! She posed in *Playboy*!"

"She was something like twenty-five years old when she did that."

"So if I pose in *Playboy* when I'm twenty-five, you'll be okay with that?"

"No, I won't. You know that."

"Dad, I don't know what I know anymore. How can you be okay with this? If I'd put that picture on my Facebook page a few months ago, you'd have gone through the roof. So why it is okay now?"

"Things have changed for you, honey. You're more in the public eye now."

"Well, I don't want to be *that* much in the public eye. Or talked about *that* way. And I don't want things to have changed so much that when I go to my father and tell him I have a problem, I can't be sure he'll be on my side." Susan Carol was trying really hard not to cry, and seeing her struggle cracked her father's resolve.

"Hey, hey, honey," he said, getting up and coming around his desk to give her a hug. "I am always behind you. Always."

"Then please, call J.P. and tell him not to talk about me that way. Not to pitch me that way."

"Okay, I'll talk to him. I'll be sure he knows how we both feel about this." He kissed the top of her head. "Now go get some sleep. There are bound to be more stressful days to come, and everything looks better after a good night's rest."

He was right about the first part of that, at least.

* * *

Stevie got an email from Susan Carol that night with the subject line *Better*. But when he got home from school the next day, there was another titled *Worse!*

Even though he was only looking at words on a computer screen, he could feel Susan Carol's agitation as he read: *So my father talked to J.P., and he swore up and down that his quotes were taken out of context and that he hadn't seen the photo or the headline that would run with them. But after he apologized for that, he convinced my dad this was all a good thing. Because J.P.'s been flooded with calls about me. And the whole point right now is to get attention. Not for my great swimming ability, apparently, but for being "marketable." According to him, the article was just what we needed. And not to worry because we can decide what offers to take or not take. And somehow my dad believes him! He's totally missing the point!*

There was more, but that was the crux of it. Stevie wasn't even sure what to say in response. He agreed with her, but somehow saying "Yes, you're right, your dad *has* gone over to the dark side" didn't sound all that comforting. So he tried a middle route:

Maybe someone your dad trusts and knows has your best interests in mind could talk to him? Not Bobby because your dad will just say "He hates agents." But he might listen to Tamara. He knows she's been a good mentor for you in journalism. And she's experienced something like this herself.

Remember the stories she told us about TV people wanting her to do on-air stuff but not do any real reporting? What was it that one producer told her? "Just smile so everyone can see your dimples and you'll be a star."

Susan Carol's response was short and to the point: *I'm calling Tamara today.*

The following evening, Stevie got a call from Tamara's husband.

"So I hear it was your idea for Tamara to intervene with Susan Carol's father," Kelleher said.

"What do you think?" Stevie asked.

"I think it's a great idea. Reverend Anderson likes her. And I think she might be able to explain why Susan Carol feels like she's being exploited—in a nice way, of course."

"So she'll do it?"

"Yup. They're setting up a lunch in Omaha on the twenty-fourth."

"The twenty-fourth? Isn't that the day before the Olympic Trials start?"

"It is. Susan Carol has to swim the 100 fly twice the next day—heats and semis."

"Is it a good idea to have a meeting that might upset her so close to her first swim?"

"We talked about Tamara flying down to Goldsboro earlier, but we thought that would only make her father feel ambushed. This is the best option: Get it out in the open before Susan Carol has to swim and hope that he listens."

"What if he doesn't? What if he just acts like there isn't a problem the way he did with Susan Carol?"

"Well, we'll see. Tamara's relationship with him is a lot

different than Susan Carol's. She's an adult, and he's not an authority figure in her life. I just hope we can rein him in now before things get worse. The pressure only builds from here."

"This just seems so crazy. I mean, Reverend Anderson is a good guy. C'mon, he's a minister."

"I know he's a good guy," Bobby said. "He's a very good guy. But I've seen good guys led astray by agents before. And being a minister doesn't mean you can't have stars in your eyes. Or dollar signs. I don't blame Reverend Anderson for hoping that Susan Carol can make the family a lot of money by swimming well. But I think he's lost sight of which part of that is most important."

"To Susan Carol, anyway."

"Exactly."

To get through the next few weeks, Susan Carol literally tried to keep her head underwater. All she wanted to do was get to the pool in the morning, get her final exams over with, and go back to the pool in the afternoon.

Only it wasn't quite that simple. She had even more obligations now. She had to go to New York twice. Once for a Speedo "shoot," as J.P. called it. Who knew having your picture taken was so exhausting? And then the week before she left for Omaha, she appeared on the *Today* show again, this time along with Michael Phelps, Ryan Lochte, and Natalie Coughlin. The other three were Olympic veterans and gold medalists. She was introduced by Ann Curry as "the newest star on America's swimming horizon."

They did their bit outside so Curry and Matt Lauer could urge the crowd to chant "USA, USA" when the swimmers were introduced.

"Welcome to the pep rally," Lochte said over the din as they walked onto the outdoor set, all of them waving to the crowd.

"More like a promo for NBC and the Olympic Trials," said Phelps, who followed them out—biggest star last so that the teenage girls could shriek when they spotted him.

After talking to the more experienced swimmers, Ann Curry turned to Susan Carol. "Now, Susan Carol, these three have been through an Olympic Trial before," Curry said. "What are you expecting when you get to Omaha?"

"A lot of people with midwestern accents," she said, drawing a laugh from everyone. "Seriously, I don't know what to expect," she continued. "I'll just be trying to keep calm and feel my way through the week."

"But you were in the World Championships last year," Lauer said. "You handled that very well."

"Thank you," Susan Carol said. "I was really happy with the way I swam. But that was different. There wasn't one race, make or break, to qualify for the World Championships. I got in by having one of the two fastest times during that *year*. For the Olympic Trials, it doesn't matter what you've done in the past or what your best time has been. It only matters what you do on the night of the final. If you don't finish in the top two, you can be, well, Michael Phelps, and you still aren't going to the Olympics."

"She's right," Phelps put in. "I think anyone who has

been through it will tell you there's more pressure at the trials than at the Olympics. At least there, you're already an Olympian. You've made the team, you're wearing USA on your suit. You've marched in the opening ceremony. With all the great swimmers we have in this country, there's no swim meet in the world that's more pressurized than the trials. Really great swimmers won't make the team."

"Thanks for making me feel less nervous," Susan Carol said, drawing another laugh from everyone.

From there, Matt Lauer launched into a promo of NBC's coverage of the trials using Phelps's line as his kicker. "The most pressurized swim meet in the world and it starts next Monday night in prime time on NBC."

When Curry threw to commercial, she dropped her microphone and headed for Susan Carol.

"You, young lady, are a *natural*," she said. "If you weren't fifteen years old, I'd be worried about you taking my job."

"Um, Ann, I've been meaning to talk to you about that," Lauer said.

For a split second Curry looked terrified, then she laughed at the joke. The swimmers were escorted back inside 30 Rock. Someone was offering them breakfast, but all the various handlers—including Susan Carol's, who had appeared magically the minute they were off the air—were insisting that their swimmer had to leave for another appearance.

Ryan Lochte, who was about as cool as anyone Susan Carol had ever met, gave her a quick goodbye hug and said,

"You've got my vote to co-host this show. See you in Omaha."

"I don't want to co-host the show," Susan Carol said, even though she knew he was joking. "I want to write."

"Write all you want," Coughlin said, also giving her a hug, "then deliver it on camera. If you're this calm on TV, you'll do fine with the pressure at the trials."

"Susan Carol, we've gotta get going," a voice said behind her. It was Susie McArthur, Lightning Fast's PR person. They were heading across town to tape an interview with National Public Radio. The angle was sportswriter turned athlete. "The car is parked on 50th Street across the plaza."

The whole crew was there: J.P. and Bill Arnold too.

As they piled into the backseat of the limo, J.P. turned to Susie as if Susan Carol was invisible. "After NPR we've got a break," he said. "I want you to take her and buy some heels. The next three interviews are on TV."

"Hello," Susan Carol said. "I'm right here; you can talk to me directly. And I don't wear heels. I'm six feet tall."

"Honey, he's right," Susie said. "We need to show off those legs of yours, and heels will be better with your outfit."

"I'm not a model," Susan Carol said. "I'm a swimmer. They're not interviewing me because they want to see my legs."

"Actually, they are," J.P. said. "Do you think USA Swimming chose you and Coughlin to do *Today* because of your flip turns?"

"I don't do flip turns, J.P. I'm a butterflyer."

"You get my point."

"Did they choose Phelps and Lochte because of *their* looks?"

"To some degree, yes. The fact that they're the two biggest stars on the men's side didn't hurt.

"Look, Susan Carol, I know you aren't liking the beauty-pageant aspects of this, but this is reality. This is how it works. And you're going to have to work with us if we're going to do the best for you. So I'd appreciate a little less attitude and a little more cooperation. We made a deal with your dad: At the meets, your coach has last say. When it comes to marketing, your agent has last say."

Susan Carol stared out the window at the New York traffic and wished she was anywhere but here. "Can we make them low heels? I can't walk in high heels and I don't want to twist an ankle before the trials."

They would be in Omaha in four days.

11: LOST IN OMAHA

Looking out the plane's window while they taxied into the gate in Omaha, Stevie could see the heat coming off the tarmac, but it didn't hit him just how hot it was until they were actually outside—then the Nebraska heat smacked him in the face.

"Welcome to summer in the Midwest," Bobby Kelleher said with a shake of his head.

"Guess I won't be needing that sweater I packed," Tamara Mearns said wryly.

Stevie had taken the train from Philadelphia to Washington so he could fly to Omaha with Kelleher and Mearns. They had landed shortly before noon.

"Think it's a hundred?" Stevie asked as a dispatcher pointed them to a cab.

"No, no," Tamara said. "More like a cool ninety-nine."

Passing a billboard en route into town, Stevie noticed

that it showed the time and the temperature. It flashed 34°C and then 98°F.

"You missed by one," Stevie said, pointing out the billboard.

The two official media hotels were on the outskirts of town, but as usual, Kelleher had pulled some strings and scored them rooms in a Courtyard Marriott within walking distance of the CenturyLink Center, where the trials were being held.

"It's supposed to be a three-minute walk," Kelleher said. "In this heat, it might feel like an hour."

Once they had checked in, the plan was for Stevie and Bobby to pick up all of their credentials and for Tamara to meet Susan Carol and her dad at a place called Spaghetti Works for their lunch/intervention.

The hotel was teeming with people when they walked in. Omaha hosted one semi-major sporting event every year: the College World Series. But Michael Phelps had almost single-handedly turned the Olympic Trials into a major event. Stevie had done some research before his trip. It wasn't that long ago that the trials had been what Kelleher called a "friends and family" event.

In 2008, USA Swimming had decided to take a chance and go big for the trials, building a temporary pool in a basketball and hockey arena. The place seated just under 18,000 for basketball, but once they'd constructed a fifty-meter pool and warm-up facilities and deck space, the capacity was reduced to just under 15,000. Phelps had won six gold medals in the 2004 Olympics and was gunning to break Mark Spitz's all-time record of seven golds in the 2008 Games, making the trials a huge draw. The arena had been nearly full to capacity for the evening sessions when all the finals were contested.

Phelps had gone on to win that record-setting eight gold medals in Beijing in remarkably dramatic fashion. Thanks to a miraculous anchor leg produced by thirty-two-year-old Jason Lezak in the 4 × 100 freestyle relay and an amazing finish in the 100-meter butterfly, Phelps had surpassed Spitz. Those Olympics had spawned a swimming boom in the United States, both in participation—half the parents in America were convinced their child was the next Phelps—and in viewership.

The London Olympics would be Phelps's last meet as a competitive swimmer. Which meant the trials here in Omaha was his second-to-last meet. Sellout crowds were expected every night. Stevie knew that the swimming facility in Shanghai had held 5,000. Swimming in front of 15,000 people would definitely be a new experience for Susan Carol.

In the meantime, Stevie's first impression of Omaha—besides the heat—was that the influx of people might be a bit overwhelming. There were two people at the front desk checking guests in, and the line stretched across the width of the lobby.

"I was really hoping to take a quick shower before lunch," Tamara said, looking at her watch.

Kelleher sighed. "I'd bet serious money that when we do get to the front desk, they're going to tell us the room isn't ready yet."

"Ah, the joys of travel," Tamara said. "Okay, I'm leaving my bags with you and heading for the restaurant to meet Susan Carol and her dad. Maybe I'll be early enough for an iced tea before the heat is on."

The thought of an iced tea almost made Stevie feel faint. Actually, the thought of eating made him feel faint because the two bags of airline pretzels he'd eaten since breakfast were not getting it done for him anymore.

All of which gave him an idea.

"Hey, Bobby, if we aren't going to get in the room anyway, why don't we leave our bags with the bellman and go get something to eat too?" he said. "Then we can pick up our credentials, and by the time we get back, the room might be ready."

"Great idea," Kelleher said. "But Courtyards don't have bellmen."

"Then who's that?" Stevie said, nodding toward the corner of the lobby, where someone was leaving his bag with a man in a hotel uniform.

"That's odd," Kelleher said. "Let's give it a shot."

"I'm going," Tamara said, giving her husband a quick kiss. "Wish me luck."

They wished her luck and Kelleher slung his wife's bags over his shoulder and they headed for the corner of the lobby.

"Is this the bell desk?" Kelleher said.

"It is this week," said the man, who wore a name tag that identified him as Lawrence Murchison, Lincoln, Nebraska. "We set it up because the hotel is so full. It isn't just that every room is booked; we've got rooms with three and four people in them."

"Yep, that's full," Kelleher said. "Can we leave our bags with you and come back later to check in?"

"Absolutely," said Lawrence of Lincoln.

Five minutes and a five-dollar tip later, they were heading for a restaurant called Spencer's. Lawrence said it had the best steaks in town and excellent hamburgers too. Stevie was in luck.

Tamara's luck was not so good. At the very moment that Stevie and Bobby were sitting down at Spencer's, Tamara was being seated at Spaghetti Works. She was also getting a text from Susan Carol. *Just leaving hotel,* it said. *Be there in 10.*

Susan Carol had trouble typing the words because she was striding through the lobby of the Omaha Hilton, where most of the top swimmers were staying. Not only was it practically on top of the CenturyLink Center, there was a sky bridge connecting the two buildings so swimmers didn't have to go outside into the heat at all. Susan Carol had used the sky bridge that morning when she had gone to work out.

It was a relief to be here and about to swim at last. She'd

thought things might get better when school let out—that she'd have one less thing to worry about. But she almost missed school. At least that was familiar.

She had felt good in the pool and would have liked to stay all day, but she was under orders from Ed Brennan not to do more than 2,000 meters. She had been in full taper mode for three weeks, and at this point all Ed wanted her to do was stretch out, get the feel of the water, and do some work off the blocks.

No two swimming pools had identical blocks even though they were all supposed to conform to standards established by FINA. They all felt just a little bit different and, especially in the 100 fly, being comfortable when you stepped up could be crucial.

She had taken a long shower at the pool, promised Ed for the hundredth time that she would stay out of the heat as much as possible, and headed back to the hotel. It was 11:30, and she and her father had plans to leave for their lunch date with Tamara at 12:45. She'd debated just pretending to run into Tamara at the restaurant but decided it was better to make a definite date. Her father had seemed surprised but happy enough when she said Tamara was working on a story for the *Post*'s Sunday magazine.

When she walked into the lobby, her dad was sitting in an armchair, waiting for her.

"I was just starting to worry," he said.

"I took a long shower," she said. "What's up?"

"We need to talk before we go to lunch."

"Okay. What about?"

"Not here," he said.

She followed him to the elevator and was surprised when they got on and he punched the button for the eighth floor.

"Dad, we're on twelve," she said.

"I know," he said. "We're going to make a quick stop to talk to J.P. and Susie."

"What about?" she said. "I thought they understood that I'm not doing anything here except swimming."

The elevator had now reached the eighth floor.

"That's exactly right," her dad said as he walked down the hall.

Confused, she followed him. Susie opened the door almost the second he knocked.

"Hey, come on in!" she said enthusiastically. "Susan Carol, how'd the workout go? You want something to drink?"

The room was considerably bigger than hers and looked out on the new baseball stadium where the College World Series was played. She wondered how they had wangled their way into the hotel. She'd been told that the Hilton was strictly reserved for swimmers who were high seeds in their events, their families and coaches, and also for some top USA Swimming officials and sponsors. As far as she could tell, agents weren't on that list.

"I'm fine," she said in response to the question. J.P. was sitting in a chair near the window.

"You look great," he said. "Ready for tomorrow?"

"I hope so," she said. "I was going to go lie down for a few minutes before lunch. . . ."

"That's what we wanted to talk about," J.P. said, indicating with his hand that she should sit in the chair opposite him. She thought about refusing but remembered Ed's constant reminder to stay off her feet as much as possible.

"You wanted to talk about lunch?"

"Honey, J.P. and Susie don't think we should be having lunch with a reporter the day before you start to swim," her dad said.

"It sets a bad precedent," Susie said, trying to sound soothing. "We're turning down one-on-ones unless they're really important—you know, NBC, ESPN, or maybe *Sports Illustrated*."

Susan Carol laughed. "You don't think the *Washington Post* is important enough to talk to me?"

"We don't think newspapers matter very much anymore," J.P. said. "But that's not really the point here. Your life is going to be very hectic from now until the end of the Olympics. You're going to have to make choices or, more specifically, we're going to have to make choices for you."

"What does that mean, exactly?" Susan Carol said.

J.P. looked at her dad. Clearly he wanted him to answer that question.

"Honey, it means that for a few weeks, you have to think of Tamara and Bobby and even Stevie as members of the media first and your friends second."

"You can't be running off to McDonald's with them the way you did in Charlotte," J.P. said.

"Or having lunch with one of them the day before the Olympic Trials start," Susie added.

"Well, that's just ridiculous," Susan Carol said.

She was angry, really angry.

"Susan Carol . . . ," her dad started.

She held up her hand. "I'm sorry, Dad. But this is going too far. I've done everything I've been asked to do until now. But I'm *not* going to just cut my friends out of my life. Stevie's been my rock through all of this. And now you want me to see less of him?"

"I appreciate your loyalty," her dad said. "I've explained to J.P. and Susie how close you guys are. But they do have a point: This is about fairness. Other reporters will see you with Stevie and Bobby and Tamara and think they're being given favorable treatment."

"Other reporters know they're my friends."

"We need to treat everyone the same," J.P. put in.

"Except for NBC, ESPN, and maybe *Sports Illustrated*," Susan Carol said.

She decided she was done talking to the Lightning Fast people. She turned to her father.

"I'm meeting my longtime friend and mentor Tamara for lunch as we planned. I'd really like you to come too, Dad. Please."

Her dad shook his head. "No, honey, I'm sorry. We're paying J.P. and Susie to tell us how best to handle all this and I think we need to listen to them. They're the pros here."

"Can you hear yourself? We're paying them to help manage my career, not to decide who I can be friends with or talk to."

There was so much more she wanted to say, but the need to get out of there was even stronger. She practically ran to the door.

By the time she reached the elevators, she was crying. How could this happen? Her dad was the best, most honest person she knew. But he seemed to have substituted the agents' judgments for his own. She barely recognized him.

When she got back to her room, it was almost one o'clock. She changed quickly and sent Tamara the text while striding out the door.

"Where's your dad?" Tamara asked as Susan Carol slid into the booth opposite her.

"Lost," Susan Carol answered. "He's completely lost."

12: THE TRIAL BEFORE THE TRIALS

Stevie and Bobby had finished eating and were walking to the arena to pick up their credentials when Bobby's cell phone began playing what Stevie recognized as the Army fight song.

"I thought you were unbiased when it came to Army and Navy," Stevie said as Bobby answered the phone.

"Can I help it if the Army song is better?" Bobby said, then, into the phone, "What's up?"

He listened for a minute and nodded. "Okay. Order some dessert and we'll be there in a few minutes."

He hung up, looking concerned.

"What is it?" Stevie asked.

"Let's go inside and I'll tell you while we're waiting for our credentials."

Actually, there was no waiting. With the first final

scheduled for the next night, most of the media had apparently not arrived yet.

"You're one of the first, actually," said the cheerful young woman whose name tag said Alexis Verdon. She had one of those flat midwestern accents that reminded Stevie of a tennis player he had written about named Evelyn Rubin. She didn't say "actually"; she said "aack-chew-uh-ly."

Bobby and Stevie showed their IDs, and she handed them credentials and booklets that said SCHEDULE and HEAT SHEETS. When Kelleher asked for Tamara's credential too, Alexis Verdon frowned.

"I think Mike Unger was going to leave a note that I was picking her stuff up," Kelleher said.

Alexis had been looking through the list of names in front of her. "You're right," she said. "There's a note right here."

She handed Bobby the credential for Tamara and asked him to sign in the space next to her name.

"Just in case you don't see her and she thinks she's supposed to pick it up here," she said.

"I'm pretty sure I'll see her," Kelleher said as he signed. "She's my wife."

"Oh!" Alexis said. "Funny, I never thought of sportswriters being married to one another."

"Well, someone has to marry us, I guess," Kelleher said, smiling.

"If this picture is accurate ("aack-curate"), it looks like you did just fine."

"He did better than fine," Stevie said.

"Well, I'll bet your girlfriend is very pretty too," Alexis Verdon said.

"You've got that right," Kelleher said. "His girlfriend is Susan Carol Anderson."

Alexis Verdon's eyes went wide. "Really?"

Stevie thought she looked a bit wobbly.

"Thanks," Kelleher said to her as they walked away.

"Did you have to do that?" Stevie hissed as the blast furnace hit them again walking out the door.

"It was worth it to see the look on her face."

"Yeah, *you* think it's funny people are shocked she'd date me, but somehow I don't."

"That's not—"

"Moving on. Will you please tell me what the call from Tamara was about?"

"Reverend Anderson wouldn't come to lunch. Susan Carol is really upset. She says her father is 'lost.'"

"Looks like we need another plan," Stevie said.

"Well, you're the boyfriend," Kelleher said. "Time for you to mount that white horse and ride to the rescue." He was grinning from ear to ear.

"Bobby," Stevie said. "I mean this with all due respect."

"Let me guess," Kelleher said.

"Yeah," Stevie said. "Shut up."

They were both grinning as they headed for the Spaghetti Factory.

There weren't any smiles once they got to the restaurant. Susan Carol was spooning some chocolate ice cream, and

Tamara was drinking iced tea. It looked to Stevie as if Susan Carol had been crying.

Kelleher sat next to his wife, and Stevie slid in next to Susan Carol. Kelleher ordered coffee and Stevie got a Coke.

"You don't want anything to drink?" Stevie asked.

Susan Carol shook her head. "I promised Ed no caffeine until the Olympics are over."

They sat in silence until the waitress came back with the drinks. Then Tamara took a deep breath and said, "Well, boys, to quote Tom Hanks, 'Houston, we've got a problem.'"

At Kelleher's urging, Susan Carol walked them through her morning. She had tears in her eyes again by the time she finished.

Kelleher sighed.

"Look, Susan Carol, I know why you feel the way you do. Let me try to cheer you up just a little: Your dad is not a pushy stage parent or a gold digger. And lots of athletes' parents are. He's a good man who has been swept off his feet by these people."

"That doesn't make this any easier for Susan Carol," Tamara said.

"I know," Bobby said. "But I think it's important to remember that you're right in saying your dad is a little bit lost. There are worse scenarios. And his condition is probably only temporary."

"But how do we fix it if he won't talk to anyone *but* those people?" Susan Carol asked.

"I've got half an idea," Stevie said.

They all looked at him, but got distracted by a commotion in the restaurant.

Pushing their way noisily between tables were three men. Stevie recognized the one leading the way—it was Trevor James, the USA Swimming guy who had been such a pain in Charlotte until Chuck Wielgus had reined him in. Stevie didn't know the other two men, but they were quite large and didn't look friendly.

James marched up to their table. Several customers who had been all but shoved aside as the trio made their way back to the booth were staring, trying to see what the commotion was about.

"Bobby Kelleher, I presume?" James said, almost in the tone of a TV cop about to make an arrest.

Kelleher took a long sip of his coffee before answering.

"Is there something we can do for you, Mr. James?"

"You can explain why I shouldn't strip you and your friends of your credentials for unauthorized contact with a participant in the trials."

"What?" Kelleher said. "What in the world are you babbling about?"

"I understand you picked up your credentials a little while ago," James said. "I would suggest you look on the back and read what it says about trying to interview athletes outside the official media areas of the arena."

"No one is interviewing me," Susan Carol said. "Do you see a notebook or a tape recorder anywhere? These are my friends."

"Not here, they aren't," James said. "They're here to cover the trials and you're here to swim. That makes them media and you an athlete."

"But not human beings, I guess," Stevie said.

James gave him a withering glare. "Make all the smart remarks you want, but we're going to take Ms. Anderson back to her hotel now." He nodded at the goons. "Mark and Ted are part of our security team. They'll make sure she gets there without being harassed any further."

Kelleher had taken his credential from his pocket and was actually reading the back of it, which surprised Stevie.

"I'm sorry, James, but you and Mike and Ike won't be taking Ms. Anderson anyplace. And if you aren't out of here in about fifteen seconds, I'm going to ask the management to remove you, and if they have to call the cops, that's fine too."

"I told you the rules, Kelleher—"

"You said I should read the back of my credential. Let me read it to you. 'There is to be no unauthorized contact between media and athletes outside the official media areas of the arena once the meet begins. Any violation of this policy may result in the loss of media privileges and access.'"

"What part of that do you not understand?" James said, sneering triumphantly.

"When does the meet begin? Did the schedule change? Or does it start at ten o'clock tomorrow morning?"

The look on James's face changed in an instant.

"See," Kelleher said, holding the credential up so James

could see it. "'Once the meet begins.' What part of that don't *you* understand? Now, are you going or am I having you thrown out?"

James's face was bright red.

"Your time is going to come, Kelleher, I promise," he said.

Kelleher laughed. "Yeah, you're really scary, James. Next time show up without the goons and we'll see how tough you are."

One of the goons seemed offended. "Hey, pal, I'm not a goon, I'm a security consultant," he said.

The manager had finally arrived to see what was going on.

"Is there a problem?" he asked.

"No problem," Kelleher said. "These gentlemen were just leaving."

The manager was about to say something when he saw Susan Carol.

"Susan Carol Anderson!" he gasped. "I didn't know you were in here. Is there anything at all I can do for you?"

"Yes," Susan Carol said, The Smile turned up to full wattage. "These men are bothering me. It would be great if they would leave."

The manager turned to James. "I will ask you to go nicely once. After that I call the cops."

James and the goons/security consultants headed for the door.

The manager turned back to the table. "I'm so sorry about this," he said. "Your lunch is on me."

"Oh, that's not necessary, but it's very sweet," Susan Carol said.

"No, I insist," the manager said. "But before you leave, would you mind if I had someone take a picture of us? I'll put it on our Wall of Fame."

"It would be my pleasure," Susan Carol said.

The manager all but bowed as he retreated.

"How do you think they found us?" Stevie asked.

"Easy," Susan Carol said. "James must be J.P.'s guy with USA Swimming. I kind of thought that back in Charlotte, now I'm sure. J.P. must have called him after I left."

"But did J.P. know where you were going?" asked Stevie.

"No . . . but my father did," Susan Carol said, slumping in her seat.

"So, Stevie," Kelleher said. "Were you saying something about an idea? We could use one."

"It's more a thought than an idea. . . . Remember in the World Series when Norbert Doyle had clearly lost his way?" he said, referring to a journeyman pitcher who had emerged as a sudden star during a World Series they had all covered. "He was a good guy—just like Reverend Anderson is a good guy. But an agent had him believing that was his one chance to really strike it rich, to take care of his kids for life. And that made him do bad things.

"What finally got through to him was seeing firsthand how sleazy his agent really was. Then he realized that the end really *didn't* justify the means, and he snapped out of it completely."

"I see the connection you're going for," Susan Carol said. "My dad needs to see firsthand that these aren't trustworthy people."

"Yes, but how?" Tamara said.

"Hey, I said it was only half an idea."

"With Norbert Doyle it was pretty much an accident that we exposed his agent. The guy thought he might be losing his gold mine and freaked out," said Susan Carol.

"So, maybe we need to freak these guys out," Stevie said.

"The only thing that would do that would be me not making the Olympic team."

"I don't think we want to go to that extreme," Tamara said.

"No," Bobby said. "Besides, if you don't make the team, then I think your agents will go away no matter what your dad wants."

"So true," Susan Carol said. "It might almost be worth it."

Stevie looked at her to see if she was even a little bit serious. She was exactly that—a little bit serious.

"Look, I want to make the team more than anything," she said. "I've worked so hard to get to this point. But I have to say: I should be more excited today than I've ever been in my life. And nervous. I'm neither. I'm just angry and hurt and, most of all, disappointed."

"Which is why you need to try to forget all of this for the next few days," Bobby said. "Your only job from now until you finish your 200 fly on Friday night is to swim and rest—nothing else."

"The agents aren't allowed to schedule anything for you until the end of the meet, right?" Stevie asked.

Susan Carol nodded.

"So, Bobby's right. You think about swimming and making the Olympic team. We'll think of a way to convince your father between now and London that J.P. and his people only care about the money."

"Which, if you think about it, makes sense," Tamara said. "Their job is to make you rich, not to protect you."

"Yeah," Susan Carol said. "It's my dad's job to protect me. Or at least I thought it was."

13: OMAHA TWO-STEP

The next forty-eight hours dragged by for Stevie.

Susan Carol swam heats in the morning and semifinals in the evening for the 100-meter butterfly, but both were routine.

There was no limit on the number of swimmers who could enter an event: If you made the cutoff time established by USA Swimming, you could enter the meet. That meant there were about 1,200 swimmers in the meet even though no more than fifty had any realistic chance of making the Olympic team.

Eager beaver that he was, Stevie was at the pool when it opened on Monday morning. Halfway through the first event—the men's 400 IM—he had figured out that there were no swimmers in the first six heats of any event who would even make it to the semifinals. When he pointed that out to Kelleher, who had arrived about an hour later, Kelleher shook his head.

"You can't be this cynical at fifteen," he said. "Do you know how *good* you have to be to make an Olympic Trials cut? You put the worst swimmers in this meet in just about any other swim meet and they're stars. If you paid some attention, you'd see there are good stories in the early heats."

"Like what?"

"Like Wally Dicks in the 100 breaststroke. He's forty-nine years old and he made the cutoff time in the 100 breaststroke. Do you know how amazing that is?"

"Amazing," Stevie said. "What place will he finish?"

Kelleher sighed. "I'm going to cut you some slack on that one because I know there's only one swimmer in the meet as far as you're concerned. But you need to decide— are you here because you still want to be a sportswriter or because you want to go out with Susan Carol?"

That stung. Stevie loved being a sportswriter. But he supposed Kelleher had a point. Normally he'd love a story like Wally Dicks, but right now it was hard for him to care about any swimmer in the meet not named Susan Carol Anderson.

"I'll admit I've got Susan Carol on my mind," he said after a long pause. "I'm worried about her. You know how she feels about her dad, so this has to be killing her. But I *do* still want to be a sportswriter."

"Good. Susan Carol is in heat seven of the 100 fly, which is up next. Wally's in heat three of the 100 breast, which won't be for a couple hours. Gives you plenty of time to watch Susan Carol and then talk to Wally after he swims."

"It sounds like you know him."

"I do. He swims on a Masters team with some friends of mine. He's a good guy. Talk to him and you'll see."

Stevie ended up having lunch with Wally Dicks, who finished forty-second among eighty-five swimmers entered in the 100 breaststroke. He was every bit as nice as Kelleher had said and had a good story to tell: He had stopped swimming for fifteen years after college and had started again because he needed something to distract him while he was going through a divorce. He had met his current wife at a swim meet, they had a beautiful little girl, and Wally was swimming faster than he had ever dreamed possible.

A perfect story to write on the first day of the meet.

Susan Carol had won her heat in the morning with ease and cruised in second in her semifinal that evening. Overall, she qualified fourth for the final the next night. Which put her in great position. But to make the team, she'd have to finish in the top two. . . .

Tuesday seemed to last forever. Stevie tried to focus on the meet, but there were no Wally Dicks stories to write and his assignment for the day was to write the lead on the women's 100-fly final anyway. Kelleher would write a column on either the 100 fly or on the men's 200-freestyle semifinals—which would be Ryan Lochte's second and Michael Phelps's first event of the week. The next night, in the final, they would go head to head.

Kelleher and Mearns were both working on other things that morning, and after watching what seemed like dozens of heats, Stevie couldn't take sitting in the stands any longer and decided to go for a walk. The heat had broken a little bit: It was still in the nineties, but the humidity wasn't quite as unbearable.

The deciding game of the College World Series was going to be played that night in the new stadium that was directly across the parking lot from the arena—which guaranteed absolute gridlock in the downtown area. Stevie decided to walk in the direction of the stadium, thinking he might be able to get a look inside.

He walked across the parking lot and began to circle the stadium to see if there was an open gate or if there were offices somewhere that might give him access to the ballpark. He wasn't planning to go very far because after ten minutes outside, he was already sweating pretty profusely.

As he rounded a corner, he thought he saw what he was looking for: ticket booths. They jutted out from the corner of the ballpark and, even if there was no one working, at least there'd be shade. Three men had clearly thought the same thing because they were standing in the shade talking. As Stevie approached, he could tell they were having an animated conversation.

He was about to veer away so as not to eavesdrop when the wind picked up the voice of the man who had his back to him and blew it in his direction. He almost gasped when he heard it because he recognized it immediately: Reverend Anderson. Instinctively, he slipped behind one of the ticket booths so he wouldn't be seen. But he could now make out the other two men. One was J. P. Scott. The other was Ed Brennan.

He took a deep breath and edged as far as he could in their direction without revealing himself. Whether it was the wind or their raised voices, he could hear pretty clearly.

"This is just the way it has to be, Ed. You're wrong. I haven't forgotten what you've done for Susan Carol and I know how much she respects you. I'm truly sorry you found out about this the way you did. I wanted the three of us to sit down when we were all back home next week."

"You think firing me in person after the trials would make it any better, Reverend? You think that would make it okay with Susan Carol?"

"Ed, be realistic," Scott chimed in. "Joe Berger has coached eight Olympians. You're a great high school coach, but this is the big time. Susan Carol needs the best."

For a moment Stevie thought the conversation had ended or that the wind had shifted because he heard nothing. Then he realized that Coach Brennan had turned away from J. P. Scott and was talking directly to Susan's dad.

"Look, Reverend, you know Susan Carol is already worried that, under this guy's influence, you're turning into another pushy, money-grabbing, teenage-jock dad. If you just let her swim and be herself, the money will come down the line."

"Excuse me?" Reverend Anderson said, clearly indignant. "My first concern is Susan Carol and you know that."

"Really?" Brennan said. "Then why would you make a decision like this with no input from her at all? Why would you go so far as to hire another coach without consulting her? Who's in charge here—you and your daughter, or this guy?"

Stevie was stunned. How could they fire Ed? Of course they were trying to fire *him* as Susan Carol's friend, so maybe it wasn't that stunning.

"Ed, look," Reverend Anderson said, reaching for Ed's shoulder. "You have done a *great* job getting her this far. We want you to be Susan Carol's friend and we really want you to support this decision—"

"Are you kidding me?" Ed said, shaking loose from Reverend Anderson. "Look, I've never tried to claim I was God's gift to swimming—unlike Joe Berger, by the way—but I know I'm the best coach for your daughter. I know her in ways that no new coach can match no matter how many Olympians he's trained.

"Why put her through this, especially now? Susan Carol's got enough on her plate without dealing with questions about why her coach got fired right after the Olympic Trials."

"That won't be a problem," Reverend Anderson said. "We'll just say Susan Carol needed higher-level coaching, which happens to be the truth. Susan Carol will see that it's necessary, I'm sure."

"NO, SHE WON'T!"

Whoops, Stevie realized the voice he had just heard shouting was his own. He had heard enough—too much.

He stepped out from behind the ticket booth. Reverend Anderson spun around while J. P. Scott and Ed Brennan squinted in his direction.

"Stevie!" Reverend Anderson said. "What are you doing here? Did you follow us?"

"Of course he followed us," J. P. Scott said. "Why else would he be here?"

"No, I did *not* follow you," Stevie shot back. "I got bored and walked over here to see the ballpark. But I did hear what you were talking about. And I can't believe you would do this to Susan Carol."

J. P. Scott stalked over to where he was standing and grabbed his arm. "How dare you? This has nothing to do with you."

"Let go of his arm, J.P.," Reverend Anderson said, coming up behind him.

"Reverend, let me handle this. . . ."

"Let go of his arm."

Scott gave Stevie a cold-as-ice look and let go.

"Stevie, J.P. is right about one thing," Reverend Anderson said. "I know you care about Susan Carol, but decisions like this aren't really any of your business. The grown-ups have to decide what's best for her."

"Like hell they do," Stevie yelled, then felt a little bit embarrassed for using the word *hell* in front of a minister. "All you grown-ups are only making her miserable when this should be the most exciting time of her life. If you'd spent any time listening to your daughter instead of these agents over the past few months, you'd know that."

Ed Brennan had walked up behind Reverend Anderson. "The kid's right."

Reverend Anderson's face was red, and Stevie was pretty sure it wasn't the heat. "Stevie, I'm asking you one last time: Don't make this any tougher for Susan Carol than it already is. There is nothing wrong with what J.P. and his people are doing. No one is lying or cheating or committing a crime. This talent she has can secure her future for a long time. If you had any athletic ability at all, your father would be doing the same thing I'm doing."

Stevie couldn't argue about his lack of athletic ability. But he didn't think for one second his father would be acting like this.

"My father would never fire my coach without talking to me about it," he said. "As if what I wanted didn't matter at all. If you do this, you're going to break Susan Carol's heart."

"She'll be fine," Reverend Anderson said. "I've talked to Joe Berger myself. He's a good man and a good coach. Ed, I'm truly sorry and I'm sorry Coach Berger said anything to you."

"I guess the fact that he couldn't wait to tell me shows what a good man he is," Ed said. "By the way, J.P., you don't happen to represent Joe, do you? He's been doing a lot of clinics lately. Plus, he's starting that swim school in Westchester."

J.P. said nothing, but he was also red in the face now.

Reverend Anderson sighed.

"Come on, J.P., it's hot out here," he said. "Let's get back inside. Ed, I'm genuinely sorry."

"No, Don, I really don't think you are," Ed said. "But I think you will be."

Reverend Anderson stared at him for a second, started to say something, then shook his head and walked away. Scott followed him.

Once they started back across the parking lot, Stevie looked at Ed Brennan. "What're you going to do?" he asked. "You have to be Susan Carol's coach."

"Don't panic," Ed said. "Clearly they weren't going to tell her anything until the trials were over, and I have no intention of saying anything either. Let's get her through this meet without any more drama if we can, okay?"

"How can you be sure they won't say something now that they know you know?"

"Because tonight is the biggest race of her life. If she doesn't make the team, all their plans go up in smoke."

"Or sink," Stevie said, thinking that was a more apt metaphor.

Ed Brennan smiled for a moment, then shook his head. "Well, we don't want our girl to sink either," he said. "Come on, I'll give you a ride back to the hotel."

Ed Brennan's instinct about Reverend Anderson and J. P. Scott keeping quiet proved to be correct. Neither of them said anything to Susan Carol about their plan to fire her coach.

Stevie told Bobby and Tamara what was going on when he met them for lunch. They seemed less shocked than Stevie had been.

"We've seen this happen before," Kelleher said. "I call it 'blinded by gold' syndrome. The agents wave so much money and glory in front of a parent's face, it's almost as if they can't see past it."

"But Reverend Anderson?" Stevie said. "Wouldn't you think with his experience working as the chaplain for the Panthers and what happened when his brother-in-law became a tennis agent, he'd be the last guy who could be blinded?"

"Yeah, I would," Kelleher said. "I guess this is proof of how powerful the syndrome can be."

Tamara nodded. "I'm sure he honestly believes he's doing what's best for Susan Carol and his family. This isn't Tiger Woods's dad turning his son into a human ATM machine. This is a father who sees a chance to make life much easier for himself and all his children in one fell swoop."

For the first time Stevie was glad that he couldn't see Susan Carol before her race that evening. He could fake it with texts, but he suspected she'd be able to see in his face that something was wrong. It was going to be a long afternoon.

They walked to the arena about an hour before the finals were scheduled to start, and the place was already jammed. With 15,000 fans packed in the stands and the fifty-meter pool shimmering on the arena floor, the CenturyLink

Center was quite a sight. Even Bobby and Tamara were impressed.

"Didn't they hold the trials in a parking lot a few years back?" Stevie said, remembering something he had read.

Kelleher nodded. "Yeah. The pool in Indy was the biggest swimming venue in the country and it seats under 5,000. So when they thought they could sell more seats than that, they put a temporary pool—like this one—in a parking lot in Long Beach and built temporary stands around it. That was '04, when Phelps was emerging as a star. But racing outside isn't ideal."

Susan Carol's 100-butterfly final was the first event of the night. Because the television window was exactly one hour—8 to 9 p.m. in the East—there was no fooling around with pre-race TV chatter. Stevie, Bobby, and Tamara made straight for their seats even though there was assigned seating in the media section. Mike Unger had told them there were 300 seats and close to 400 accredited media.

"If there's an empty seat, someone will grab it," he said. "Unless you want to wrestle with them for your seat, give yourself a few extra minutes."

Stevie could feel his stomach churning when they sat down. He knew how much this meant to Susan Carol. He remembered something she had said to him after her win in Shanghai: "It was just incredible to swim that well and to win. But when you're a swimmer, you don't grow up dreaming of the World Championships, you grow up dreaming of the Olympics. Now I really have a chance to get there."

This was it. This was her chance. But it wouldn't be

easy. There were two swimmers in the race who had gone under 57 seconds before—Christine Magnuson and Dana Vollmer. Four others—Susan Carol, Kathleen Hersey, Felicia Lee, and Elizabeth Wentworth—had been under 58.5, led by the 57.88 Susan Carol had gone in Charlotte. Wentworth, who was sixteen and came from Florida, had actually qualified first with a time of 58.04—her best time by more than a second.

Stevie figured these six swimmers of the eight in the race all had a shot at the two spots on the Olympic team. The field was that tight.

Stevie heard a roar go up and saw the swimmers emerging from the tunnel that led from the pre-race ready room into the arena. There was no waving at friends or family as they marched to the blocks. Each was trying to stay calm and focused.

Susan Carol had her head down, her long brown hair tied into a ponytail that he knew she would unknot and push up on her head when she put on her bathing cap. Off to the side, Stevie saw Ed Brennan standing with the other coaches, ever-present stopwatch in his right hand.

"Doesn't look like there's any doubt who Susan Carol's coach is right now," he said, pointing him out to Kelleher.

"That's good," Kelleher said. "But right now there's nothing he can do for Susan Carol. It's all up to her."

Stevie took a deep breath. The race would take less than a minute once the starter's horn went off. It would feel a lot longer than that.

14: LOSING?

The swimmers had a moment to get ready before they were introduced. This was not an uncomplicated process since it involved taking off sweats (top and bottom) and a T-shirt, footwear—flip-flops for some, sneakers for others—and, in some cases, baseball caps. All of that was placed in a basket that was scooped up by a volunteer to hold until after the race. Then came the race preparation: hair put under caps, goggles adjusted, suits pulled as tight as possible. Stevie often wondered why the swimmers couldn't walk out more ready to go, but it was all part of the ritual.

The swimmers were introduced from lane one to lane eight. The biggest roar, without doubt, was for Susan Carol, who was in lane six as the fourth qualifier. Magnuson, who had qualified second, would be next to her in lane five, and Hersey was on the other side in lane seven. Wentworth was in the middle, lane four, as the top qualifier. Vollmer was in lane three, and Lee in lane two. The swimmers in lanes one and eight—Penny Bates and A. J. Block—were long shots.

As loud as it was when the swimmers stepped onto the blocks, Susan Carol was convinced everyone in the building could hear her heart pounding. She reminded herself of what Ed had said shortly after warm-ups had ended: "Everyone in the pool will be just as nervous as you." But as she bent down in response to the starter's instruction to "take your mark," she was convinced Ed was wrong. No one could be as nervous as she was at that moment.

The start came so quickly that Susan Carol was almost startled by the sound. She felt herself flinch as she left the block and was convinced she had cost herself time even before she hit the water.

As she kicked her way to the surface, with her arms extended as far in front of her as possible, she told herself to forget the start and focus on her stroke. She knew she couldn't win the race in the first fifty meters, but she could certainly lose it. As she always did when the pressure was greatest, she tried to hear Ed's voice in her head.

Stay low, her Ed voice reminded her. In a pool this deep, with lanes that were nine feet wide, there was almost no wash from the other swimmers to worry about, so she visualized her chin barely clearing the water every time she came up to breathe. Instinctively, she counted her strokes. If she was pacing correctly, she should hit the wall on her twenty-first stroke. She would get a little extra air at the wall by getting there on an odd number since she breathed every second stroke.

As she reached the flags five meters from the end, she could tell she was going to hit the wall correctly; mentally she breathed a small sigh of relief. She dropped her shoulder going into the turn—which had once been illegal—and, as she lifted her head out of the water to make the turn, she could see that Magnuson was already into her push-off, meaning she was about a half second ahead of her.

Don't panic at the fifty.

There was Ed's voice again, reminding her she shouldn't concern herself with what the other swimmers were doing until the last ten meters. She had no idea what Magnuson's strategy was—maybe she was hoping to get out fast and make the others try to catch her too early. It didn't matter. Susan Carol had to focus on the way *she* felt and not be affected by what anyone else was doing with half the race left.

She pushed off hard, staying under the water for one comfortable beat before kicking her way up. She liked to breathe after the first stroke on the way back, just to steal some extra air after being underwater coming off the turn. A thought flashed through her mind: *In less than thirty seconds you'll know. . . .*

She flushed it quickly. Her stroke felt good halfway back, but she could sense that Magnuson was still ahead of her. If it was just Magnuson, that was okay. In the Olympic Trials, second place was just as good as first place. Third place, however, meant heartbreak.

Stay patient was Ed's next counsel as the flags started to come into view when she came up to breathe. She didn't want to pick up her kick too soon and find herself slowing at the finish. In a sprint like this, the race was usually won or lost in the last five meters. She could see that Hersey, on her left, wasn't close. There was no sign of the forward splash a butterflyer makes when taking a stroke, which meant Susan Carol had to be at least a half body length ahead of her.

The flags loomed directly in front of her. For the first time since she had left the blocks, she was aware of the noise. She could feel her body tingling with exhaustion from the effort and adrenaline from the moment. There was no more time to think. She took one more breath, which she knew would get her to the flags, and then she put her head down. She *had* to get to the wall in three strokes or she would almost certainly get touched out at the finish.

One—two—three . . . She kicked as hard as she possibly could and stretched her arms to the wall and felt her hands reach the touch pad. At the very least she knew she hadn't been touched out because of a poor finish. She pulled her head out of the water, trying desperately to see the scoreboard. There was shrieking all around her, and she saw that Magnuson had buried her head in the gutter, clearly devastated.

Susan Carol's heart sank. She yanked off her goggles so she could see the board. At the same moment that she was able to read it, she heard Ed's voice over the din: "You're an Olympian, Susan Carol. You're an Olympian!"

The board confirmed it: Elizabeth Wentworth, the other teenage sensation, had won in 56.81—her best time by more than a second. Susan Carol had finished second in 56.99. She had barely beaten Magnuson to the wall thanks to her perfect finish. Magnuson had gone 57.02. The difference between being an Olympian and being an also-ran was three one-hundredths of a second. The two kids had beaten the veterans for the Olympic team spots.

Susan Carol didn't know what to say or do. Without thinking, she went under the lane line to comfort Magnuson. Wentworth had done the exact same thing. Magnuson still had her face in the gutter and was sobbing.

"I'm so sorry," Susan Carol said, because she could think of nothing else to say.

"Me too," Wentworth said.

Magnuson pulled her head up and then did something remarkable. Hanging on to the wall with one hand, she first took Wentworth's hand and held it up in the air. Then she put Wentworth's hand down and grabbed Susan Carol's hand and held it up in the air. The crowd was going nuts.

"You two better promise me," Magnuson said, still gasping for breath. "You better *promise* me to go one-two in London, or I'm going to come looking for you."

The three of them had a group hug, then they climbed out of the water. A USA Swimming official was standing there. "Elizabeth, Susan Carol, congratulations. You have to come with me to NBC right away," he said, pointing in the direction of a mini-podium where Andrea Kremer was waiting to interview them.

"Can I get a towel?" Susan Carol asked.

"We'll get you towels," the man said. "Come on."

He began herding the two new teenage stars in the direction of their close-up. Christine Magnuson was left standing by herself on the deck. No one offered to bring her a towel.

Stevie actually thought his head might explode as the swimmers approached the flags. From the angle where he was sitting—standing, actually—it was impossible to tell who was winning. The first five swimmers appeared to be matching one another stroke for stroke. Susan Carol had been closing ground (or water) since the turn, when she had been fourth, but there was no way to tell who was first or who was fifth.

He remembered what Susan Carol had told him about how important it was to put your head down once you got to the flags. "There's plenty of time to breathe when the race is over," she had said.

He held his own breath when he saw her put her head down and take her last three strokes into the wall. It was impossible to tell where she had finished until he—like everyone else in the building—looked at the giant scoreboard. When he saw the 2 next to her name, he forgot that he was supposed to be a dispassionate journalist and jumped into the air yelling, "YES, YES!"

Kelleher gave him a look, and he quickly got ahold of himself.

"Sorry," he said.

Kelleher had a huge smile on his face. So did Tamara. "It's okay," he said. "It isn't as if we're trying to pretend you're unbiased in your stories. Just don't go too crazy. No need to call attention to it."

Stevie nodded, still a bit breathless. "What a race!" he said. "Look at those times, how close they are. I still can't believe she did it."

Kelleher nodded. "The best story is Christine Magnuson, which is what I'm going to write. There are few things worse in sports than finishing third in the Olympic Trials. Especially since this was her only event. Susan Carol at least would have had another shot in the 200 fly if she didn't make it."

"You weren't rooting for . . ."

"No, no," Kelleher said, laughing.

"Come on, guys, let's get down there," Tamara said. "It'll be a madhouse, you can bet on that."

They made their way from the press section down to the pool level. Fortunately, most of the crowd had stayed in their seats since Michael Phelps was getting ready to swim a semifinal in the 200 freestyle, and there were three more finals right afterward.

But down in the bowels of the arena there was chaos. Mike Unger raced past them, talking into a walkie-talkie. "Wentworth and Anderson in the interview room ASAP," he was saying. "No Phelps unless he somehow doesn't qualify. Breaststrokers after they get their medals. Can't rush these two girls."

Tamara nodded approvingly as Unger moved out of earshot.

"Good to have Mike back in control," she said.

"Yeah, but I need to talk to Magnuson," Kelleher said. "I doubt if she's going to volunteer to come to the mixed zone."

The swimmers who qualified for the team would nearly always be brought into the interview room to answer questions from the media. But journalists didn't only want to talk to the qualifiers. Like Kelleher, some might want to talk to a swimmer who had just missed qualifying. More often, reporters wanted to talk to swimmers from their local area.

But as Trevor James had pointed out when he had Bobby read his credential, access to the athletes was pretty tightly controlled. The mixed zone was an area at the end of one of the hallways near the locker rooms, where media and athletes were allowed to "mix." The problem for the journalists was that the swimmers were not required to go there. You could ask for an athlete to come, but they could say no. If Magnuson didn't feel like talking at that moment, she didn't have to.

"I'm going to find Mike Unger and ask if he can get one of his people to find out if Magnuson is willing to speak," Kelleher said. "I'll catch up to you guys later."

He picked up his pace to catch Unger. Stevie followed Tamara into the interview room.

The first person he noticed was J. P. Scott, standing in a corner. He had his arms folded and was whispering to someone else in a suit. If he was overjoyed that his client had made the Olympic team, he wasn't showing it. Curious as always, Stevie told Tamara to save him a seat and made his way over to Scott—who was clearly not happy to see him.

"Are you coming to eavesdrop on another conversation?" Scott said in a nasty tone.

"Not this time," Stevie said. "I'm just wondering why you look like Susan Carol finished third. Your client's going to London."

Scott's face twisted into a sneer and he shook his head.

"I thought you were supposed to be smart," he said. "She *lost*. And she lost to another teenager. I can't market a loser."

"A *loser?*" Stevie said, genuinely angry. "She just made the Olympic team at the age of fifteen, and you're calling her a loser?"

"In a marketing sense, she's a loser."

Stevie really and truly hated this guy. "I would think that, in a marketing sense, she was an *Olympian.*

"Maybe you can still sign Wentworth," Stevie went on. "You might get lucky and find another family to buy into your BS the way Reverend Anderson did."

"There you go again—not so smart. Have you seen Wentworth's face? And those shoulders . . . But it's not over. We've still got the 200 fly. And if she wins in London, everything will be fine."

"You'll love her all over again, right?" Stevie said.

"You got it, kid."

Stevie stared at him for a moment and thought about how satisfying it would be to wipe the arrogant smirk off Scott's face.

He settled for a parting shot. "Talk about being a loser," he said.

He turned around and went to find Tamara. Susan Carol had just made the Olympic team. She had never needed her friends more.

15: WANTING IT

Three hours later, Susan Carol knocked on Bobby and Tamara's door. After texting back and forth, she and Stevie had arranged to meet there since anyplace public would be jammed and technically she shouldn't be fraternizing with the media.

"Remember," Kelleher said. "It's all good. No talk of coaches or scumbag agents. At least not until after the 200."

They had just ordered room service, which fortunately was on call twenty-four hours a day that week. Kelleher had needed longer than usual to write. "Christine Magnuson broke my heart," he said. "She says she's retiring. That was her last race. Some columns are tougher than others. . . ."

He was sitting in a chair next to the round table that served as his desk, with his feet up on another chair. Tamara was sitting on the bed, and Stevie was on a small couch near the window. When he heard a light tap on the door, Stevie practically fell off the couch as he scrambled to get up and answer the knock.

"Easy, big fella," Kelleher said with a smile.

Susan Carol came into the room to a hearty round of applause from Bobby and Tamara. She smiled, but just a small one that told Stevie all wasn't right in her world.

"Do you have the medal with you?" Tamara said.

"Yes, I do," she said. "I hope you guys like it more than my dad and the Lightning Fast people did."

Great, Stevie thought, Scott and company had already convinced her dad that Olympian or not, Susan Carol was a loser.

She had her swim bag over her shoulder, and she put it down on the floor and rummaged through it for a second before pulling out a case and opening it to reveal the medal. It was huge, the size of a coaster, and had the Olympic rings on it. The writing on it said UNITED STATES OLYMPIC SWIM TRIALS 2012—OMAHA, NEBRASKA. There was no need for the words *second place*. The silver color of the medal made that clear.

"Wow," Stevie said when Susan Carol handed the medal to him. "*Wow*. Do you understand how amazing this is? Has it sunk in yet? I am so proud of you!"

Now Susan Carol did give him The Smile. "You're so sweet sometimes," she said. "I appreciate that. But I know J.P. talked to you before we got to the interview room. And I know you know what they're trying to do to Ed."

"Oh, honey." Tamara sighed. "We're so sorry. This should be the happiest night of your life."

"Tell us everything," Kelleher said, pulling his feet off the chair and indicating that Susan Carol should sit. "And, just for the record, Stevie's not being sweet. That was an amazing race. For anyone to say you shouldn't be proud to have made the Olympic team is crazy."

"Oh, they said it was okay to be proud," she said. "Just as long as I understand that in London, second isn't good enough."

"Tell us what they said," Tamara said. "Don't leave anything out."

She nodded and took a deep breath.

"Once we finished with the media and the medal ceremony, I had to go to drug-testing," she said. "Fortunately, that didn't take too long. J.P. has a corporate box upstairs, so we went up there to 'celebrate' and 'make plans.' The races were over by then, so the building was pretty quiet, but J.P. was there and his partner Bill and the insipid Susie, who I can't stand, my dad and this guy Joe Berger, who for some reason had made a big point of introducing himself to me when I was warming up. They told me he was going to be my new coach while I get ready for the Games."

"Just like that?" Stevie asked.

She nodded.

"They said Ed had done a great job getting me this far, but I needed a big-time coach who'd been to the Olympics before, and Joe was that guy," she said. "I'm afraid I kind of lost it then. I started *screaming*. I told them Ed was my coach, he was my only coach, and no one else was going to coach me. My dad said this wasn't my decision; that the grown-ups knew what was best, and they had done a lot of research before hiring Joe.

"And then I said things to my father I can hardly believe. I told him that he didn't know a damn thing about swimming—"

"You said *damn* to your father?" Stevie said, earning himself a sharp look from Kelleher, who always reminded him to never interrupt someone in mid-story, no matter who it was.

Susan Carol nodded, starting to tear up. "I did. I can't believe it, but I did. I told him I was the swimmer, not him, not J.P. Me. And that the only reason I was here and doing this well was because of Ed and that I still needed his support.

"He said it was done. He'd already told Ed about Joe and that Ed was upset but that he understood. I said, 'Well, I don't understand. I don't understand why you are trying to cut me off from everyone who cares about me. Anyone I can rely on. Because I clearly can't rely on anyone in this room.'

"I just left. I practically ran out of there. I don't know if I can do this anymore. I don't know if I *want* to do this anymore. It's not worth it."

She was sobbing by the time she finished. Stevie couldn't help but wonder how many young athletes had been put through something like this. He wrapped his arms around her and looked at Tamara and Bobby, hoping they had some kind of answer. Bobby was leaning forward in his chair, hands under his chin.

"Have you talked to Ed since this happened?" he asked.

Susan Carol composed herself and nodded. "I called him on the way here," she said. "He told me to be calm and to be at the practice pool at noon tomorrow just like we planned. That we'd worry about all this when the trials were over. He said he'll be my coach in London if he has to pay his own way there and not to worry about it."

Bobby nodded. "Ed's a good guy," he said. "I think you've put your trust in the right person. I'm surprised they sprang this on you tonight, though. I guess they figured Ed or Stevie would tell you anyway."

Stevie looked at Susan Carol, who was nodding.

"I wouldn't have, I don't think," Stevie said. "I don't know if that's right or not. I didn't want to upset you before your race. But I don't like the idea of lying to you either. And really, you are the toughest person I know."

She looked at him and raised an eyebrow.

"I mean, if anyone can perform under pressure, it's you," Stevie said.

"Thank you," she said. "Thank all of you."

They figured that Susan Carol's team would back off as she prepared for the 200 fly, and they were right. Ed Brennan was waiting for her on the deck the next day as usual. She wrapped him in a big hug, and he gave her a squeeze too.

But then he straightened up, gave her his usual swat on the back of the head, and said, "Okay, then. Into the pool," and they got on with her workout.

But even though her father and agents weren't hovering, Susan Carol couldn't clear her mind the way she knew she had to. She swam so poorly on Thursday that she barely qualified for the final—finishing seventh among the semifinalists, meaning she would be swimming in lane one the next night. The top qualifier was Elizabeth Wentworth, who was quickly becoming the star of the meet.

"It's actually not all bad that everyone is focusing on Wentworth," Ed Brennan said, biting into a piece of toast late on Thursday night. Stevie, Bobby, and Tamara had driven to the outskirts of town to meet Susan Carol and Ed at an all-night diner once they had finished their stories.

"My dad is barely speaking to me," Susan Carol had told Stevie when he asked if he knew she was meeting them. "I think they've all decided this isn't the time to push me. Joe Berger *did* come up to me on the deck tonight after I warmed up to ask if I felt better than I did in the morning."

"What'd you say?" Stevie asked.

"I told him it wasn't really any of his business."

"You can bet that'll get reported back."

"I really don't care at this point."

Stevie knew she meant that. The problem was that she didn't care about *anything* at the moment. Susan Carol's greatest strength was her passion. She cared about doing what was right and not letting the bad guys win. But now the best guy she had ever known—her dad—appeared to have thrown in with the bad guys. And clearly it was affecting her swimming. And if Susan Carol had taught Stevie anything about swimming, it was that you could not fake the 200 fly. With a sprint you could just hit the water, blank out your mind, and go as hard as you possibly could. The 200 fly required being in great physical *and* mental shape. If you weren't thinking with absolute clarity when you stood on the block, there was no way you could swim your best.

Dinner was quiet—clearly they all had a lot on their minds.

"What do you mean it's better if everyone is focusing on Wentworth?" Kelleher said, picking up Coach Brennan's thought.

"He means I should be able to concentrate because I won't have people coming at me all day long," Susan Carol said. "And he's right. I just have to get my head cleared of all this so I can swim tomorrow night."

"Maybe you should sit down with your dad and just tell him exactly how you feel, get it all out," Stevie said.

"Bad idea," Ed Brennan said. "Too complicated. That's for later, before we leave for London. This right now is pretty simple, actually. Susan Carol, you have to decide if you *want* to swim the 200 fly in the Olympics. I don't mean 'Yeah, I'd sure like to.' I mean you want it more than anything you've ever wanted in your life. That's the way you swam the 100. If you don't feel that way, you should scratch, let the first alternate swim because being in the final will be the thrill of a lifetime for her. If you're not *thrilled* to be swimming tomorrow night, you shouldn't swim."

Stevie was a little shocked.

"Ed, has anyone ever been *thrilled* to swim a 200 fly?" Kelleher asked half joking, trying to lighten the mood.

Ed looked him right in the eye without a hint of a smile when he responded. "Only the great ones," he said.

Maybe it was Ed Brennan's tough-love, post-midnight talk, but something clicked for Susan Carol the next morning. Unlike Wednesday night, when she had tossed and turned and had nightmares most of the night, she slept soundly and didn't wake up until after ten o'clock. For someone accustomed to being up most mornings at 5:30, that was major.

She went to the pool to meet Ed for her late-morning warm-up swim and was bursting with energy, wishing she could swim the race right then.

Sitting in the ready room that night with the other seven swimmers, she was convinced she was going to win. The others all looked nervous, which was perfectly normal. They were swimming for the chance to race in the Olympics. Only she and Wentworth already had spots on the team clinched.

They marched onto the deck to huge cheers, Susan Carol leading the way since she was in lane one. That's the way it should be—qualifying times aside—she told herself because when this was over, she was going to be leading the way again. The introductions seemed to take about an hour because Susan Carol was dying to get on the block. Finally she heard her three favorite words: "Take your mark . . ."

And they were off. Susan Carol was swimming next to Penny Bates. The only thing she knew about Bates was that she would probably go out slow and come back fast. If Bates was close to her at the 50 or the 100, that would be a bad sign.

She wasn't worried. The first 50 felt easy. She found her rhythm quickly and reminded herself to stay low and stay smooth—that was her mantra for the first 150 meters most of the time. But she wasn't going to let Wentworth or any of the other swimmers in the middle of the pool get out too fast on her. That was the disadvantage of being in an outside lane: The only time she could really see the top qualifiers was when she turned.

The way she saw it, five swimmers had a chance to finish in the top two: Aline Wylie, Jane Blythe, Teresa Crippen, Elizabeth Wentworth, and herself. The other four were in lanes three to six. As she stretched to the wall at the 50 and swiveled her legs to turn, she glanced at the middle of the pool and saw that no one else had reached the wall. She couldn't even see Bates.

Normally, leading at the 50 of a 200 would have semi-panicked her. Now she smiled as she pushed off. She knew—just knew—she hadn't put anything extra into the first length and she was still out front. She wouldn't really get another look at the other swimmers until the 150, but that was okay; they wouldn't be seeing her out here in lane one either. Her second length normally took twenty-five strokes. This time she only needed twenty-four, which meant she was doing a good job of keeping her stroke long.

As she turned at the 100-meter mark, she could hear the drumbeat of noise in the arena rising. She assumed it was because the race was close. She reminded herself not to get caught up in racing anyone on this length. It was way too soon. *Stay low, stay easy,* she kept repeating as she closed in on the 150 wall.

As she picked her head out of the water at the turn, she could hear very clearly that the building was going crazy. When she glanced across the pool, she could see that she still had the lead. By how much she wasn't sure—she just knew no one else was on the wall when she was and if someone had been ahead of her, she would have seen her pushing off.

Now, she told herself, now *the race starts.* This was what all those early mornings were about, the sets of 200s, the crawling out of the pool and lying on the deck too tired to even stand. The next fifty meters were what all of that had been for.

Halfway home, for the first time all night, she felt her arms starting to tighten. It was okay, though, she could handle tightness. It wasn't the piano, just a small piano bench. She began to pick up her kick and made certain that each stroke was stretched out as far as she could get her arms to go. She knew her stroke was shorter now in the final meters—but she wanted to get everything she could out of each one.

Then she was under the flags and she knew she had never gone this fast in the 200 fly before. The question was, how fast had the other girls gone? Just about out of air, she forced herself to stay down for the last three strokes. As she always told Stevie, she would have plenty of time to breathe later.

One stroke, two, three, and she was on the wall—gasping as she pulled her head out of the water. She gasped again when she looked to her right just in time to see Wentworth and Crippen hit the wall. Then came the others—behind them. She almost didn't want to look up at the board, but when she did, she gasped again.

Next to her name was the prettiest sight you could see in swimming: the number 1. She had blown away her best time and had blown away the field, finishing in 2:01.96—a new American record, less than a second away from the world record. Wentworth had finished second in 2:03.44—Susan Carol's exact time in Shanghai. Crippen was third in 2:03.97. No one else had broken 2:05.

From out of the cauldron of sound, she heard Ed's voice saying, "Unbelievable, just unbelievable." Blinking up at him, she saw tears in his eyes. She had never seen that before.

Wentworth and Crippen had both come under the lane lines to congratulate her. When she climbed out of the water, she saw the NBC people and the USA Swimming people and the photographers rushing at her.

Ed managed to get five seconds alone with her before they spirited her away.

"That break you got the last couple of days from all the attention?" he said, talking into her ear so she could hear and no one else could.

"Yeah?" she said.

"It's over." He grinned.

"Soon as you finish with Andrea Kremer, we have to get you right to Costas," someone was saying.

Ed was right. The real work was just beginning.

16: LONDON CALLING

Stevie hadn't thought it possible that a city could feel more crowded and more intense than New York. But London quickly proved him wrong.

Maybe it was just the out-of-sorts feeling he had watching traffic go by on the wrong side of the road during the cab ride from Heathrow Airport to the Gloucester Hotel.

"Do you get used to it?" he asked Bobby Kelleher, who had covered fourteen Wimbledons and had spent a good deal of time in Great Britain.

"No," Kelleher answered. "Every instinct you have driving a car or even crossing a street is wrong when you're here. You have to stop and think about it all the time."

Most of the media were staying in rooms set aside by the International Olympic Committee, which, according to Bobby, were little more than glorified dorm rooms.

"The media isn't exactly the IOC's main priority, so the

accommodations are usually lousy," Kelleher had said. "If it's a night or two, no big deal, but when you're going to be someplace for a couple weeks, it makes a difference."

Kelleher always stayed at the Gloucester when he covered Wimbledon and had become friends with the general manager over the years. He'd made arrangements a long time ago for him and Tamara to stay there during the Olympics. And when Stevie had been added to the traveling party, he had been able to get bumped to a junior suite, meaning Stevie would be sleeping on a pullout couch in a sitting room—which was fine with him. He was just excited to be here.

"Once we get to the hotel, we'll take the subway to Olympic Park every day," Kelleher had explained. "The Gloucester is a block from the Gloucester Road underground station. That's what's great about it—location. It's right in Kensington: lots of restaurants, not too far from Harrods, where we'll have to shop at some point so you can tell people you were there, and, most important for you, twenty-four-hour room service."

That sounded perfect to Stevie.

The first thing he wanted to do when they got to the hotel was eat. The plane had left New York just after 10 a.m., and with the five-hour time change they had landed at Heathrow at a few minutes before 10 p.m. It had been close to 11 by the time they had wended their way through customs, gotten their luggage, and found the taxi line—or, as Kelleher explained, the taxi queue. "In London there are no lines," he said. "But there are plenty of queues." By the time they pulled up to the Gloucester, Stevie was starved.

He knew he would have to wait until morning to call Susan Carol. She had flown over with the rest of the American swim team a week earlier, on July 18. The opening ceremony was now just two days away, and Susan Carol would swim her first race—a 100-butterfly heat—the day after that.

There had been many scuffles with her dad and the Lightning Fast people since the trials, and many desperate emails and texts and phone calls as she vented her frustrations. The latest drama was about whether she should take part in the opening ceremony.

They don't want me to do it, she had written. *Apparently you have to be on your feet for quite a while waiting to march in and they're nervous about that. A lot of people who are swimming on Saturday aren't going to go, so they aren't being completely crazy. But who knows if I'll ever be on an Olympic team again? How could I possibly miss it?*

Ed is okay with it. He checked, and apparently while you're waiting, they have seating areas reserved for athletes who have to compete the next day so you don't have to stand for too long. And really, I don't have to swim all that fast to make the semis.

The best news of all had come earlier: The Joe Berger-as-coach experiment had ended before it even began. After Susan Carol's incredible swim in the 200 fly in Omaha (and after her refusal to be coached by anyone else), Don Anderson had decided to stick with Ed Brennan. Plus, he had asked J. P. Scott directly if he did in fact, represent Joe Berger.

Turns out Ed had that one exactly right, Susan Carol had written. *And the best part is that I think the whole incident finally made my dad step back and take a fresh look at J.P.*

Shortly before boarding the plane in New York, Stevie had gotten a text from Susan Carol saying she had also won the opening ceremony battle. After receiving assurances from the US coaches that she wouldn't have to stand for too long, Reverend Anderson had sided with her against the Lightning Fast folks.

"Maybe her dad is coming around," Stevie said, showing Kelleher the text while they were boarding. "This makes two wins in a row for the good guys."

"I wouldn't count on it," said Kelleher, always the last skeptic standing. "We'll know more after she swims the 100. Sarah Sjöström is looking really strong. I think she's got the edge over Susan Carol in that race. So let's see how they react if she gets beaten."

"What if she does win?"

"Well, then the pressure's off. Or on. If she wins, Susan Carol will officially be the It Girl of the Games."

Kelleher was right. She was already a huge headliner star of the games. She seemed to be in every pre-Olympic profile show or article or photo spread. Stevie had her on Google alerts for a while but finally turned it off. There were several fan sites dedicated to her, and Stevie had had his fill of reading about all the boys (and men) who were in love with Susan Carol. He knew jealousy was pointless.

And Susan Carol had proven in the past that she wasn't wowed by looks or money or star athletes.

Still . . .

He was off in Stevie-world getting ready to fight off . . . well . . . everyone for Susan Carol's affections when they pulled up to the hotel. Before he was even out of the cab, the doorman was hugging Tamara like a long-lost relative.

"Bonus for us this summer, having you two back again," he was saying to Tamara and Bobby. "Feels like you were here for Wimbledon last week."

"Well, it was only three weeks ago," Kelleher said. "So you aren't far off. Edward, meet our friend and colleague Steve Thomas."

"Pleasure, Mr. Thomas," Edward said.

He turned to Tamara, smiling. "I presume this is the young man you've told me about who is a young Bobby Kelleher."

"He's a lot better than that," Bobby said with a laugh.

"But his partner won't be working this fortnight, will she?" Edward said. "Be a bit busy in the pool."

"That's right," Stevie said. "You're well informed."

"Well, she's made quite a splash here, if you'll forgive the pun. Pretty girl, that," Edward said. He clapped Stevie on the shoulder. "I'd keep a close eye if I were you."

"He does, Edward," Kelleher said. "He does."

They made their way into the lobby.

"What about our bags?" Stevie asked as they walked to the front desk.

"Edward will take care of them," Kelleher said.

"But he didn't give you a ticket or . . ."

"Stevie, Bobby is the mayor of the Gloucester," Tamara said. "Don't worry about it."

The rest of the check-in confirmed that. It seemed as if everyone who worked in the hotel came out to greet them. Much to Stevie's relief, they headed straight to the hotel restaurant once they had their key cards. There, the night manager simply told them to order whatever they wanted, regardless of what was on the late-night menu.

After they'd eaten, everything seemed better still. Kelleher leaned back in his chair with a smile. "I love the morning flight," he said. "Means we can get a good night's sleep and be ready to go in the morning instead of walking around like jet-lagged zombies."

"But what are we going to do?" Stevie said. "The opening ceremony isn't until Friday night and there's nothing important going on until Sunday."

Tamara and Bobby both laughed.

"First trip to London and he's bored already," Tamara said.

"In the morning we'll pick up our credentials," Bobby said. "That will kill half the day. Then we have to find the media center and figure out the lay of the land. And then we have to fill out all the paperwork so we can get into the athletes' village. That'll kill the rest of the day. Friday, if we're lucky, we'll get to do some sightseeing."

"Half a day to pick up credentials?" Stevie said.

"If we're lucky," Bobby said. "If you think security was

tight at the Final Four or the Super Bowl, think again. This is a whole new world."

Susan Carol already knew what Bobby was talking about. She had arrived in London ten days before the opening ceremony, flying on a charter that included all forty-nine American swimmers plus the men's and women's water polo teams. Coaches and officials quickly filled the plane to capacity.

As luck would have it, Susan Carol was seated next to Elizabeth Wentworth. Or maybe it wasn't luck. Apparently USA Swimming thought it was a good idea for swimmers who swam the same stroke to get to know one another better.

Elizabeth Wentworth wasn't anything like Susan Carol had expected. In their brief encounters at the trials, she had seemed like a nice girl. And she'd been genuinely excited about Susan Carol's record-breaking time in the 200 fly. But when they started talking on the long flight across the Atlantic, Susan Carol found herself thinking that her problems with her dad and her agents were pretty minor.

Elizabeth had grown up just outside Pensacola, Florida. She was the youngest of her parents' four children and her dad had left when she was five. To this day she had no idea what had caused her parents to split, but her older siblings had told her that her father's drinking had been a major issue.

Left alone with four kids ranging in age from eleven to five, Elizabeth's mom had often worked two jobs: one at

Walmart and another one on weekends and sometimes at night manning the front desk at the local YMCA. That was where Elizabeth started swimming. Her mom had enrolled her in swimming classes so Elizabeth didn't have to sit around the day-care center while she was working.

"I was always the biggest kid in my class," Elizabeth said. "Not just tall, but big." She shrugged. "The Y coach took one look at my shoulders and said, 'You're a butterflyer.'" She smiled. "Why'd they make you a butterflyer?"

"Because I was tall like you," Susan Carol said. "And I'm pigeon-toed. I always had the kick."

Elizabeth began winning meets when she was six, easily swimming twenty-five meters of butterfly when other kids her age couldn't swim the length of the pool yet. By age eight she was nationally ranked, and at ten she was being recruited for top age-group teams around the state.

"Even though home wasn't the greatest place in the world, my mom didn't want me to leave," she said. "It wasn't until a couple of years ago that she sent me to Orlando to swim with Mike Schulte. That was when I really started to get good. But even though it's nice there, I do get homesick."

"Where do you live?"

"With Mike and his family. It's okay, but I have to share a room with two of his daughters and sleep on the top bunk."

She laughed. "Of course, I'm up at 4:30 to work out every morning, so it isn't as if I get to sleep that much anyway."

The two girls talked for at least half of the trip before falling asleep. Once they had arrived at the hotel north of London where they were going to stay until they moved into the athletes' village, Susan Carol sent Stevie an email detailing Elizabeth Wentworth's story.

She's the best story on the team, she wrote. *You should write something on her as soon as you get here. I feel terrible—she's so nice, and incredibly talented, but she's not that pretty, and it seems like that's why no one's really paying attention to her. It's so not fair! I'd almost like to see her win more than me.*

Stevie had written back and said, *You're kidding about wanting her to win, right?*

Susan Carol thought a long time before she answered. *Honestly,* she wrote, *I'm not sure.*

The team had spent a week at a hotel outside London, getting bused to a nearby health club that had apparently just built a fifty-meter pool for workouts. The Chinese and the Russian teams were using the facility too because there weren't many fifty-meter pools in the London area.

Susan Carol knew enough from her history classes to realize that even just twenty years ago, the thought of American and Chinese and Russian athletes sharing a practice facility would have been impossible.

The schedule was the same each day: The Chinese team had the pool at seven and again at three. The Americans had it at 8:30 and 4:30, and the Russians had it at ten and six. The workouts were hardly taxing. Everyone was tapering heavily. There were times in the middle of winter when

Susan Carol would swim 12,000 meters a day. Now, in a long-course pool, she was barely cracking 3,000.

There were all sorts of team meetings, but the silliest by far was when the ever-annoying Trevor James from USA Swimming was brought in one evening to go through the rules with them. How could they have come this far without knowing the rules? The butterflyers and breaststrokers knew they had to touch every wall with two hands and that their hands had to be parallel to one another. The backstrokers knew they were allowed one stroke on their stomach before flipping. Everyone knew they couldn't kick underwater for more than fifteen meters.

But James went over the rules so thoroughly, and so officiously, that for several days the swimmers had mimicked him during practice. "If you allow a hand to drop making a two-handed turn, you *will* be disqualified!" . . . "Ooooh, looked like you were trying to beat the starter there. Wait until you hear the beep before moving. Don't think you can outsmart the officials!" . . . "That was more than fifteen meters underwater—clearly you are a fish and must be disqualified!" In an odd way it helped bring the team together. They were all so focused and keyed up, it felt good to laugh.

It was on Monday, four days before the opening ceremony and two days before they were all scheduled to move to the athletes' village in London, that Susan Carol met Liu Zige, the Chinese world-record holder she'd just touched out to win the World Championship. They hadn't spoken in Shanghai beyond nodding at one another before climbing onto the blocks.

Susan Carol was standing off to the side of the pool stretching with Elizabeth Wentworth when she saw Liu climb out of the pool. She had noticed her on other mornings, but protocol seemed to dictate that the swimmers not speak to one another as one team exited the pool and the other entered it. Now, though, Liu was walking directly toward them.

She was easy to distinguish from the other Chinese swimmers because she was just about six feet tall. Her walk, Susan Carol noticed, was full of confidence, the kind of strut—for lack of a better word—befitting an Olympic gold medalist.

"Miss Anderson," she said, in very clear English, her hand extended. "I thought perhaps it was time we meet."

Susan Carol had stood up straight when she saw Liu approaching. They were almost the same height.

"It's a pleasure," she replied, taking Liu's extended hand. "This is—"

"Elizabeth Wentworth," Liu said, turning to Elizabeth with a bright smile. "The two of you have certainly become stars very quickly."

"A star is someone with an Olympic gold medal," Susan Carol said.

"Perhaps so, but you beat me fair and square last year in Shanghai," Liu said. "I very much look forward to our meeting again next week."

The way she said it took Susan Carol aback. Not the idea that they would be competing again but that it would be *next week*. It was all happening very fast now.

"I guess we all have a lot of swimming to do before that," Susan Carol said.

Liu nodded. "I know you will both swim the 100 butterfly too," she said. Then, with a smile, she added: "I'll wish you both the very best in *that* event."

Elizabeth had been staring at Liu almost since she had first approached. Now, finally, she asked the question Susan Carol hadn't wanted to ask: "Where did you learn to speak such good English?" she said.

Liu laughed. "It is taught in our schools," she said. "But if someone shows potential as an international athlete, they're put into a special program to accelerate their studies."

Susan Carol was keenly aware of how monolingual most Americans were. Covering tennis, she had met a number of athletes from other countries who spoke English that ranged from passable to perfect.

A whistle blew, and Susan Carol and Elizabeth realized it was time to get in the water and warm up. They shook hands with Liu again. "Perhaps we will see each other when we are all in the athletes' village," Liu said. "I will buy you both a Coke."

Whether it was because of Liu's boldness or just a coincidence, Susan Carol met another major threat in the butterfly later that day. Svetlana Krylova was a Russian swimmer and in much the same boat as Susan Carol and Elizabeth. She had just emerged on the international scene in the last year at age seventeen. Her swim at the Russian trials in April had announced her arrival. She had won the 200 in a time of 2:01.91—just one-tenth of a second shy of Liu's world record.

Susan Carol had just finished her last 50-fly sprint of the day and was about to warm down when she noticed Krylova standing at the far end of the pool, clearly watching her. Krylova was impossible to miss. She had already been dubbed "swimming's Maria Sharapova." She was tall and blond and, according to Stevie and every other boy in the world, stunning. Mary Carillo had done a feature on her for NBC that had aired during the Olympic Trials. In the piece, Krylova had laid out her plans to Carillo very clearly: "I will win at the Olympics twice, this year and then again in four years, and then I will move to the USA and become a model and an actor," she had said. "I think people will give me this chance, don't you?"

No doubt people would give her that chance. But Susan Carol wasn't going to let her win her first Olympic gold medal without a fight. (Rooting for Elizabeth was one thing, but this girl . . . no way!) Now, seeing Krylova eyeing her, she climbed out of the pool fifty meters sooner than she had planned so she could introduce herself.

Krylova saw her coming and put her hands on her hips as Susan Carol walked up.

"Svetlana, hi," Susan Carol said, trying to keep her tone friendly. "I'm Susan Carol Anderson."

"Yes, I know," Krylova said. "Congratulations on your race in the trials. It was quite something to watch."

There wasn't a hint of a smile on her face, and she never moved her hands from her hips. It might have been Susan Carol's imagination, but it seemed as if she was standing as straight as possible so she could look down at her. She *was* tall—easily three inches taller than Susan Carol.

"Well, thanks, I didn't go quite as fast as you did in April, though," she said.

"I suspect you will do better here," Krylova said. "I think we all will have a good race, two good races, in fact."

She was . . . polite. But unlike Liu, who seemed genuinely friendly, there was a coldness to Krylova. She had heard from her friend Evelyn Rubin, who was a top-ten-ranked tennis player, that Maria Sharapova wasn't very friendly. It seemed as if Krylova had that in common with her as well as her looks.

"Well, I just wanted to introduce myself," Susan Carol said. "I'm sure I'll see you around the next few days."

"Most important, you will see me in the water on Sunday night, no?" Krylova said with that icy smile. That was when the 100-butterfly final was scheduled.

Susan Carol decided two could play this game. "Yes, you will," she said. "You most certainly will."

She didn't bother shaking hands before walking away. She needed a hot shower.

17: OLYMPIC HURDLES

As usual, Stevie had to admit that Bobby Kelleher was right. Getting their credentials on Thursday took the entire morning. First they rode the subway—or, as it was called in London, the Underground—to the Stratford Station stop. From there they walked several blocks to the entrance of Olympic Park, where they had to go through a lengthy security check and show letters confirming they were credentialed to cover the Games.

From there they were directed to the check-in area at the main press center, where they waited in line for forty-five minutes and then endured what felt like an interrogation before being given their badges.

Once they had their badges, they went inside the vast press center, which looked like a giant warehouse, and began looking for the cubicle assigned to the *Washington Herald* and the *Washington Post*.

They walked forever—or so it seemed—before they found where they were going.

"Pretty grim place," Stevie commented. He had kind of expected bright lights and glitter. This was, after all, the Olympics.

Tamara said, "Ah, budget cutbacks. There were supposed to be a couple of restaurants and bars in here, but now there's apparently just a tent with cafeteria food. Cost overruns and the tough economy forced them to economize and, no surprise, the first thing they cut was amenities for the media."

"Not necessarily a smart move," Kelleher added. "The Atlanta people are still hearing about how bad the food was, and that Olympics was sixteen years ago."

The *Post-Herald* cubicle had ten desks: five on one side of the "room"—there were no walls, just partitions separating them from the cubicles along the same row—for the *Post*, five more for the *Herald*. The only person inside was Matt Rennie, the *Herald*'s sports editor.

"Welcome to paradise," Rennie said as Stevie, Tamara, and Bobby trooped in.

Kelleher shrugged. "No big deal," he said. "After all, we're not going to be spending much time here once the Games begin."

"Speak for yourself," Rennie said. "Someone has to edit what you write into readable English."

Rennie was a classic editor. His attitude toward his writers was simple: If you don't have something sarcastic to say, don't say anything at all. Stevie knew Kelleher loved Rennie because he was smart, funny, and knew what he was doing.

"We want to go over to the athletes' village," Kelleher said. "How tough do you think that will be?"

"No tougher than getting your credentials," Rennie said. "What'd that take you, about three hours?"

They had to fill out a form requesting access to the village that explained who they were, who they wanted to see, and how long they intended to stay. They had to sign another form in which they agreed that if they spoke to any athlete *other* than the ones they said they were going to see, they could be stripped of their credentials.

Stevie had texted Susan Carol to let her know they had arrived and wanted to come see her. That was necessary because she had to send an email through the Olympic computer system saying she was willing to be interviewed by the three reporters who had requested to see her.

When they had finally cleared all the various hurdles, they were directed to a shuttle bus that would take them to the front gate of the athletes' village. The "Guide to the Games" they had been given earlier said the village was within walking distance of all the venues in the park, but apparently they had a pretty liberal interpretation of the phrase "walking distance."

Traffic around the Olympic Park was gridlocked, so it took the shuttle twenty-five minutes to go what couldn't have been more than two miles. They had to go through another lengthy security check at the gate, and when they were finally cleared, they were greeted by an unsmiling thirty-something guy who studied their badges, their faces, and their paperwork before saying, "Peter Brooks, IOC Communications. I'm your escort to Miss . . ." He paused to look down at his paperwork. "Anderson."

There were brief handshakes, and then Peter Brooks began leading them through a plaza that had modern apartment buildings surrounding it. Each building looked to be about eight stories high.

Brooks was giving them a tour-guide spiel as they walked, explaining how designing the village so that the apartments surrounded several plazas "was done to give the athletes of the world a place to gather and come together and learn from one another."

Gag me, Stevie thought.

The village wasn't all that crowded, which, according to Brooks, was because teams were still arriving. "By Friday, when we have the opening ceremony, ninety percent of the athletes will be here. Though some who don't compete until the second week will arrive later."

They finally reached building 14C, which, like the other buildings, had several flagpoles in front of it, one of which was flying an American flag. Susan Carol, dressed in a T-shirt with a USA logo on it, was sitting on a bench next to the entrance, talking to another girl. When she saw them approach, she jumped to her feet and ran straight to Stevie, shrieking, "You're finally here!"

She gave Stevie a hug and a kiss, then did the same for Bobby and Tamara. Peter Brooks looked as if someone had said all future Olympics should be canceled. He recovered and, almost as if he hadn't seen anything, said, "Are you Ms. Anderson?"

"She better be," Kelleher said. "Because if she's not, the real Ms. Anderson is going to be pretty upset when she hears someone else has been kissing Stevie."

Stevie wasn't sure who reddened more, Susan Carol or Brooks.

Brooks was still trying to perform his duties to the letter. "Ms. Anderson, this is Ms. Mearns from the *Washington Post* and Mr. Kelleher and Mr. Thomas from the *Washington*—"

"*Herald,*" Kelleher said, trying to be helpful.

"*Herald,*" Brooks repeated.

Stevie began to wonder if perhaps he was really a robot who could only respond to what was in his programming.

Susan Carol turned to the girl who had been sitting on the bench with her. She was standing now and looked very familiar.

"Stevie, Bobby, Tamara, this is Elizabeth Wentworth. I'm sure you remember her from the trials."

"Sure do," Kelleher said, shaking hands. "That was great swimming. I'm Bobby. This is my wife, Tamara, and I'm guessing Susan Carol has told you about Stevie."

Before Elizabeth Wentworth could respond, Peter Brooks began to hyperventilate. Or something close to it.

"There is nothing . . . on my paperwork . . . about you interviewing a second athlete today. . . . You must have read the form. . . ."

Kelleher put his hand on Brooks's shoulder to steady him.

"Really, it's okay," he said. "We're here to see Susan Carol. I promise that we won't ask Elizabeth to reveal any state secrets to us."

Brooks was taking deep breaths, trying to regain his composure.

"There's no authorization for this."

"Is there actually a form that authorizes athletes to say 'hello' to journalists?" Susan Carol said. She was giving Brooks The Smile, but, being a robot, he wasn't affected by it.

He was frowning and shaking his head.

"Ms. Wentroth—"

"Wentworth," Elizabeth corrected him.

Stevie was completely convinced that Brooks's head was going to explode.

"Ms. WentWORTH," he said. "I have to warn you that if you speak to these people in any official way, there could be repercussions for you with your organizing committee."

"I'll risk it," Elizabeth said.

Brooks decided he'd had enough. He pointed at his watch. "It is 4:10 p.m.," he said. "Your passes expire at 6 p.m. If you aren't back at the front gate by then, security will come and find you."

Tamara gave him her version of The Smile and shook

his hand. "Mr. Brooks, we just want to thank you for making us feel so welcome. Being with you these past few minutes has enveloped us in the Olympic spirit."

If Brooks picked up on the sarcasm in the slightest, he didn't show it.

"You're welcome," he said. "Six o'clock."

He turned and walked away.

"Is it always like this?" Stevie asked.

"Oh no," Kelleher said. "Most of the time it's worse."

Susan Carol had finished her first workout in one of the Olympic Aquatics Centre's practice pools at three o'clock and hadn't eaten lunch, so she suggested they all go get something to eat.

Elizabeth begged off, saying she'd promised her mother she would Skype with her. "It's eleven o'clock back home," she said. "They like to talk to me in the morning so they know everything is going okay."

As they walked through yet another plaza en route to the nearest dining hall—apparently there were two in the village—Susan Carol was sending a text.

"So I gather there are computers in the room," Bobby said. "Cell phone service pretty good?"

"Actually, it's great," Susan Carol said. "They have every piece of technology you could hope for. We're four to a suite and there are four computers in each suite. You can Skype, video-chat, pretty much anything you want."

"Who were you texting?" Stevie asked.

"You'll see," she said mysteriously.

They walked into the most massive cafeteria Stevie had ever seen.

"Place is open twenty-four hours a day," Susan Carol said. "You wake up at three in the morning with an ice cream craving or you're just nervous and want a snack, you can walk over here."

"Have you done that yet?" Stevie asked.

"No. But we just got here yesterday."

There were food stations all over the place. Stevie grabbed a tray and was headed for a line that said GRILL when Susan Carol gently took his arm.

"I'd advise you against your usual burger," she said. "Not the best thing over here. Their version of rare is our version of extremely well done."

"So what's good?" he said.

She pointed in another direction. "I'll bet the fish and chips are good."

"Okay. But do you think there's somewhere I can get fries?"

Susan Carol laughed. "Stevie, you're going to have to start learning the lingo. Chips *are* fries."

"Then why do they call them chips?"

"They would ask you why we call chips French fries. I'm going to get some pasta. Find a table near a window if you get there first."

Even though the place wasn't crowded, Stevie could hear several different languages being spoken while he waited for his food. When he stopped to take a bottle of

Coke out of a giant-sized container, Kelleher came up behind him.

"Good thing you don't like Pepsi," he said. "If someone tried to bring a Pepsi in here, Peter Brooks of the IOC might have them shot."

"Why?" Stevie asked.

"Official sponsor. Everything you will see for the next ten days—sodas, food, sweat suits, sneakers, you name it—comes from an official sponsor. No food is fed to an Olympic athlete and no clothes are worn by an Olympic athlete unless someone has paid the IOC or their country's Olympic committee for the right to do so."

"Just like the NCAA Tournament," Stevie said, remembering the logoed cups that had been handed to anyone who wanted to bring a drink courtside.

"You got it," Kelleher said.

Susan Carol and Tamara, both holding plates of pasta, arrived a moment after Stevie and Bobby sat down at a table by the windows. Stevie was digging into his fries—chips—when he heard a voice say, "Susan Carol, you were right, he is cuter than ever!"

Stevie did a double take. Evelyn Rubin, also with a plate of pasta on her tray, was standing there with a huge grin on her face.

She put her tray down, and she and Susan Carol embraced like long-lost friends.

Evelyn had been involved in one of Stevie and Susan Carol's early adventures—at the US Open tennis tournament. She was now the eighth-ranked player in the world. Stevie had completely forgotten that she'd be competing in the Olympics.

Evelyn was now looking at Stevie, who was still paralyzed in his chair.

"Remember me?" she said.

"Of course I do," Stevie said, trying not to sound too defensive. He finally remembered how to stand up, and Evelyn gave him a warm hug. "I'd just forgotten that you'd be here."

"Ah, yes, only one Olympian is on *your* mind, I'm sure."

Stevie blushed, but Evelyn breezed on.

"I just got in yesterday," she said. "We don't start playing until the middle of next week, but I wanted to get here early to take the whole thing in. I think I'm the only tennis player here already. Actually, I may be the only one staying in the village. I've heard all the big names will be staying in luxury hotels."

"Typical," Kelleher said. "I bet most of them are only coming because their agents told them an Olympic medal could help their sponsorship deals."

Tamara elbowed him, but Evelyn just laughed. "To be honest, my deals have bonuses for Olympic medals too," she said. "I would have made *more* money if I had played World Team Tennis. But this is a once-in-a-lifetime opportunity."

Everyone sat down, and Evelyn and Susan Carol began comparing notes—Susan Carol telling stories about swimmers, Evelyn dispensing tennis gossip. Stevie felt left out. Now that Susan Carol was a world-class athlete, she was traveling in different circles than he was.

Evelyn was telling a story about Serena Williams bringing four different outfit changes into the locker room one day at Wimbledon when Stevie, eyes and mind wandering, saw a familiar figure across the room.

"Susan Carol," Stevie said, interrupting Evelyn in the middle of a description of one of Serena's outfits. "Isn't that one of your agents over there?"

He nodded in the direction of the man—who stood out like a sore thumb because he was in a suit.

Susan Carol, looked and nodded. "Ah, good old Bill. I wonder what he's doing here. He didn't say anything about coming over when I saw him at the pool."

"Maybe he heard the food here is good," Kelleher said. "Or, maybe he's here to see her."

Stevie saw a very tall blonde with her long hair tied back in a ponytail walking to the table where Bill Arnold had sat down. She was followed by another man in a suit.

"She looks familiar," Stevie murmured.

"She should," Evelyn Rubin said. "She's been on about fifteen magazine covers in the last month. That's Svetlana Krylova. She's staying in the same building I am. All the Russian women swimmers are there. I met her. That other guy is her dad."

"But what's she doing meeting with your agent?" Stevie said, turning back to Susan Carol.

Susan Carol shrugged. "They must have other clients. Why wouldn't he want her as a client? God knows if she wins here, she's going to make a lot of money."

"Yeah, but don't you feel just a little uncomfortable that he's chatting up one of your main competitors?" Tamara said.

"Plus, doesn't she already have an agent?" Stevie said.

"She has a Russian agent, I know that," Kelleher said. "But she might want someone based in the US. That's where the biggest sponsorship dollars are."

"I'm going over there," Stevie said, standing up.

"What for?" Susan Carol demanded, her eyes narrowing into her familiar "what are you up to now, Steven Thomas?" look.

"Maybe I just want to meet Krylova," he said.

"Maybe you should sit down right now," Kelleher said, his voice about as stern as Stevie could remember it. "How many times have I told you that you don't tip your hand to an opponent?"

"Okay, okay." Stevie sat back down. "But what do you think that sleazebag is up to?"

"Who knows?" Susan Carol said. "Maybe nothing."

"Or maybe," Stevie said, "not nothing."

18: THE "GAMES" BEGIN

If Bill Arnold and the Krylovas spotted their group, they didn't show it. The room was filling up pretty quickly, but Stevie kept an eye on *them* until they left.

Evelyn volunteered to be super-friendly with Krylova and see what she could find out. As it closed in on six o'clock, they decided they'd better head for the front gate rather than risk the wrath of Peter Brooks and the IOC thought police.

They walked outside and exchanged hugs. When Susan Carol hugged Stevie, she said quietly, "Stay calm. Everything's going to be fine."

"Isn't that what I'm supposed to say to you?"

Susan Carol laughed and gave him another squeeze. "Maybe, but I know that look on your face—like you've smelled a rat. I think you're reading too much into one meeting. How could it possibly affect me?"

Stevie didn't know exactly. But he had a bad feeling about it. It *didn't* smell right. And this time he wouldn't have Susan Carol working with him to figure it out.

"We need some kind of strategy," Kelleher said.

They were back in the media center, thinking about their stories for the day. It was after seven o'clock, but since it was only two o'clock in Washington, they had some time before starting to write. Kelleher and Mearns were going to write about some of the pre-Olympic glitches that were still being ironed out, and Stevie was going to do a first-person piece on his impressions of London and the Games to come.

"A strategy for what?" Tamara asked. "An agent back-dooring a client isn't exactly a story. It happens all the time."

"What's back-dooring?" Stevie asked.

"It's when you go after someone who is in direct compe-tition with one of your clients," Bobby said. "It'd be like Tiger Woods's agent suddenly showing up with Phil Mick-elson. It's kind of sleazy, but it happens."

"Two days before the Olympics start?" Tamara asked.

"Now you're making my argument for me," Bobby said. "That's why it feels weird. It could be that Lightning Fast wants to be covered no matter who wins the two fly events."

"What if Liu wins? Or Elizabeth Wentworth?" Stevie asked.

"Then they've got troubles. Liu has an agent, so they're

out of luck there. And Elizabeth is a great story, but she isn't going to be the new It Girl."

"It's kind of sick that so much of what an athlete can earn depends not on their talent but on their image," Stevie said.

"I know," Tamara said. "It's really glaring sometimes. I mean, Chris Evert made millions of dollars as a tennis player because she was America's sweetheart. Martina Navratilova was a better player, but she made next to nothing because she was from Czechoslovakia and was open about being gay."

"Right," said Bobby. "It's been this way for a long time."

"Okay, but what I don't get," Stevie said, "is why all this focus on the butterfly events? Aren't there swimmers in other events Lightning Fast could glom onto?"

"Not necessarily," Kelleher said. "There aren't that many swimmers who win gold medals to begin with. There are—what?—fifteen individual events for men and fifteen for women. A lot of swimmers win multiple events. Some are repeat winners—Phelps, Lochte, Coughlin—so they have agents and deals already in place. Throw in the cute factor and it's a short list."

"So," Stevie said, "Bill and J.P. could want to sign Krylova to increase their chances of having a gold medalist."

"*If* they're trying to sign her."

"What else could they want?" Stevie asked.

"That's the question," said Tamara.

Kelleher leaned forward to put his drink down on a

table. "I think you need to go back to the village tomorrow—alone," he said. "Susan Carol, or maybe Evelyn, can set you up with what they call a 'one-on-one' pass. It gives you four hours instead of two."

"And then what?" Stevie said.

"Once you're in there, they seem to leave you alone. So try hanging around the building where the Russian swimmers are staying. Maybe you'll see something or hear something. Or get a chance to talk to Krylova. Something always seems to happen when you're around; maybe you'll get lucky."

"Okay," Stevie said. "And if I see Bill Arnold again, I *am* going to talk to him. The direct approach might work."

"Just be sure to think like a reporter," Tamara said. "Not a boyfriend."

As it turned out, Stevie ended up with *two* four-hour passes the next day. After he had texted Susan Carol to tell her what he wanted to do, she texted back to say that Evelyn would "accept" his request for a one-on-one too. Both she and Evelyn had practice sessions in the morning, so Stevie was supposed to request time with her from noon to four and with Evelyn from four to eight.

So on day two in London, Stevie headed out to Olympic Park on his own. Kelleher had gone out to Wimbledon because Andy Roddick, who was also in town early, had agreed to talk to him after his practice session. Tamara had headed to IOC chairman Jacques Rogge's pre-Olympics press conference at eight a.m.

With a little bit of trepidation, Stevie walked the one block to Gloucester Road Station and took the long escalator down to the platform. He had to change trains at Piccadilly Station but there were so many signs to the "Javelin Line," the special train set up to get the expected hordes of spectators to Olympic Park, that it would have been difficult to get lost.

There was a light rain falling as he made the fifteen-minute walk from the train station to the corner of the park where those with media credentials could enter without having to reclear security. At the media center he went to the "interview request" desk and filled out two forms asking for one-on-ones with Susan Carol and Evelyn.

When he handed them in, the IOC guy behind the desk frowned (surprise) as he looked over the forms.

"Problem?" Stevie said. "Did I get something wrong?"

"Are these two athletes aware that you are requesting these interviews?" he asked.

"Yes."

"It's unusual for us to allow a journalist to be in the village for that long."

"From what I understand, though, it's within the rules."

"I don't know if it's within the rules," said the man, whose name tag read ROBIN ALLRED. "I'll have to check."

"Well, if there's any problem, please let me know. I'll contact the USOC right away if need be."

Kelleher had told him to drop the US Olympic Committee into the conversation if there was any hassle and had given him a specific name, Mike Moran, to use if he had to. Apparently the IOC didn't like to get into any more battles than necessary with the USOC since it was American television money that paid most of the IOC's bills.

"The USOC has no jurisdiction in this," Allred said.

"Oh, I know," Stevie said. "But Mr. Moran said if I had any trouble getting access to American athletes, I should contact him."

"Mike Moran said that?" Allred said.

For a second Stevie thought he had dropped the name of someone he had never met a little too quickly.

"Sounds like something he'd say," Allred added, so Stevie exhaled. "We'll page you after we confirm with the athletes."

Stevie decided to wait in the media dining area since he was nearly always hungry. There weren't many options, so he settled for a second breakfast of some dicey-looking scrambled eggs and toast.

He was picking at the eggs, thinking he should've just waited for lunch, when he heard a voice behind him say, "Wow, Steve Thomas. Wilbon, you were right, this *is* an important event."

He turned and saw Tony Kornheiser and Michael Wilbon, the hosts of ESPN's one watchable show, *PTI*, approaching. He had run into the two of them on various occasions in the past but was surprised to find them here: Kornheiser notoriously hated to fly, and since NBC had the TV rights, Stevie hadn't expected ESPN to bring them here.

He stood up and shook hands with both men.

"May we join you?" Kornheiser asked. They were both

carrying trays. "This way when we both die trying to eat this food, there will be a witness."

"It isn't that bad," Wilbon said as they sat down.

"You're right," Kornheiser said. "It's much worse than that."

"The food in the athletes' village is pretty good," Stevie said.

"You've been there?" Kornheiser said. "You see, Wilbon, real reporters, you know the ones who actually go out and talk to athletes? They get to eat better food."

"Speaking of that, where's your partner in crime?" Wilbon asked.

"Susan Carol?" Stevie asked. "Right now she's swimming."

"Working out, huh?" Wilbon said. "Good idea. Where'd she find a place to swim?"

Stevie was confused. "The practice pools in the Aquatics Centre are open," he said.

"She got them to let her work out *there?*" Wilbon appeared stunned.

Kornheiser dropped his fork and leaned forward. "Wilbon, are you not aware of the fact that she's *on* the Olympic team? Do you pay attention to *anything* other than the NBA? She's one of the best stories going over here."

Wilbon looked completely confused. "She's *on* the swim team?" he said. "Really?"

"She's swimming the 100 fly and the 200 fly," Stevie said.

"Seriously, Wilbon, you didn't know?" Kornheiser said.

"Even I knew about this. She could be one of the big stars here. She's gotten massive coverage."

"The only swimmer who matters here is Michael Phelps," Wilbon said. "We'll talk about swimming when he's in the pool. That's it."

"You're an idiot," Kornheiser said.

If that bothered Wilbon, it didn't show. He was dumping about eight sugar packets into a small cup of tea.

Kornheiser took two bites of the eggs on his plate, declared them inedible, and then explained that ESPN had sent *PTI* to the Olympics because lack of access affected their show less than most. "We just blather and yodel anyway, so we're perfect for this."

"But you don't fly," said Stevie.

"I fly if I'm heavily drugged and heavily overpaid."

Wilbon looked up from the tabloid newspaper he had been reading.

"So I see where Barack is coming to the opening ceremony," he said.

"Really," Kornheiser said. "I figured you'd be sitting with him. . . ."

He paused because the PA system was blaring Stevie's name. "Steven Thomas, *Washington Herald,* report to the interview request desk. Steven Thomas, if you please."

"Sounds like I have to get going," Stevie said.

"Shame you can't go back for seconds," Kornheiser said, nodding at Stevie's uneaten food.

"All the more for you," Stevie said. He shook hands with both of them.

Wilbon's cell phone was buzzing.

"Probably Barack." Kornheiser winked as Wilbon answered.

Stevie heard his name again. The entertainment portion of his morning was over. It was time to get to work.

Whether it was dropping Mike Moran's name or just his lucky day, Robin Allred had two four-hour passes waiting for him when he reported back to the interview request desk.

"No problems, I take it?" Stevie said, unable to resist a light jab.

"Both athletes confirmed that they had accepted your request," he said. "Sign here and here."

Stevie rode the shuttle bus again and was escorted by a female IOC-bot who recited the same speech he'd heard the day before.

"I was here yesterday," he said when she got to the part about being shot on sight if he happened to speak to, as she put it, "an unauthorized athlete."

"I know the drill."

"We're required to remind you regardless of how many times you've been here," she said. "Can't have someone claiming they weren't properly warned."

"No, can't have that," Stevie said, which earned him a withering look.

Susan Carol and Elizabeth Wentworth were again waiting outside their building. Stevie was officially handed over to Susan Carol, and the IOC-bot managed not to short-circuit when Stevie and Elizabeth actually said hello. Alone at last, the three of them headed straight to the cafeteria.

"We're starved," Susan Carol said. "We figured we'd get some food and talk strategy while we eat."

Stevie was surprised that she was talking so openly in front of Elizabeth. Susan Carol, as she had done almost since the day they'd met, read his mind before he could say anything.

"Don't worry. Liz knows everything. She's about as big a fan of J.P. and his people as you are."

"Really?" Stevie said. "How come?"

"After the trials my coach, Mike Schulte, sent out letters to all the big-time agents," Elizabeth said. "Most of them wrote back and said, 'Let's talk after the Games,' which is agent-speak for, 'If you win a gold medal, we *might* be interested.'

"I mean, I get it. If I looked like Susan Carol or Krylova, there'd be more interest in me. So fine. But one agent wrote back and said, 'We're too busy right now to consider taking on any new clients.'"

"And—oh, let me guess," Stevie said.

"Exactly right," Susan Carol said. "Liz told me last night after I mentioned seeing Krylova and her dad eatin' with Bill. I swear, I wish I'd never signed with Lightning Fast. Worst thing I've ever done."

She was in full southern accent mode. Which in this case meant she was mad.

"You shouldn't sweat it," Elizabeth said. "It's not as if

finding out that agents are idiots is a surprise to me. And really, the more you tell me, the less appealing that whole side of things looks. I'm here to *swim*. And I don't need the distraction or the extra pressure."

"It still makes me mad," Susan Carol said as they pulled open the doors to the dining hall. As they walked inside, she pointed her finger at Stevie.

"If you don't write a story about Liz in the next couple of days, I will never speak to you again," she said.

He put his hands up. "Don't shoot. You don't have to convince me. I'm on your side, remember?"

She picked up a tray and shook her head, still upset.

"I thought my dad was on my side too," she said. "Look how that's turned out."

"But . . . hasn't he been better lately?"

She glared at him in a way that told him he had better cut his losses then and there. It was not a good idea to mess with Susan Carol when she was mad.

19: THE CHARMING PLAN

While Elizabeth went in search of some protein, Susan Carol and Stevie waited in line at the pasta bar. The room was a lot more crowded than it had been the day before, and you could almost feel the electricity building among the athletes with the opening ceremony that night.

"I'm sorry I jumped on you like that," Susan Carol said when Elizabeth was out of earshot. "It just makes me angry that in the year 2012, female athletes are still valued more for their looks than for their ability."

"It's true of men too," Stevie said. "Do you think Tiger Woods and Michael Jordan would have been such iconic figures if they weren't considered good-looking? Same with Phelps."

"Okay, first of all, you're talking three men who were arguably the best *ever* in their sports. Second, none of them are to die for, exactly."

"What about Roger Federer?" he said, pausing long enough to ask for spaghetti with marinara sauce and some meatballs on the side.

"Now *he's* gorgeous," Susan Carol said. "But he also may be the greatest tennis player in history. The point is this: Unless J.P. is flat-out lying to my father, if I win a gold medal here, I'll make *at least* five million in the next *year*—maybe a lot more. Elizabeth might win two gold medals and not make a penny. How is that fair?"

"It's not," Stevie said. "You're right. But what about this?—and don't bite my head off. Is it fair that a gorgeous fifteen-year-old who swims fast *can* make millions? Think about your mom the teacher and your dad the minister. They won't make that kind of money ever. And that doesn't seem fair either."

Susan Carol stared. "So, do you think I shouldn't take the money?"

"No, I don't mean that at all. I'm just saying—we've both seen enough in the sports world to know that money is everywhere, but fairness is harder to come by."

Susan Carol was quiet, and Stevie was afraid he'd made her feel worse. When would he learn to keep his mouth shut? But he couldn't stand the silence either, so he tried again. "Don't beat yourself up about it. You didn't make the rules. It's not your fault that you have opportunities Elizabeth doesn't. And *neither* of you is here for the money anyway. You're both here to *swim*."

"I know. I always feel much better at the pool. . . . Everything else is just so confusing."

"So, do you want to just drop this? Forget about Bill and Krylova? It's probably nothing, and you should be concentrating on swimming."

"Well, I'm as ready to swim as I can be already," Susan Carol said slowly, considering. "Do you really think there's nothing funny going on?"

Stevie laughed. "With the two of us here, Scarlett? Of course there's something going on."

They were now searching for a table in the midst of a blur of sweat suits with the flags of different countries on them—along with corporate logos, of course.

"Too true," she said. "By the way, did you know that Vivian Leigh was English?"

"Um, no. But probably because I have no idea who Vivian Leigh is."

She gave him her "you're too stupid to live" look.

"She *played* Scarlett O'Hara in *Gone with the Wind*. Both she and Olivia de Havilland, who played Melanie, were Brits playing southern belles."

"And you're a southern belle in Britain right now. Is there some deep meaning in that nugget of useless information?" he said as they finally found an empty table.

"Useless? That's a laugh coming from someone who takes pride in knowing who the tenth man is on Villanova's basketball team."

"What does this have to do with Maurice Sutton?" he said.

They were both still laughing when Elizabeth Wentworth, carrying a plate that had a steak the size of Stevie's room on it, joined them.

"What did I miss?" she asked.

"Nothing useful," Susan Carol said, The Smile lighting up her face.

"So, have you guys got some kind of plan?" Elizabeth said, digging into her steak.

"I promise you, Elizabeth, she has a plan," Stevie said, nodding at Susan Carol. "She always does."

"Matter of fact, I do," she said. "But it involves a little bit of risk for you, Mr. Big-Shot Reporter."

"Risk is my middle name," Stevie shot back, although a little shiver had just run through him.

"Okay, then, Steven Risk Thomas, listen up."

Susan Carol's plan involved a fairly major risk: the potential loss of his media credential. But it also had a good deal of possible upside: He might be able to find out what Bill Arnold had been discussing with Svetlana Krylova.

Apparently Susan Carol was convinced that Stevie would go along with the idea because she had already enlisted Evelyn Rubin's help. Evelyn arrived back from Wimbledon at 1:30 and joined Stevie and the two swimmers at the table soon after Stevie had gone to the ice cream bar and returned with a massive ice cream sundae.

"So," Evelyn said as she sat down. "Are we on?"

"Mr. Risk Is My Middle Name says he's in," Susan Carol said.

"Which means we should be back at my building by two o'clock," Evelyn said. "We don't want any of the other Russian athletes who might be around to think we're rushing over to meet up with Krylova."

"Right," Susan Carol said. "Their practice session is wrapping up soon, so we should get going."

The building where the Russian female swimmers and the American female tennis players were staying—the Americans represented solely by Evelyn at that moment since none of the others had arrived—was on the far side of the village, a solid ten-minute walk from the dining hall. Stevie and Evelyn dropped Susan Carol and Elizabeth off at their building on the way since Susan Carol had promised Ed she would try to nap, or at least stay off her feet, before the opening ceremony that night.

She pointed a finger at him and said firmly: "Do not do anything stupid, Steven Thomas. If it looks like it won't work, just forget about it. We'll figure something else out."

"So now you're worried about me?" he said.

"Not a bit. You always figure your way out of trouble."

"Seems to me he always figures his way *into* trouble," said Evelyn.

Susan Carol rolled her eyes. "He just does that for attention." She gave him a quick kiss, and she and Elizabeth went inside.

Stevie fell into step as Evelyn led the way through the various plazas to her building. The flagpoles all seemed to have flags flying now, indicating that most teams had officially arrived in the village.

"So, you and Susan Carol are still an item?" Evelyn asked as they went.

"I guess so," Stevie said. "I mean, we don't see each other all that often, living 500 miles apart. But the last few months I don't think I've had fifteen minutes alone with her, so it's kind of difficult."

"I know what you mean," Evelyn said. "With my travel schedule it's really hard to date anyone on a steady basis. When I'm at home, guys at school ask me out, but then I'll be gone for a month and not there the entire summer. What are they supposed to do, sit home and wait for me to show up?"

Stevie understood a lot better now what her life must be like. She'd just turned seventeen and was considered the American most likely to succeed the Williams sisters as a genuine threat in major championships. She'd made it to the quarterfinals at both the US Open and Wimbledon.

Like Susan Carol, she was extremely attractive: not as tall, at about five-eight—which meant Stevie was actually an inch taller than she was—but with piercing blue eyes and a devilish grin and dimples. And, not surprisingly, she'd made a lot of money off the court.

"Here's my building," Evelyn said. "If we sit on this bench, I'm sure we'll see Krylova come back."

Susan Carol's plan was simple: When Krylova returned after her workout, Stevie would have his notebook out, "interviewing" Evelyn. Evelyn would wave her over and introduce her, and the rest would be up to him.

"Okay," Stevie said, pulling out his notebook as they sat down. "What should I interview you about?"

Evelyn smiled. "You're the reporter. Why don't you ask me about all the sightseeing I've done in London?"

"Have you done much?" he asked. "I haven't been anywhere yet."

"Some," she said. "I've been to the Tower of London, Buckingham Palace, Parliament, Big Ben . . . and Harrods, of course!"

Evelyn spent the next several minutes talking about London and some of the sights she had seen in her travels around the world. "When I can, I try to get to places a couple of days early, or stay a day after, so I can see the sights," she said. "This year I made the final at Eastbourne, so I didn't get to London until the day Wimbledon started. I'm glad to be back to see—"

She broke off in mid-sentence. Stevie looked up from the notes he had been scribbling and saw a group of young women dressed in red sweat suits with the word *Russia* across the front approaching them. Even walking with other swimmers, Svetlana Krylova stood out. She was easily the tallest of the group and her golden-blond hair, hanging straight down and still a little bit wet, was impossible to miss.

"Here we go," Evelyn said softly. She waved at the approaching swimmers, who waved back.

"Hey, Svetlana, you have a minute?" she said. "I want you to meet someone."

Krylova broke off from the others and walked over.

"You are being interviewed, Evelyn?" Krylova said. "I do not want to interrupt."

"No, no, it's fine," Evelyn said. "I thought you'd like to meet Steven Thomas. He works for a very important American newspaper, the *Washington Herald*."

Stevie stood up to shake hands with Krylova, which was a mistake. She was tall enough to block the sun.

Krylova smiled down at him.

"You are young for a reporter, no?" she said.

"He is," Evelyn said. "But he won a writing contest when he was just thirteen and he's worked for the *Herald* ever since. He's broken a lot of big stories."

"Evelyn should be my PR person," Stevie said, blushing. "It's a pleasure to met you, Svetlana."

Krylova smiled again—a dazzling smile, Stevie had to admit, if you could see that far up.

"The *Washington Herald*. This is not the famous one, right?" she said. "That is the *Washington Post*. They find out the American president Nixon was a liar."

"Yes, that's true," Stevie said. "The reporters who covered that story were Bob Woodward and Carl Bernstein. I've met Mr. Woodward."

"So, you are doing a story on Evelyn?" Krylova said, clearly not overly impressed that Stevie had met Woodward. "You think perhaps she can beat Sharapova?"

"She's done it before," Stevie said.

"True. But not on the grass court, right, Evelyn?"

"I have to win a lot of matches before I worry about playing Sharapova," Evelyn said. "Stevie, did you know that Svetlana and Maria have become good friends?"

This was Stevie's cue.

"Really? That's interesting especially since you do, if you don't mind my saying so, look quite a bit like her."

Krylova smiled, clearly not minding the comparison at all. "I am actually a little taller. We have measured. She has been very helpful to me, advising me on how to deal with so much attention so fast."

Stevie nodded with what he hoped didn't come across as false enthusiasm. "That's actually a great story." He paused, as if thinking. "You don't think . . . I mean I know this is sudden . . . but could I maybe talk to you for a few minutes?"

"But what about Evelyn?"

"We were just finishing when you walked up," Evelyn said.

"Well," Krylova said, clearly not accustomed to such a sudden request. "I was going to go and eat. . . ."

"Maybe I could just take a few minutes while you're eating?" Stevie said.

Krylova nodded, having made a decision. "Yes, it's fine," she said. "I need to go inside to drop my bag off. Washington, DC, the US capital. Yes, sure, I can talk to you about this. Give me five minutes."

She walked inside, leaving Stevie with Evelyn.

"Well played," Evelyn said.

"I think she just liked the idea of being written about in

a Washington paper, even if it isn't the famous one," Stevie said, flattered nonetheless by the compliment.

"That and your charm," Evelyn said.

Stevie reddened for a moment. "Probably her pal Sharapova told her that the more publicity she can get from the American media, the better. Now if only I can figure out how to get her to tell me what's going on with our Lightning Fast pals."

"Oh, Stevie, I am *certain* you can charm the story right out of her."

She had Susan Carol's southern accent down cold.

"I'm begging you," he said. "One Scarlett O'Hara in my life is enough."

Krylova was walking back out the door. She had changed from her sweats into shorts, and Stevie was convinced she'd grown another six inches. The sooner they could sit down, the better. It was hard to be charming with a crick in your neck.

20: RISKY BUSINESS

Fifteen minutes later, Stevie found himself seated across from Svetlana Krylova in the now-familiar surroundings of the athletes' dining area. She had gone the pasta route. Stevie, who had explained that he had eaten earlier with Evelyn, decided a jolt of caffeine wouldn't be a bad idea and opted for coffee.

"So, what is it like to live in the American capital city?" Krylova said as she dug into her pasta.

"Oh, I don't live there," Stevie said. "I live in Philadelphia, which is about two hours away."

Krylova frowned. "I don't understand. How does this work?"

Stevie explained briefly how he had come to work for the *Herald*—leaving out all the parts involving Susan Carol: He had won the writing contest, gone to New

Orleans, met Bobby Kelleher, and started freelancing for the *Herald*.

Stevie could see Krylova's eyes wandering around the room as he told his story. She was being polite, he realized, in asking the question and wasn't all that interested. He pulled out his notebook and tape recorder.

"Okay if I tape the interview?" he asked. "I'm more accurate that way."

"This is a good thing," she said, smiling.

Stevie started with easy, innocuous stuff, knowing it was the best way to get someone comfortable enough to then tell him something they probably shouldn't. He lobbed softball questions at Krylova about her upbringing, how she'd gotten into swimming, when she first thought she might someday be an Olympian, how she and Sharapova came to be friends and what kind of advice she had. Her answers were lengthy; she was trying to make a good impression. As long as an NBC crew didn't show up and steal her, Stevie sensed Krylova would talk as long as he wanted her to.

At last she gave him the opening he was looking for when she mentioned that she hoped to travel to the US sometime after the Olympics were over. Still going slowly, Stevie said that of course she'd want to go to New York, but she should definitely come to his hometown of Philadelphia as well. It turned out she was a basketball fan. "I like Dirk Nowitzki," she said. "Even though he is German. He's very tall and a great shooter too."

Stevie enthused about how Philadelphia was a great

basketball city. He told her a little about the Palestra and the Big Five and then, almost in mid-sentence, he said, "But maybe you won't have so much time for being a tourist. You'll probably be meeting with many American companies and agents. I hear lots of them are interested in you."

She beamed when he said that. "You've heard this?" she said. "I'm surprised. I haven't talked to very many people yet at all."

"No? *I'm* surprised. I mean, I feel like I'm hearing about you everywhere—you're such a favorite. And after your ter-rific interview with Mary Carillo on NBC, where you said you might be interested in modeling . . ." Stevie blushed but then stammered on. "Well, you're so beautiful, I just figured people would be clamoring for you already."

She looked confused. "Clamoring?"

"Fighting over you."

"Oh yes. Well, thank you. I hope this will be true, but I think I have to win. American companies like winners, not second place."

Now that sounded like a line that had come straight from J. P. Scott's mouth.

"Where did you hear that?" he asked.

She leaned forward as if she didn't want anyone else to hear what she was about to say. "My father and I have met with a very important American agent," she said. "He says if I win one gold, he can make me ten million American dollars next year. Two gold and it will be much more."

Since he already knew who the agent was, Stevie didn't

ask for a name, though he noted they were promising a lot more money to Krylova than to Susan Carol. Instead, he nodded and said, "Wow," intentionally using a word he usually tried to avoid.

She nodded just as eagerly. "Yes, and I know he is telling the truth. Already one very important company has told my father if I win gold, they are willing to pay me into the millions."

That name Stevie really wanted to know. His first guess was Nike. Speedo already had Phelps, Susan Carol, Lochte, and Coughlin, so they seemed less likely.

"Wow, that's amazing," he said again. Then, as casually as possible, added, "Which company?"

She looked around again. "If I tell you this, you must not put it into your newspaper," she said. "They would be very mad, I think."

Stevie looked around too. "I promise," he said, since he had no interest in naming the company in print at this point.

"It is Brickley," she said. "They want to go international, and the man we talked to says I will be their . . ." She paused looking for a phrase. "Poster girl."

Stevie was stunned. He had read about Brickley chang-ing its name from Brickley Shoes to just Brickley to be more like Nike and Adidas and Reebok. He knew they were trying to expand out of the basketball world, where the company had started, but he had no idea they were thinking about swimming or any Olympic sport or that they wanted to recruit international athletes.

"That's really interesting," Stevie said. "I thought Brickley was mostly a sneaker company."

"But they are expanding. Clothing, swimwear . . . big exposure." Svetlana smiled.

"Wow," Stevie said again, thinking three *wows* should definitely be his limit. "So, did you meet with the Brickley people here?" he asked.

"Yes, when we were still training north of London," she said. "Mr. Maurice came to our practice one day and then he had lunch with us when it was over."

The name Maurice rang a distant bell in Stevie's memory. Then it came to him: New Orleans, the Final Four. He had been the Brickley rep who was hovering around Chip Graber, then the star player at Minnesota State, now the point guard for the Minnesota Timberwolves. And, Stevie just remembered, a member of the US Olympic basketball team. That could be helpful. But he had to concentrate on this conversation now.

"Bobby Maurice?" he said. "Is that who you met with?"

She looked surprised. "He called himself Robert," she said. "But in the US that name becomes Bobby sometimes, no? How are you knowing him?"

Stevie said, "I've met him covering basketball."

"Oh yes, that's right," she said. "He said he was a basketball person until he was promoted to this new job."

"Oh. I didn't know he had a new job."

"Yes. I don't remember the exact title, but he is in charge of finding international athletes to promote Brickley around the world. They want to sign two or three athletes here and start something they will call the Brickley Gold Line."

"Ah. So they must want athletes they think will win gold—like you."

She smiled. "I guess so."

"Your agent must be pleased. . . ."

She shook her head. "I don't have an American agent yet, remember? I only *spoke* to one. Mr. Maurice asked us not to mention it to anyone. He doesn't want anyone talking about it until my events are over."

She reached across the table and put her hand on his. "I can trust you?" she said. "You won't tell anyone? Even Evelyn?"

This was getting more intriguing by the minute. "Of course," he said, feeling just a little bit guilty. "This is totally off the record." As he didn't want to print what she said, he wasn't strictly lying.

Strictly.

He parted ways with Krylova outside the dining hall. She said she was going to walk over to the village souvenir store to see if there were people around, trading pins. Stevie knew from some of his pre-Olympics research that pin-trading was a very big deal at the Olympics—even among the athletes. Stevie thanked her, repeated his promise not to write or say anything about the Brickley deal, and headed off to find Susan Carol so he could break that promise as soon as possible.

He texted Susan Carol, who said she would meet him outside her building. It was a warm day, the morning's drizzle had cleared away, and Stevie took a minute to look around in wonder—he was in an Olympic village! In London! He was rounding the corner onto Susan Carol's square when he heard someone behind him calling his name.

"Mr. Thomas!"

The tone, even in just two words, was clearly unfriendly. Stevie turned to see Peter Brooks, the IOC Communications guy, walking briskly in his direction, talking into a walkie-talkie. This wasn't going to be good.

"Mr. Thomas," Brooks repeated as he reached Stevie. "I'm informed you were just seen in the dining area with"—he stopped to look down at a piece of paper in his hand—"Svetlana Krylova of the Russian swim team."

He mispronounced her name, calling her Kree-lova. Instinctively, Stevie corrected him. "It's *Krylova* as in 'cry like a baby,'" he said.

Brooks's eyes narrowed. "You can pronounce it any way you like," he said. "According to your request for access, you were to see"—he looked down at the paper again—"S. C. Anderson and Evelyn Rubin."

"I saw Ms. Rubin earlier and I'm on my way to see Ms. Anderson," Stevie said. Looking across the plaza, Stevie could see Susan Carol coming out the door. "Look, there's Ms. Anderson right now."

Brooks was shaking his head so emphatically Stevie thought it might fall off.

"No, no, you are missing the point," he said. "You have broken *two* rules. One, you are walking around in here unaccompanied, which you know is forbidden. And two, you were talking to an athlete you did *not* make a request to interview."

"But I did," Stevie said. "I asked her if I could interview her, and she said yes."

He was going to play this as dumb as he possibly could. If he was going to go down, he might as well get to see Brooks's head explode too. Even so, his heart was pounding. If he lost his credential, he was in big trouble.

Susan Carol arrived on the scene. "Is there a problem here, Mr. Brooks?" she said—somehow remembering his name. "I was just comin' to meet Mr. Thomas for our interview and saw you talkin' to him."

She was in full Scarlett O'Hara, the drawl rolling off her lips, The Smile somehow brightening the already-sunny day. But if there was a human being on earth who might *not* be charmed by Scarlett, this was the guy.

And yet, when he looked at Susan Carol, smiling brightly, dressed in a USA T-shirt, shorts, and flip-flops, looking about as close to the ideal all-American girl as you could get, even Peter Brooks melted just a little.

"Ms. Anderson, I'm afraid there is a bit of a problem," he said. "Mr. Thomas has been flouting the rules— interviewing another athlete without authorization, walking around the village unaccompanied—"

Susan Carol interrupted by shaking her head and putting her hand on Brooks's arm. "Oh, Mr. Brooks, I do apologize," she said. "It's really my fault. I had to go to my room to do a couple of interviews back home that USA Swimming asked me to do? And Steve hadn't eaten, so I asked my friend Svetlana to take him over to the dinin' hall while I finished up. I hope you'll forgive me. He was just doin' what I asked him to do."

Brooks was clearly confused. On the one hand, he had Stevie dead to rights and was very much looking forward to taking him by the arm and escorting him to the gate and perhaps stripping him of his credential altogether. On the other hand, here was this charming girl—one of the athletes, no less—giving him this big smile and saying *she* was the one who had gotten it all wrong.

"All right, then, all right," Brooks finally said, digging deep for his inner bureaucrat even as he continued to look dazzled by Susan Carol. "Since Ms. Anderson has vouched for you, Mr. Thomas, I will let you go with a warning *one* time. If there is a repeat of this sort of behavior, I promise you there will be repercussions regardless of explanation."

"Oh, thank you for understandin'," Susan Carol said, patting him effusively on the shoulder all the while giving Stevie a look that said, "Back me up here, pal."

This was actually harder for Stevie than trying to be charming. But he managed to say, "Yes, thank you. I didn't realize it was such a big deal, but I see now that it is. It won't happen again."

Brooks gave them both a curt nod and turned on his heel. Susan Carol had her hands on her hips.

"I declare, Steven Richman Thomas, you can find trouble—"

"I was carrying out *your* plan, remember?" he said.

She waved a hand. "Yes, well. Shall we find Evelyn so you can fill us in?"

"There's one other person we need to find," he said.

"Who's that?"

"Chip Graber."

She gave him a look, said nothing, and waved at him to follow her. The village had become crowded. They needed to find a quiet place to talk.

They met in the suite that Evelyn was "sharing" with Venus and Serena Williams. The two sisters were going to be staying at The Savoy when they got to London, so Evelyn had the entire place to herself.

The problem was getting Stevie into the building. Only athletes, coaches, and family were allowed in. Evelyn explained to the guard on her door that, even though Stevie had a media badge, he was her cousin. Another lie, and so soon after they'd promised Peter Brooks to be good . . . Oh, well.

Stevie filled the two girls in on what Krylova had told him about Brickley.

"So is Chip still with Brickley?" Susan Carol asked.

"Definitely," Stevie said. "There was a story in the Minneapolis paper a few weeks ago that kind of went national. Apparently Brickley wanted him to pull a Michael Jordan and wrap himself in the American flag if the US wins, and he said he wouldn't do it."

He was surprised that he knew something Susan Carol didn't. Then again, her life had been a bit hectic the past few months.

"What is pulling a Michael Jordan?" Evelyn asked.

"Back in '92, the first year NBA players were allowed to play in the Olympics—the year of the original Dream Team—the USOC had a contract with Reebok that said all the American players had to wear Reebok sweats during medal ceremonies. But Jordan had his own contract with Nike and didn't want to be seen wearing a Reebok logo. So Jordan accepted his medal with an American flag draped over his shoulders to cover it up. And he got the rest of the team to go along with him."

"It was pretty cheesy," Susan Carol said.

"We weren't even born," Stevie answered.

"I've seen tape," she said.

Of course she had.

"The point is, Chip may be able to tell us more about *Robert* Maurice, as he now calls himself. He was the one who recruited Chip in the first place."

"Yeah, I guess Bobby Mo doesn't sound quite as international," she said.

"So our next problem is finding Chip. I know the American basketball players aren't staying in the village," Stevie said.

"Probably they're in the most expensive hotel London's got," Susan Carol said.

"That would be the Wyndham Grand," said Evelyn, "I think it's the only five-star hotel in London. It's where all the top players stay during Wimbledon. It's elegant, right on the river, and near lots of good restaurants."

"Then why aren't Venus and Serena staying there?" Susan Carol asked a split second before Stevie did.

"Because they *never* do what everyone else is doing. They like to be different."

Susan Carol was giving Stevie a look he had seen before. It was her "you have to do something that's going to be hard" look.

"Let me guess," he said. "You have a plan."

"Not really. All I can think is that you need to talk to Maurice. And Chip could be your in. I mean, I don't think calling a Brickley PR person is going to get you a meeting."

"You think Maurice is going to tell me what he's planning for Svetlana Krylova and whether your agent is in on it?"

"No. But if you imply you know that *something's* going on, I think he might get upset enough to make a mistake and tell you something. But you'll have to figure a way to rattle his cage without ratting out Svetlana . . ."

Right. This was going to be hard.

21: OPENING CEREMONY

Stevie managed to find his way back to the media center without getting into any more trouble and found Bobby Kelleher and Tamara Mearns banging away on their computers in the *Herald-Post* office area.

"Nice of you to check in with us," Kelleher said when Stevie walked in.

"We were getting a little worried," Mearns confessed. "But Susan Carol sent us a text saying you were en route back."

Stevie apologized for forgetting to stay in touch but said he had lots to tell. So they walked through the maze that led to the dining area and had official Cokes in official cups.

They sat at a corner table, and Stevie told them everything—including his close call with Peter Brooks.

Kelleher leaned back in his chair when he was finished.

"Huh. That's all very interesting. But, really, we've got

nothing," he said. "An agent talks to a prospective client. A shoe company rep makes a pitch to the same athlete and asks her to keep it quiet. It's nothing."

"But, Bobby—" Stevie said, even as Kelleher put his hand up to tell him to wait.

"And yet, it *feels* like something. We all feel it, including Susan Carol, and she's the one closest to it in a lot of ways."

"Okay," Tamara said. "But what is *it*?"

"Exactly," Kelleher said. "Stevie, do you have Chip's cell number?"

Stevie shook his head. "I had it, but he changed it about a year ago, and I've never gotten the new one. I haven't talked to him in a while."

"Well, that needs to change," Kelleher said.

He pulled out his own phone and got the number for the Wyndham Grand hotel.

"Mr. Graber, please," he said when someone answered.

Apparently the operator didn't find anyone under the name Graber because Kelleher said, "He could be under a separate rooming list. He's on the US Olympic basketball team."

He listened for another minute, then nodded. "I understand," he said. "Thank you."

He snapped the phone shut. "They won't even confirm that the team is staying there. But I know they are because Mike Krzyzewski told me that's where they're staying."

"You've got *his* cell," Tamara said. "Why not call him and tell him you need to get in touch with Chip?"

"That's plan B," Kelleher said. "Plan A is we talk to Chip in person tonight at the opening ceremony."

"In that crowd? How?" Stevie asked.

"Each American team has been asked to make a couple of athletes available in the mixed zone after the ceremony is over," Kelleher said. "The swimming media are going nuts because Phelps isn't going to be one of the Americans. But Mike Moran from the USOC told me that the basketball players are going to be Kobe Bryant, Kevin Durant, and Chip."

"Why did that even come up in conversation?" Tamara asked.

Kelleher smiled. "I was ninety-nine percent sure LeBron wouldn't be one of the players because he would be worried about playing second fiddle to Kobe. So just to be a hundred percent sure, I asked Mike. Little did I know the answer would be so useful."

"The mixed zone will be a zoo, though," Tamara said.

"It will be," Kelleher said. "But we've got a secret weapon when it comes to getting to Chip."

"What's that?" Stevie said.

Kelleher laughed. "You," he said.

Deciding to take part in the opening ceremony over the objections of J. P. Scott and her father was the best decision that Susan Carol had ever made.

The security checks were a pain, beginning with being wanded and having everything they were carrying checked even before they got on the bus at the athletes' village to make the ride to the Olympic Stadium. The traffic was brutal even for so short a ride. Then there was more security before they were allowed to go to the area where they lined up. And then there was an hour wait before they marched in.

But the rest of it was magical. Putting on her official USA uniform had given Susan Carol chills. Everywhere she turned, she saw great athletes. She'd have to find the official count later, but there must have been close to five hundred athletes, just for the American team. She was surrounded by divers and fencers and rowers and cyclists. The women's gymnasts looked so tiny standing next to the weight lifters. She recognized a lot of the sprinters and the beach volleyball players and all the swimmers, of course. But which were the sailors and which were the water polo players? There were wrestlers and badminton players and equestrians. Suddenly she was overwhelmed by it all. By all that talent and all that ambition and longing in one small space.

She ran into Mike Krzyzewski, who was coaching the men's basketball team and who had written her a note when he found out she'd qualified. She was always happy to see him, but somehow here it was even better, and she gave him a big hug.

Then she heard a voice behind her say, "Well, if it isn't the greatest girl reporter/swimmer in history."

She turned and saw Chip Graber with a huge smile on his face.

"Oh, Chip, I'm so glad to see you!" she said as they hugged.

"My God, Susan Carol, will you please stop growing?" he said. "You're making me look bad."

She blushed. Chip was only five-foot-ten, easily the shortest member of the Olympic basketball team. Even in the low-heeled shoes all the women were wearing, she was a good three inches taller than he was. Still, he looked the same as ever: the floppy hair, the easy smile.

Stevie had texted her that he was going to try to talk to Chip later in the mixed zone and that if she saw him, to please give him a heads-up.

"Chip, I hear you're going to the mixed zone tonight after the ceremony," she said.

"Yeah, I'm the guy everyone who can't get close to Kobe and Kevin will be talking to," he said, grinning.

"Well, there's one person I really need you to talk to," she said.

"Who's that?"

"Stevie."

Chip gave her a look.

"Please don't tell me the two of you have somehow found trouble *here*," he said. "You're here to swim, to win a gold medal, to be a star. For one week can't you stop being a reporter?"

"This could involve my swimming," she said. "I'm just not sure."

His smile faded. "Are you in trouble somehow?"

"No," she said. "Well, we don't know. Maybe we're all overreacting because Stevie and I always seem to find trouble. . . ."

She was about to tell him more when a USOC official came up and said, "We need everyone lined up with their teams right away. We're getting ready to march in."

"I'll make sure to find Stevie," Chip said to Susan Carol. "Don't worry. Whatever it is, I'll help."

He gave her another quick hug before the official practically dragged him over to join the other basketball players. And she went and found her own team.

Marching into the stadium was one of the great moments of her life. Even before they came out of the tunnel into the sea of lights and people and flashing cameras, Susan Carol could hear the noise building. She was walking in the second row of swimmers—the women went first, then the men—in between Elizabeth Wentworth and Natalie Coughlin.

"I've done this three times before, but it's amazing every time. This does not get old," Coughlin said as they approached the end of the tunnel.

Susan Carol could see why. The cheers for the American team swept through the massive stadium as they circled the track and waved at the stands where people frantically waved back, pausing only to snap photos.

She watched Michael Phelps, who had been chosen as the American flag bearer, march past the box where Queen Elizabeth and other members of the royal family were standing. Other countries dipped their flags as they went by, but not the US. By long-standing tradition, the American flag didn't bow before royalty or any heads of state.

Somewhere in the stands she knew her entire family

was watching. They had flown in that morning and had spent the day recovering from the overnight flight. One thing that made Susan Carol happy was that the money she was making made it possible for her mom and dad and both her brothers and her sister to come to the Games. No matter what disagreements she'd had with her dad in the past couple of months, she knew he was in the stands with the same lump in his throat that she had in hers.

As the Americans passed the staircase that led up to the Olympic torch, she heard the PA announcer say, "Ladies and gentlemen, please welcome the athletes, coaches, and officials from the United States of America!"

She didn't think it was possible, but the noise grew even louder. Susan Carol had tears in her eyes. She looked to her right and saw Elizabeth was crying. So was Coughlin—as she no doubt had three times before.

When all the athletes from all the nations were gathered in the middle of the field, one shard of light revealed Sebastian Coe as he entered the darkened stadium with the Olympic torch. Coe was a great English runner who had won gold medals in the 1,500 meter in 1980 and 1984, and he had also headed London's Olympic bid. You could hear a pin drop as he climbed the steps and turned to face the crowd, holding the flaming torch in his right hand.

He stood that way for a moment, then dipped the torch into the giant cauldron. The minute the flames leapt up, the stadium went crazy, and Coe stood still, drinking in the cheers.

If I finish dead last in all my races, Susan Carol thought, *it will be okay because I got to be part of this.*

Stevie was just as thrilled to be there, sitting—or more accurately standing because everyone was on their feet.

The ceremony—all the dancing and singing and performing that had gone on before the entrance of the athletes—had been way too long in Stevie's opinion. But once the athletes began marching in, the wait was more than worth it.

Seeing all the athletes together in the stadium, Stevie was hit by just how *big* the Olympics were. He had been so focused on one sport and one athlete since arriving that he'd kind of lost sight of it. Stevie knew that more than 11,000 athletes had taken part in the 2008 Games in Beijing. Closer to 12,000 were expected in London, and most of them were marching in right in front of him. It was a mind-boggling sight, especially with all the colorful outfits they were wearing.

Kelleher seemed to sense his thoughts. "Look at them all," he said at one point. "Thousands and thousands of athletes. The best in the world. And the next two weeks are crucial for all of them."

They were close enough that they spotted Susan Carol among the Americans. That was thrilling, as was the introduction of the American team. But the moment that really got to Stevie was when the last team—the hosts from Great Britain—came marching in.

When the PA announcer formally introduced them, the ovation wasn't just loud, it was lengthy. The media section was close enough to the royal box that Stevie could look over and see that the queen was applauding with a good deal of enthusiasm and Prince William and his wife, Kate, had their arms over their heads, waving to the athletes who were waving back.

When the stadium went dark just before the torchbearer entered, you could feel the anticipation. There was no introduction, just a spotlight finding the lone runner as he stepped onto the track carrying the torch.

There was a roar when the spotlight confirmed that it was Coe with the torch. And once the flame was lit, the roar was louder still. Then they played "God Save the Queen," and the queen herself formally announced the beginning of the Olympics. "I declare the Games of London to be open," she said to more wild cheering.

It was well after eleven o'clock by the time the ceremony was over, but everyone in the stadium was still adrenaline-pumped. No one was allowed to leave their seats until the queen and the other royals had departed.

"Who does she think she is," Tamara said with a smile as Elizabeth waved a final goodbye, "the queen of England?"

"She's only had the job for sixty years," Kelleher said. "I don't see what the big deal is."

Then they headed downstairs—along with a huge horde of media—to the mixed zone. There would be no formal interviews since technically nothing had happened. Athletes had been "requested" by their various Olympic committees to pass through the mixed zone on their way out. There were signs overhead that told journalists which athletes would be where, and Stevie headed for the one that said MEN'S BASKETBALL. Sadly, half the TV cameramen in the world were already there, jockeying for position.

Kelleher had gone to try to talk to a soccer player who was from Washington, and Mearns was headed for the swimmers just in case she could see Susan Carol.

Stevie hung back as Kobe Bryant, Kevin Durant, and Chip Graber were led to the gates that separated the athletes from the media. Stevie thought the whole thing was humiliating—all the pushing and shoving just to talk to someone across a gate—but apparently the IOC had done it this way for years. It was easy to see Bryant and Durant from the back because they were so tall, but Chip was swallowed up almost instantly.

Stevie had seen mob scenes in post-game locker rooms, but nothing like this. He knew he'd have to wait until the various TVs got their sound bites, but the crowding was intense. He was convinced some kind of fight was going to break out at any second.

Sure enough, a few minutes in, Stevie heard shouting coming from the front. Someone with an American accent was shouting, "Let him answer in English first, dammit. He can talk in your language later."

"The language is Italian, you idiot," someone answered in what Stevie imagined was an Italian accent. "He can answer in any language he wants."

Stevie remembered that Bryant had spent much of his

boyhood in Italy and was fluent in Italian. Apparently he'd been asked a question in Italian and was answering it when the American got frustrated. There were more raised voices, and finally Stevie heard someone on the other side of the fence say, "English questions *first*, please."

Whether that made everyone happy or not—Stevie suspected it didn't—it stopped the shouting match. The crowd had packed in to get close to Bryant and to a lesser extent Durant, and Stevie saw a little bit of an opening to the outside. There was another row of steel separating those trying to talk to the basketball players from those talking to several soccer players, and Stevie edged along the fencing until he was close enough to the front to actually see Chip, who was standing with his arms folded, talking to about four reporters. Stevie got close enough so that Chip could see *him*—and he nodded and smiled to let Stevie know he had spotted him.

The small group talking to Chip finally dispersed, and Stevie was able to get right up against the fence separating them.

"Stevie Thomas, I swear you're as tall as I am," Chip said, leaning across the fence to give Stevie a hug.

"I just wish I was as tall as Susan Carol," he said.

"Me too," Chip said, laughing. "I understand we need to talk. You guys have somehow found trouble again?"

"Yeah, well, we think so," Stevie said.

He was about to launch into the story when a TV guy with a cameraman in tow raced up, light shining in Chip's face, and without so much as an "excuse me" asked Chip something about the US playing Turkey in its first game—a rematch of the 2010 World Championship final.

Chip looked right at the camera and the microphone and said in a pleasant tone, "I'm in the middle of something here. Give me a minute."

The TV guy looked miffed, but said nothing.

"Look, we'll never be able to really talk here," Chip said. "I don't leave for practice until noon tomorrow. Can you meet me at the Wyndham Grand at eight for breakfast? It'll be quiet."

"I'd love to, but how am I going to get through security?" Stevie said. "I hear it's intense."

"Yeah, I know," Chip said.

He reached into his pocket and pulled out a pin with the Olympic rings on it and lettering underneath it that said USA FAMILY.

"We each get four of these," he said. "My parents and Anjie (my girlfriend) aren't coming in until next weekend. So put this on your shirt or jacket and *don't* wear your media credential. I'll meet you in the lobby at eight." They exchanged cell numbers, and Chip went back to the TV guy, who had now been joined by several others.

Stevie happily worked his way out of the scrum, thankful he didn't need a quote for a story tonight. What a zoo! He found Kelleher leaning against a wall near the exit.

"I'm getting too old for this," Kelleher said. "I gave up after the second fistfight nearly broke out. Did you get to Chip?"

"Yup. I'm having breakfast with him in the morning at his hotel." Stevie pulled out his family pin and showed it to Kelleher. "He says this will get me in there."

Kelleher nodded. "Good work. Now let's hope he can tell us something about his old friend Bobby Mo."

22: PRELIMINARIES

Stevie was in a cab at 7:30 the next morning, still yawning.

The security outside the Wyndham Grand looked a lot like the security had looked at the Olympic Stadium the previous night. For a second, Stevie wondered if the queen might be coming to have breakfast. When the doorman opened the cab door for Stevie, his first comment wasn't "good morning" or "welcome," the way it always was at the Gloucester, but "hotel guest?"

Stevie paid the cabdriver and flashed the family pin at the doorman, who said, "Of course, sir. You can go right inside. Just show the pin to the gentleman inside the door."

Stevie actually had to show the pin twice more before he was safely in the lobby, where Chip was waiting for him.

"Little tired this morning?" Chip said, seeing the look on Stevie's face.

"I'm okay," Stevie said. "It's just like walking the gauntlet getting in here."

Chip laughed. "You're in the inner sanctum now, man. Come on, let's go to the restaurant in back."

The restaurant had a spectacular view of Chelsea Harbor and beyond to the Thames River. It was early enough that the restaurant wasn't crowded yet, so they were given a table near a window. There seemed to be about four waiters for every table, so they ordered quickly.

Stevie asked Chip if he was surprised he had made the team given that just about everyone else on the roster had been an All-Star forever and in some cases—Bryant, James, Durant, Dwyane Wade, Dwight Howard—were probably lock Hall of Famers.

"Yes and no," Chip said. "Clearly I'm not in the same class with some of those guys—most of those guys, maybe *all* of those guys. But I knew Krzyzewski wanted someone on the team who would distribute the ball on offense and didn't mind being an attack dog on defense. I don't have to score a point to make him happy. I just have to keep all the other scorers happy."

"Not so easy, I'd think," Stevie said.

"Not as hard as you might think either," Chip said. "These guys know that being unselfish worked in '08, and they want to win. Sharing the ball is the best way to win."

He poured coffee from the pot they had ordered. "So, tell me what's going on and how I can help."

Stevie added milk and sugar to his coffee, took a long

sip, and told Chip the whole story, dating back to Charlotte. When he finished, Chip shook his head in disbelief.

"Wow," he said. "I feel for Susan Carol. It's one thing if an agent is pushing you around, or a shoe guy or officials. But her father? That hurts."

"Well, I think the whole aborted coach-swap thing opened his eyes a little. But Susan Carol still seems like things aren't totally fine. . . ."

Chip frowned. "My guess is he's just overwhelmed by what this could mean financially. Now, the agent and Bobby Mo—"

"What do you know about Bobby Mo?"

"Enough to know he's not to be trusted."

"But you're with Brickley."

Chip shrugged. "I have to be with someone, and Bobby Mo always seemed like a relatively small fish. Plus, it isn't like the other companies are run by Mother Teresa's protégés. They're all pretty much the same. You're talking about people who pay middle school kids, or at least pay their parents, to get them to play on AAU teams they sponsor."

Stevie sat back as the waiter delivered his eggs, toast, and bacon. Chip had asked for French toast. When he saw his eggs and Chip's French toast, he knew he'd ordered the wrong thing.

"That looks good," he said.

"Go ahead and order some," Chip said.

"But they'll charge us. This is fine."

Chip laughed. "Stevie, my salary for next season is eight and a half million dollars. I can swing an extra breakfast."

Stevie wasn't going to argue. He called the waiter back and asked for French toast.

"Something wrong?" the waiter asked.

"No, it's just that the French toast looks really good."*

The waiter gave him a look that screamed "spoiled American teenager!" but took his plate away.

Stevie was about to ask Chip more about Bobby Mo when he heard footsteps behind him. He looked up to see an extremely tall man with blond hair and an easy smile approaching with a boy who looked to be about twelve.

"Chip, you certainly seem relaxed," the man said as he reached the table.

Graber laughed and said, "Mark, you played long enough to know a game-face can be hidden."

"Especially when you're playing Angola, right?" the man said.

Chip nodded. "Steve Thomas, this is Mark Alarie and his son, Christian."

Stevie stood up to shake hands and immediately wanted to sit down again. Mark Alarie was at least six-foot-eight.

"Mark was on Coach K's first great team at Duke back in '86. First round draft pick that year. Of course the real talent in the family is Christian. Right, Christian?"

Christian Alarie wasn't interested in talking about his own game.

"How many do you think you'll score today, Chip?" he asked.

"Not as many as Kobe or LeBron," Chip laughed.

"Yeah, but they're nothing without you," Christian said. "You set up the offense."

"Mark, your son is obviously a basketball genius," Chip said.

"He's got a point guard's mentality in a power forward's body," Mark Alarie said. "Just like his dad."

"As I recall, his dad shot it pretty well," Chip said.

"I'm a good shooter too," Christian Alarie said. "But Coach K told me I better learn to pass."

"Good advice," Chip said. "You'll never go wrong if you listen to Coach K."

Stevie groaned. "Now you sound like Susan Carol."

Chip was laughing. "You'll have to excuse Stevie—unlike his friend Susan Carol, he's not such a Duke fan."

Mark Alarie looked shocked. "Say it ain't so, Steve! It's never a good idea to bet against K. Did you know that David Falk is out in the lobby right now telling everyone he's going to put together some kind of joint deal for Coach K and Susan Carol since she's such a big fan?"

Now Stevie and Chip both groaned. "Oh God. Will these agents stop at nothing?" asked Chip.

"Obvioulsy not," Alarie said. "Come on, Christian. Let's get some breakfast."

But Christian was still eyeing Stevie suspiciously. "You're not a Duke fan?"

"It's okay," Mark Alarie said. "We're happy to meet him anyway. Chip, we'll see you at shoot around. Coach K invited Christian."

They all said their goodbyes, but as the Alaries walked away, Stevie heard Christian whispering to his dad again, "What do you mean he's not a Duke fan?"

"He really was a great player," Chip said. "Would have played fifteen years in the NBA if he hadn't gotten hurt."

Stevie's French toast arrived then and after the two of them had dug in, Chip said, "But back to Bobby Mo. Lately he seems to have grown into a much bigger fish. Their competitors have cashed in big-time overseas. Brickley hasn't yet, and they've put Maurice in charge of getting their name out over here."

"And Svetlana Krylova is who he's betting on?"

Chip shrugged. "I don't know what his plan is. But she's certainly got the looks. You said she speaks good English, so they can market her here and in the States. But no matter how good-looking she is or smart or articulate, she's not going to move product with a silver or bronze medal dangling from her neck."

"Yeah, well, if Bobby Mo is recruiting athletes for something called the Gold Line, I guess a silver medal won't do it," Stevie said.

"Exactly," Chip said. "You have to figure he's scoping out the gymnasts and the runners too. The tennis players are all locked up. But he really only needs two or three athletes as long as they're the right ones."

"Krylova's hardly a lock to win," Stevie said. "I mean in the 100, you've got Susan Carol and this girl Elizabeth Wentworth, not to mention Sarah Sjöström, who may be better than all of them. And in the 200 you've got Susan Carol and Elizabeth and the Chinese woman, Liu."

"The fact that you know this much about swimming scares me a little bit," Chip said.

"I know a lot about Susan Carol's events," he said.

"In that case, it's okay." Chip laughed. "So if you're right and Krylova's no lock to win, then Bobby Mo must have something more up his sleeve. Maybe the reason he wants to keep his talks with Krylova secret is that he's selling the same dream to other swimmers too. Whoever comes out of here as the biggest star gets the biggest Brickley contract."

"He hasn't talked to Susan Carol."

"Are you sure?" Chip said. "He may have talked to the agents or to her father. Or both."

Stevie hadn't thought of that. "But how would Susan Carol get him into Europe?" he asked.

"Yeah, it's a stretch," Graber said. "But in case you hadn't noticed, your girlfriend's a knockout too. You're right, though—Krylova is the ideal winner for Bobby Mo."

"So what can I do?" Stevie asked.

"First, eat your French toast. Second, keep an eye on the agents and Reverend Anderson. They might do something that tells you what's going on. And I'll poke around with Bobby Mo. Keeping secrets isn't his best thing. So if I find anything out, I'll let you know."

Stevie decided to take Chip's advice. He devoured his French toast.

Susan Carol was amazed how calm she felt before her first race as an Olympian.

It had been after midnight by the time she got back to the athletes' village, but she'd slept more soundly than any night since she'd been in London. She and Elizabeth Wentworth met Ed Brennan for breakfast, and then he had driven them to the swimming venue in one of the official vans the coaches had been given by USA Swimming.

Even after swimming in the practice pools for several days, Susan Carol was still awed by the sheer size of the building. It held two fifty-meter pools—one for warm-ups and one for competition—along with a twenty-five-meter diving pool and seating for 17,500 spectators. The building had an enormous swaybacked roof, and there was actually a bridge over part of the building that people used to walk into the Olympic Park, so it was like the gateway to the Games. Everywhere she looked, there were people in action.

"We're a long way from Goldsboro High School," she said to Ed as they approached the entrance. They had left extra time to go through security, but there was almost no one ahead of them, so they breezed right through.

"How do you feel?" Ed asked.

"Actually, I feel great," she said. "Maybe I'll get nervous on the blocks or something, but right now, I'm just excited."

He nodded. "Good. You look more relaxed. I'm not sure why, but I'm not complaining."

Ed saw both swimmers safely to the locker rooms and then went out on deck to wait.

As Susan Carol changed in the crowded locker room—there were three events going on for women with about eighty swimmers entered in each—she felt much the same as she had the night before: proud to be there. This wasn't a locker room full of age-group swimmers back in North Carolina. These were Olympians, and she was one of them.

The only bad moment of the morning came when she walked onto the deck headed for the warm-up pool and saw J. P. Scott walking in her direction. *Not now,* she said to herself. Scott was waving as if they were meeting for a friendly lunch.

"How do you feel?" he said, giving her an awkward hug.

"I'm fine," she said. "What are you doing on deck?"

"Oh, I have friends in the right places," he said. His credential said USA SWIMMING on it. "I'm working on getting one for your dad too."

"Please don't," she said. "Just let my dad sit in the stands like he always does. I need some space."

"Come on, Susan Carol, lighten up," he said. "Try remembering we're all on the same team."

She had a lot of answers for that but—fortunately—Ed showed up, waving a hand at her. "You need to get in the water, no time for small talk," he said.

She left J.P. without another word, wondering who from USA Swimming had given him a credential to get on the deck and whether she could get it revoked without causing a major scene. The swimmers had been told on a daily basis how tight space on the deck was going to be, especially during the heats.

Fortunately, J.P. went straight out of her mind as soon as she slipped into the water. She knew she had hit her taper perfectly: She was rested and strong and completely ready to swim. Ed wanted her to swim 1,500 meters to get loose. By the time she flipped after her first easy 100, she was ready to get on the blocks and go.

She went through her entire warm-up routine, pausing on the wall a couple of times to chat with Elizabeth, who also seemed to be enjoying the experience. As she was finishing, she noticed Svetlana Krylova one lane over, relaxing on the wall.

"Good luck," she said with a wave.

"To you too," Krylova said. "Today we can hope each other swims fast. It is tomorrow when it gets serious."

"It's the Olympics," Susan Carol said. "It's all serious—but fun too."

Krylova shook her head. "There is nothing fun when millions of dollars are at stake."

Susan Carol just smiled and pushed off with another quick wave, ducking her head under the water. But she thought about what Svetlana had said. Clearly someone—or perhaps several someones—had made it clear that there were huge contracts riding on her performances over the next few days. Susan Carol willed herself back to the atmosphere of the opening ceremony. The Olympics hadn't felt like a giant money grab then. Those were the Games she wanted to play in.

All she wanted to do now was swim the best races of her life. If she could do that, she'd walk away happy.

Stevie was a lot more nervous at that moment than Susan Carol. He was sitting with Kelleher and Mearns, filling them in on his breakfast with Chip.

"Sounds like Chip thinks Maurice isn't exactly an upstanding guy," Kelleher said.

"No doubt," Stevie said. "But what can he *do*, really? This isn't like the Final Four, where you can blackmail someone to throw a game."

"Why go all the way to blackmail?" Tamara said. "How about a simple bribe?"

"Could you really bribe an Olympian . . . to lose?" Stevie couldn't quite imagine it.

The last heat of the men's 400 IM was in the water. The place had gotten loud because Ryan Lochte was blowing away the other seven swimmers and wasn't that far off Phelps's world record as he started the freestyle leg.

"And where does Lightning Fast fit in?" Stevie asked. "Are they working with Maurice?"

"Or *against* Maurice," Kelleher put in.

They sat in silence while Lochte finished his race, coming up less than a second shy of the world record.

"Too bad Phelps decided not to swim this," Tamara said. "That would have been a great race to see."

The announcer was saying something about a short break before the heats began for the women's 100 butterfly. There would be eleven heats, and Susan Carol was in the eighth.

"Okay," said Kelleher said once the PA had quieted. "Just speculating wildly . . . If I'm Bobby Maurice, the one swimmer I might be able to control is Wentworth. Her family's not well off at all. And even if she wins *both* butterfly events, she isn't going to make much money out of the water."

"She didn't strike me as someone who could be bribed when I met her," Stevie said.

"Did Susan Carol's father strike you as the type who could be snowed by an agent?" Kelleher said.

"Good point," Stevie said.

Once they started, the 100-butterfly heats moved along quickly—it was such a fast race. Stevie heard heat seven being called to the blocks and suddenly felt nervous. He knew the heats shouldn't be a problem for Susan Carol. All she had to do was be one of the sixteen fastest swimmers to make the semifinals. But this was it now—the real thing. In a race that was only about a minute long, one mistake or bad break—a poor start or turn, swallowing water, your goggles leaking—could knock you out.

"I'm nervous," Stevie said as the swimmers in heat seven approached the wall. He could see Susan Carol standing behind the lane-four block, shaking her arms to get loose.

"She'll be fine," Kelleher said. "She's always done her

best swimming under pressure. I'll bet that right now the water is where she feels most comfortable."

Then the seventh-heat swimmers were out of the water, and Stevie heard the whistle ordering the swimmers for heat eight onto the blocks. He looked around for a second. The massive building was full—even for the heats. There was media seating for about 500. The media section was less than half full. At night, when finals were being contested, he knew it would be packed.

"Take your mark," he heard the starter say, and then, almost instantly, he heard the beep for the start.

Susan Carol arched her back gracefully leaving the block and seemed to slide into the water without making a splash. As always, she stayed underwater for several kicks. By the time she took her first stroke, she was in the lead. From there, she made it look easy. Stevie could tell she was on cruise control because her pullout from the turn was longer than usual, meaning she knew she had a comfortable lead.

She splashed into the wall in 59.06, making her the first swimmer in the competition to break a minute. The smile on her face as she climbed out of the pool told Stevie she was satisfied and—like him—glad to have the first race out of the way.

"She does the same thing tonight, she'll be in perfect position for the final," Tamara said.

Stevie was texting Susan Carol during the final three heats. The biggest cheers were for Sarah Sjöström in heat nine, although Krylova got some serious whistles and hoots when she stepped onto the block, stretching her arms above her head in a way guaranteed to make sure everyone in the place noticed her. Sjöström, with nothing to prove, won her heat in 59:77. Elizabeth Wentworth also won her heat, going just a tad slower than Susan Carol: 59.22. The only one who posted a faster time than Susan Carol was Krylova, who charged home in 58.55, meaning she would be in lane four for the second heat that night with Wentworth next to her. Susan Carol would be in lane four of the first heat with Sjöström next to her. There seemed little doubt that the three medalists on Monday night would come from these four swimmers.

"Let's go eat," Kelleher said. "Then we can walk around for a while. I need to get a look at more than just the swimming venue."

To Stevie, the entire Olympics would take place in the swimming venue between now and the final of the 200 butterfly on Wednesday night. He knew he shouldn't feel that way, but he did. As they walked outside onto the plaza, his phone buzzed. Susan Carol had texted back.

Felt great, she wrote. *Never hurt at all. Need to know re Chip. Have something to tell re J.P. Having dinner with my fam tonight after semis. Get a pass to have bfast w/me tomorrow? I will get you clear on my end. Xoxoxoxo.*

23: GOING FOR GOLD

The semifinals had gone just about perfectly as far as Susan Carol was concerned. She and Ed had decided the best strategy was to sit right on Sjöström's shoulder and let her set the pace.

"She knows exactly what she needs to do because she's been through it a million times," Ed said. "Let her do the mental work, and then turn it on at the end."

Susan Carol did just that, picking up her kick with ten meters to go. Sjöström still touched her out, going 58.06 to Susan Carol's 58.12, but she was through to the final with no problem. In the second heat, Krylova blasted through the first fifty meters, opening up a lead of almost a body length on Wentworth before tiring at the finish. She touched in 57.44—awfully fast for a semifinal. Wentworth was second in 58.24, meaning that Krylova would be in lane four for the final with Sjöström in lane five, Susan Carol in lane three, and Wentworth in lane six.

That was fine with Susan Carol. She knew Krylova would set the pace, and she was happy to let her go out fast and fade.

And she was very happy to be having breakfast with Stevie now.

"So how do you feel this morning?" Stevie asked as he dug into a plate of French toast that looked like it could feed four people.

"Fine," she said. "Usually when you swim two races in a day, the one at night is a final and you go all out. I held back a little in both, so I'm not feeling spent at all."

"You looked like you were cruising the whole way," he said.

She smiled. "It's a *very* fast pool," she said. "Everyone is saying it may be the fastest pool ever. Even without the rocket suits, I think there will be lots of world records this week. Whoever wins our race tonight will probably break fifty-six."

The rocket suits, as swimmers called them, almost literally lifted a swimmer in the water because of the materials they were made from. They had been banned in 2009, and there had been a dearth of world records for most of the next two years. Now, in a super-fast pool with Olympic gold medals at stake, it seemed likely that people would start breaking world records again even in regular suits. Susan Carol *knew* she could go a good deal faster than she had the night before and assumed the other three primary contenders could too.

"Okay," she said when all the French toast had miraculously disappeared. "Tell me about Chip."

He filled her in on the news and speculations. Remembering Bobby Maurice and his sinister black beard from their meeting in New Orleans made Susan Carol shudder a little bit. She took a long sip of her orange juice and folded her arms.

"Well, that almost fits with what J.P. said after my heat yesterday morning," she said.

"What'd he say?"

"That if I won either gold medal—100 or 200—there was going to be a bidding war for me."

"Hasn't he said things like that before?"

"Yes, but there's a new twist now."

"What?"

"Now he says it's okay with him if I win 'only' one gold as long as Krylova doesn't win the other."

Stevie almost spit out the coffee he was drinking. "So Lightning Fast must be totally up to date on the Brickley deal. If Krylova wins gold, Brickley goes with her," he said. "You win gold and she doesn't—"

"Then Brickley will want me. And if Brickley makes a big offer and Speedo decides to invoke the matching clause in my contract—"

"It could get completely crazy."

"Exactly."

"You know, that also might mean Krylova's going with another agent."

"Maybe. Or the whole thing is a smoke screen because he's worried I may have heard he met with Krylova. Or he's spinning her a similar story about how she needs to beat me. . . ."

Susan Carol spotted Elizabeth Wentworth approaching and waved her over.

"Steve, you're spending more time here than in the media center," Elizabeth said as she sat down. Stevie noticed she was having French toast too—although considerably less than he had eaten.

"Is it really okay to eat French toast on the day of a big race?" he asked.

She laughed. "Well, to begin with, we all burn so many calories in a day we can pretty much eat whatever we want to—as long as it's early. I'll eat some pasta about three hours before we swim but only fruit between now and then. Second, it isn't as if anyone is going to ask me to do any bikini modeling when this is all over—unlike some people."

"Stop it," Susan Carol said, smiling but clearly embarrassed. "I will *not* be doing any bikini modeling."

"Oh, I was talking about Krylova." Elizabeth grinned. "What made you think I was talking about you?"

Susan Carol laughed. "I told you she was funny," she said to Stevie.

"Speaking of when this is over," Stevie said, plowing ahead as always. "Have you been approached by anyone? Agents? Swimwear companies?"

"I'm guessing that was directed at me since you already know Susan Carol is doing all the morning shows, *Letterman*, and *Leno* from here tomorrow if she wins tonight," Elizabeth said. Then she turned serious. "Actually, I do have an agent who is interested in me. I think his last client was Johnny Weissmuller."

That one was lost on Stevie. "Johnny who?"

Susan Carol sighed. "Oh, Stevie. You really should read more. Johnny Weissmuller was an Olympic swimmer about ninety years ago. He then went on to play Tarzan in the movies."

"So, that was a joke about the agent, then, right?" Stevie said.

"Can't fool you." Elizabeth smiled.

Susan Carol was still irked. "If you win, I guarantee there will be agents and swimwear companies after you."

Elizabeth shrugged. "I doubt if I'll have *two Sports Illustrated* photographers trailing me after a semifinal like you last night, not to mention that HBO guy who wants to do a documentary on your 'Olympic experience,'" she said, smiling. "Honestly, I don't care. I never got into swimming to make money."

"Neither did I," Susan Carol said, feeling at that moment very, very sad.

The two girls were headed for the pool for a light workout after breakfast. Stevie gave Susan Carol a hug and kiss goodbye and wished her luck. Then he went to pick up Kelleher at the media center. They saw the US men's basketball team beat up on Angola 123–54 for their first win. It was a pretty boring game, but mostly Stevie just wanted a chance to see Chip in person again to find out if he'd had any contact with Bobby Maurice. Sadly, all Chip knew was that Maurice would definitely be at the Aquatics Centre for the finals that night. Hardly breaking news.

Riding back to the media center to meet Tamara, Stevie thought about what Elizabeth Wentworth had said that morning about not getting into swimming to make money. He doubted that any swimmer got into the sport to make money. But what if Bobby Maurice offered her a lot of money *not* to win? Considering she could try her absolute hardest and not win anyway, it might be tempting. His gut told him she wouldn't play that game. But his gut wasn't always right.

They tried hashing over what they knew—but it was all so nebulous. Kelleher said, "Well, if Svetlana or Susan Carol wins tonight, there will be a huge scramble to get their names on contracts—even before the 200-fly final on Wednesday. At the very least, one of them will be buried in offers. If Sjöström wins, I imagine her value in Europe would go up, but not by much—she's already a champion."

"And if Elizabeth wins?" Stevie asked.

"Then things may get interesting," Tamara said. "It's what none of the agents or marketers want. . . . Who knows what they might get up to if it happens."

Kelleher's cell phone was ringing. He answered, listened for a few seconds, and then his eyes went just a little bit wide.

"That *is* interesting," he said, and then hung up. "Looks like the stakes keep getting higher."

"Who was that?" Stevie asked.

"Matt Rennie," he said. "Apparently, Bobby Maurice isn't the only apparel rep who is planning on attending the swimming tonight. Phil Knight is going to be there too."

"The founder of Nike is hardly what you would call a swimming *rep*," Tamara said.

"Even so, why is that a big deal?" Stevie asked.

"Because Phil Knight doesn't show up someplace unless he's got an athlete competing or unless there's an athlete competing he doesn't have but wants. I'm telling you, the plot's thickening."

"I just want Susan Carol to win," Stevie said. "I don't care about the rest of it."

"Spoken like a truly objective reporter." Kelleher smiled. "Let's get something to eat before we head over. I have a feeling it's going to be a long night."

Susan Carol actually brought a book to read because she knew it was going to be a long wait before she swam. The swimmers had been told to please be in the venue before the evening events began at 7:30 just in case some logistical issue delayed them on their way over from the athletes' village.

So, even though the 100-fly final was the second-to-last event on the program and wasn't scheduled to start until nine o'clock, she and Elizabeth were in the locker room by 6:45. That would give them time for an easy, stretched-out warm-up, and then, as she always did, Susan Carol would jump in the pool and swim 200 meters about fifteen minutes before they were taken into the ready room.

Her first experience with a ready room had been in Shanghai, and she hadn't especially liked it. Almost everyone put on headphones and sat with their eyes closed. Susan Carol found this disconcerting: eight people trying not to look nervous who were all dying inside, wishing the race was already over.

So she had brought a book, along with her headphones, hoping for a bit of distraction. She'd chosen *All the President's Men*, which was one of her favorites and one that reminded her of the career in journalism she was hoping for—a little last-minute dose of perspective, maybe. It was also a book that reminded her of Stevie because they'd discussed it so often. And that helped too.

The swimmers were actually asked to sit in chairs with their lane numbers on them in the ready room. That meant Susan Carol had Krylova next to her. As soon as she pulled out her book, Krylova pulled off her headphones.

"You *read* before you swim?" she asked.

"Sure," Susan Carol said. "It keeps my mind occupied."

Krylova shook her head. "I just close my eyes and see my race in my head. What is that called in English?"

"Visualizing," Susan Carol said. "I used to do that. It made me tired. Swimming the race once is enough for me."

Krylova laughed.

The other swimmers, even wearing their headphones, were giving them looks—except for Elizabeth, who was clearly into whatever she was listening to and had a dreamy look on her face.

A stern-looking official marched into the room a couple minutes later.

"Ladies, it's time," she said.

They all stood up and gathered their swim bags, stuffing headphones (or books) into them. As they filed out, the swim bags were handed off to runners—there was one assigned to each lane—who would return them once the race was over.

They walked down a hallway, led by Nadia Antonopolis, an Australian who would swim in lane one, before emerging into the brightly lit pool area to cheers and some overly dramatic music that Susan Carol didn't recognize. For the first time since she'd gotten to London, Susan Carol suddenly felt her nerves jangling. She gazed around at the packed arena. It looked completely different than it had the night before for the semifinals. Or at least it *felt* completely different.

Then she hadn't noticed that the place was packed. But now . . . She had spent most of her life swimming in front of crowds of maybe 100—many of whom weren't even paying attention when she stood up on the blocks. Now every one of the 17,500 seats was filled. And everyone seemed to be standing. The night before, for a semifinal, there wasn't much buzz. This was a final: Olympic medals would be handed out when the race was over. Someone would become a part of swimming history.

And, she knew, someone might become very wealthy.

She was instantly embarrassed for thinking that. She wondered if Krylova, walking a couple of steps behind her, had that on her mind at all. She knew Elizabeth didn't.

Once they reached their spots behind their lanes, they began the ritual of taking off their sweats. She put her things in a basket, and her lane runner literally ran by and scooped it up. Then came the introductions, starting with Antonopolis. The cheers for the four swimmers in the middle lanes—Susan Carol, Krylova, Sjöström, and Wentworth—were deafening.

Susan Carol could pick out the media section at the far end of the pool because the seats had desks in front of them. Right next to the media section was the family section. For a moment she was able to pick out her father. And she saw her little sister, Anna, waving a miniature American flag.

She glanced the other way and saw her teammates in the team section. A little chill went through her when she saw that Phelps and Lochte, having finished their 200-freestyle semifinals and the 4 × 100-meter relay final, were right there, standing and pointing toward Susan Carol and Elizabeth as if to say, "Come on, you guys can do it."

Jane Vessels, the British swimmer in lane eight, had just been introduced to huge cheers. Susan Carol heard the double whistle calling the swimmers to the blocks. She carefully placed her goggles on her eyes and took a deep breath. A moment later came the single whistle telling the swimmers it was time to step onto the blocks.

If Elizabeth had been next to her, she would have looked

at her and said softly, "Good luck." She always did that with friends before climbing onto a block. But Elizabeth was miles away in lane six. Krylova had jumped onto the block as soon as the whistle had blown. Susan Carol stepped onto the block and pressed the mental button inside her head so she could hear Ed's voice. First instruction: "Up first, *then* out on the start." Her starts tended to be flat, so Ed wanted her to push off upward first so she would enter the water more smoothly.

"Take your mark."

She slowly got into position, not wanting to have to stay in the starting position any longer than she had to. "BEEP!"

She arched her back to get up into the air and pushed off the block. As always, it took a few seconds to change over from sheer instinct—muscle memory got her through the start and the first few strokes—to thinking about what she was doing. In the 100, there wasn't all that much to think about. It wasn't an all-out sprint, but you couldn't afford to hold much back on the first fifty or you would be swamped—literally and figuratively.

Halfway down the pool she could tell that Krylova was using the same strategy as in the Semifinal: Swim as fast as you can for as long as you can and hope you can hang on. Ed had told her to expect that and not to worry about it.

"She's gonna die if she does that—with the adrenaline she'll be out too fast."

Krylova was almost a body length ahead at the turn,

which was fine. When Susan Carol picked her head out of the water, she could see she was almost dead even with Sjöström. She couldn't tell where Elizabeth was. Right with them, she guessed.

She pushed hard off the wall, wanting to conserve as much energy as possible with a long pullout. Once she had taken her first two strokes and come up for air, she began to consciously pick up her kick. Even with thirty-five meters to go she knew she wasn't going to die. She felt strong. But could she reel Krylova in?

The noise was so loud now that even underwater Susan Carol could hear it clearly. *Stay down!* she screamed at herself, knowing that adrenaline could cause her to come out of the water too high when she breathed and cost her time. The flags were approaching. She could see Krylova coming back to her. She was convinced she would catch her. Just before she reached the flags, she decided to take one last breath and stay down. It was the Olympics: One breath could be the difference, she knew, between first and fourth.

She put her head down and took three strokes. Her touch wasn't absolutely perfect, but it was close. She picked her head up and could see that Krylova, Sjöström, and Elizabeth were all on the wall. The noise was beyond deafening.

She couldn't hear Ed up above her, but she could see him clapping. Finally, she looked at the scoreboard. All four swimmers had broken the world record. Krylova *had* died and finished fourth at 56:01—out of the medals. Sjöström had finished third in 55:92—fourteen hundredths of a second under her world record—but not quite good enough to beat the two young Americans, who had finished one-two.

Elizabeth had won the race. She had gone 55.79—four hundredths faster than Susan Carol, in 55.83. When Susan Carol realized they had finished one-two, she let out a shriek. Her first thought wasn't to bemoan losing by the tiniest of margins, it was to celebrate: She had won an Olympic silver medal and her pal had won gold.

Krylova had her head in the gutter and was crying. Susan Carol ducked under the lane line and went through Krylova's lane and Sjöström's to get to lane six. Sjöström was already there, congratulating Elizabeth. When Elizabeth saw Susan Carol's head pop out of the water, she screamed, "WE DID IT!" and the two young Americans embraced.

Sjöström, totally gracious in defeat, put her hand on Susan Carol's head and said, "Greatest race I have ever been in."

Elizabeth was crying. So was Susan Carol. If she had won gold instead of silver, she honestly wasn't sure she could have been any happier.

24: ONE IS SILVER

Stevie wasn't sure how to feel when he saw the times go up on the board. The finish had been so close, there was no way to tell from the stands who had finished first and who had finished fourth. From where they were sitting, it almost looked as if all four swimmers touched at the same time.

Even so, he was a little bit surprised when he realized that Elizabeth Wentworth had won. She had looked like a non-factor for most of the race. At the fifty she had been half a body length behind Susan Carol and Sjöström and almost two behind Krylova.

With twenty meters to go, it still looked like a three-woman race. Stevie hadn't been paying any attention to Elizabeth until over the din he heard Kelleher say, "Here comes Wentworth!" Sure enough, she was closing in on the three leaders—Krylova fading with every stroke,

Susan Carol and Sjöström matching strokes, and Wentworth suddenly looking faster than all of them.

The sight of Susan Carol and Elizabeth hugging and crying on each other's shoulders choked Stevie up. Wentworth had been going just that little bit faster at the finish to touch Susan Carol out. So ridiculously close! Even so, no matter what else happened, Susan Carol was going to come home with an Olympic silver medal. That was mind-boggling.

He could see Susan Carol's family in the stands going nuts—jumping up and down and waving flags. . . .

He was jolted from his reverie by the sound of Kelleher's voice. "Come on, we need to get downstairs. The game is really on now for the 200."

Oh, right. J. P. Scott didn't have a gold medalist to pitch, and Brickley still needed a poster girl.

Scrambling through the stands to get downstairs for the post-race interviews, Stevie saw Elizabeth and Susan Carol being interviewed together by NBC's Andrea Kremer. Both wore bright-as-the-sun smiles as they talked. He wondered if Susan Carol had thought about what might be coming next.

Probably not. That was the way a reporter would think. At this moment she wasn't a reporter. She was an Olympic silver medalist. And he hoped she was soaking up every minute of it.

Sarah Sjöström had agreed to go to the mixed zone to talk to reporters. Svetlana Krylova, the media was told, would not be there. The two Americans would come to the inter-view room together.

"Look, I know you want to see Susan Carol and you will," Kelleher said to Stevie once the announcements had been made on which swimmers were showing up where. "The medal ceremony is in thirty minutes, and we'll see that for sure because it's cool even if you've seen it a hundred times."

"Which you have."

"At least. Still gives me chills. I miss the old Soviet anthem, though."

"Whaa?"

"The old Soviet anthem was the best I've ever heard. Better than 'Le Marseillaise' and better than 'O Canada,' which is saying a lot. Sorry, rambling. Right now I want you to take a walk around here and see what you can find out."

"Take a walk?"

"Yes. Tamara is trying to find out if there's any way to talk to Krylova. She's got a friend who works for FINA who might be able to help. All our players are in this building somewhere right now—J.P. for sure; Bobby Mo almost for sure; hell, Phil Knight is here somewhere. Go find them. See who they're talking to, what they're doing. If there's something going on here, they'll all be refiguring their strategies given how this race turned out."

"But what am I supposed to ask; what would I do if I saw them?"

Kelleher gave Stevie a look.

"This your first rodeo? No. You've got the best reporting instincts I've seen in ages. Go use them." He practically pushed Stevie out of the room. The hallway outside was teeming with people. Chockablock, he'd heard the British call it. The last event of the night, the women's 400 freestyle, was in the water. Stevie knew that because there were TV screens on the walls everywhere, and he could see a 200 split time on the screen, meaning the women had just passed the halfway point of the race.

He walked in the direction of the mixed zone, remembering from past experiences that agents and other hangers-on could get access to it, although there was no reason for anyone he might be looking for to be there. J.P. would no doubt be attached to Susan Carol, and Krylova might be out of the building by now, for all he knew.

He turned a corner and almost bumped into Ed Brennan. If Ed was disappointed by Susan Carol's near miss, he didn't show it.

"Can you believe that race?" he said, once he saw it was Stevie he'd almost collided with. "Four swimmers under the world record! My God, that was great. I still can't believe Wentworth came from so far behind to win. She is so strong. I think she'll be tough to beat in the 200."

He was talking so fast that Stevie was almost out of breath just listening. But that last comment got his attention.

"You think she's better than Susan Carol in the 200?"

Ed shrugged. "Who knows? Susan Carol beat her in the

trials. The 200 is about being in shape and swimming a smart race, but sometimes it's also about sheer strength at the finish. Susan Carol's in great shape, but *that* girl is as strong as anyone I've seen in years."

He looked up at the TV screen. "I need to go make sure Susan Carol got through drug-testing okay. Sometimes a hard sprint like that and all the nerves can dehydrate you. Where are you going? Interview room's the other way."

"I know," Stevie said. "Bobby's got the interview room. I'm looking for other people to talk to. Have you seen our guy J.P. or Reverend Anderson?"

Ed gave him a look as if to say, "Why would you want to see them?" Then he shook his head. "No, haven't seen them. I'm sure the Andersons are in the stands, waiting for the medal ceremony. But I did see J.P.'s partner, Bill what's his name, hanging around with that Brickley guy who's been nosing around all week."

"Robert Maurice?"

"Yeah, that's him. Boy, he's the worst one yet. There's just something so . . . oily about him. I saw them walking into the Coke hospitality room a couple minutes ago."

"Thanks."

Ed shrugged. "I don't know why you'd want to talk to those guys if you didn't have to. Though I suspect we *won't* have to if Susan Carol doesn't win the 200 on Wednesday. I want her to win, but if some of these people disappeared, I'd be very happy."

"Me too," Stevie said.

On that note they each rushed off in opposite directions.

Stevie needed to figure out a way to get himself into the Coke hospitality room.

The various corporate hospitality rooms for the moneyed set were all at the far end of the building, and you needed a special pass to gain entry. The pool deck level—which was also the locker room, interview room, and mixed zone level—was on the ground floor. The far end of the building had three stories of rooms all with great glass walls looking out over Olympic Park.

Stevie hadn't been in any of them but had walked past them and looked in from the outside.

As he turned the corner and began passing various signs with corporate names on them—Speedo, Nike, Adidas, Rolex, and NBC all had rooms—his mind was racing to figure a way into the room that was coming up fast on his right, the one that said COCA-COLA.

Maybe he could claim he was desperate for a Coke. That wouldn't work. There was plenty of Coke in the media workroom. Walking past the NBC sign he braked to a halt. Maybe . . .

There were two guards on either side of the door checking passes. He knew his would be rejected, so he stopped in front of the younger of the two guards and said, "I wonder if you can help me."

The guard eyed his media credential and said, "Are you lost? Media room is way at the other end of the building."

"No, not lost, but searching," Stevie said. "I've just now been assigned to do a feature on Andrea Kremer from NBC that has to be written *tonight*. I can't find any of the NBC PR people, and Andrea will be finished with her work for the night in a few minutes. I've *got* to find someone from NBC who can help me."

The guard looked a little confused, so Stevie pushed on. "The people in there from NBC who are actually working all have walkie-talkies—see?" He pointed at a young woman inside the room walking by them. "If you can just get one of them to come over here and talk to me outside for a minute, I'll bet they can help get me to the right person." He looked at his watch as if semi-panicked. "I'm really desperate."

He knew Susan Carol would be better suited for this job than he was. By now, the guard would have been under her spell and probably would have been personally escorting her to talk to Mark Lazarus, the president of NBC Sports.

Maybe it was the fact that he asked to talk to someone outside the room—making it clear he wasn't trying to crash—that sold the guard. In any event, he turned to his partner and said, "Martin, cover for me for just a moment, will you?"

There wasn't a huge crush to get into the room at that moment, so Martin nodded.

"Stand over here to the side," his new friend said. "I'll see what I can do."

He walked into the room. A moment later, he was back with the young woman Stevie had spotted before with a walkie-talkie.

"Sabrina McGregor," she said, shaking hands. "And you are?"

"Steve Thomas," he said. "I'm from the *Washington Herald*. I'm terribly sorry to bother you, but—"

"You need someone who can help you get a minute with Andrea Kremer," she said.

"Exactly."

"Hang on, I've got just the person for you."

She suddenly bolted into the room again, leaving Stevie and the security guard standing there. No more than thirty seconds later, having melted into the crowd for an instant, she was back with a short, middle-aged man in tow.

"Jon Miller, this is . . ."

"Steve Thomas," Stevie said, shaking hands with Jon Miller.

"Among other things, Mr. Miller oversees our communications division."

"You need Andrea?" Jon Miller said, pulling out his walkie-talkie.

Now Stevie had to make his move.

"Can we talk for just one moment?" Stevie said. "I want to explain my story to you."

Miller shrugged. "Sure." He turned back to the young woman. "I'll take it from here, Sabrina," he said.

Stevie thanked her and the security guy, and he and Miller walked a few steps down the hall for privacy.

"Look, Mr. Miller, I know you don't know me from Adam—"

"Sure I do," Miller said. "You and Susan Carol Anderson are the kids who keep breaking big stories at big events. So why in the world do you need to talk to Andrea? I would think you'd be writing nothing but Susan Carol right now."

Stevie took a deep breath.

"I don't really need to talk to Andrea," he said, causing Miller to raise an eyebrow, "but I do need a favor. I can't really explain, but there *is* a story going on and Susan Carol can't help me—"

"No kidding," Miller said, smiling.

"So I'm working it alone. And I need very, very much to get into the Coke hospitality room right now."

Miller looked at him as if making some kind of decision.

"Follow me."

They walked up to the guards at the door of the Coca-Cola suite, and Miller turned and pointed Stevie out to the guard. For a split second Stevie's heart jumped: Maybe he was just turning him in for lying to get his attention. Before he could contemplate that any further, he heard Miller say, "Young man is with me."

The guard nodded. Stevie noticed that Miller's pass had every possible letter on it, meaning he could go, he guessed, just about anywhere.

He followed Miller into the room. Miller led him through the crowd a bit and then stopped.

"Okay, you're in," he said. "But you're on your own from here."

"I can't thank you enough," Stevie said.

"Thank me by getting the bad guys, whoever they are," Miller said. "Your track record tells me you know when something is up and that you're trying to do the right thing. Good luck."

"Thanks. I'll give it my best," Stevie said, shaking his hand.

Okay, Stevie thought, *now to find the bad guys.*

He started circling the room slowly. He was dressed a lot less formally than most people, so he tried not to make eye contact with anyone. He moved slowly, not wanting to bump into anyone or draw too much attention to himself.

There was a bar at the midway point of the room, and he stopped to ask for a Coke. That gave him a chance to stand and take in the room without looking too suspicious. The bartender handed him his Coke, and he moved to the side of the bar so he could keep looking and get out of the way at the same time.

And then he saw them.

They were standing in a corner with drinks in their hands. Stevie wondered why they had come in here to talk but then decided this was the place they were least likely to run into someone from a competing company. How they had gotten in was another question—but not his problem.

His problem was different: how to get some clue what they were up to. He sipped his Coke as if that would somehow inspire him.

Remarkably, it did.

"Mr. Maurice?" he said, clearly startling both men when

he approached. They were so intent on their conversation they didn't even notice him until he opened his mouth.

"Huh? Yeah?" Maurice said, giving Stevie a "Who are you and why are you bothering me?" look. The look on Arnold's face wasn't nearly as friendly. Susan Carol would have called it withering.

He plowed ahead, trying to channel Susan Carol's charm.

"Steve Thomas," he said, sticking his hand out. "We met a couple years ago in New Orleans at the Final Four. You were helping Chip Graber out by loaning him a car. . . ."

Recognition finally flashed in Maurice's dark eyes. "Oh yeah. You're the kid who was with Susan Carol Anderson, right? The two of you were running around with Grabes because of that blackmail thing."

"Yeah," Stevie said. "The blackmail thing."

The urge to say "The blackmail thing we got Chip *out of*" was almost overwhelming, but he resisted.

"Mr. Arnold, how are you?" Stevie said, turning toward Bill's withering glare.

"How'd you get in here?" Arnold said in response.

Stevie remembered Susan Carol saying that the reason J. P. Scott was the out-front guy for Lightning Fast was that he was better with people. Arnold was the deal maker, the numbers guy. He could see why.

"Probably the same way you did," Stevie said, choosing to brush off the challenge. "Some race, huh?"

"You aren't disappointed your girlfriend lost?" Maurice said.

Stevie tried to look shocked. "My girlfriend's an Olympic silver medalist. I think that's amazing! And how can you feel bad after a race like that? And Elizabeth is *so* nice. What a great story she is, huh? You can't help but feel happy for her."

Maurice grunted in disgust.

"If you feel happy for her that she might be costing your girlfriend millions, that's fine."

"I don't think Susan Carol is worried about that," Stevie said.

"Yeah, well, her father is," Arnold put in. He shook his head. "Do you know how many deals we have that rise or fall based on her winning a gold?"

Stevie saw an opening. He turned to Maurice. "That true, Mr. Maurice? Brickley's not interested in silver medalists?"

"No one is interested in silver medalists, kid," Maurice said.

"So you might be going after Elizabeth Wentworth, then?"

Arnold had just taken a sip of his drink and almost coughed it up.

Maurice actually smiled—a sinister smile, but a smile nevertheless.

"You seem smart enough," he said, "so I'm surprised you'd say something so dumb. Elizabeth Wentworth looks like a bodybuilder. Maybe she can get a commercial for one of those home gyms or something, but that's about it."

"So it's looks *and* a gold medal."

"You got it."

"So Svetlana Krylova would work for you too then, right?"

Maurice's eyes bugged out a bit as soon as Stevie brought up Krylova, but he recovered quickly. And he was looking at Bill Arnold pointedly when he said, "Krylova choked tonight. Blew it."

"She went under the world record."

"And didn't even medal. Going under the world record and finishing fourth will get you a Coke in this room—if you ask nicely."

"Well, she's better in the 200. And so is Susan Carol. Maybe you'll get the result you want in the next race," Stevie said.

Bobby Maurice gave him a look that scared him.

"I feel sure I will," he said.

25: THE OTHER GOLD

Susan Carol was on a roller-coaster ride.

After she and Elizabeth finished their poolside inter-view with Andrea Kremer, they were shuttled a few yards down the deck to a BBC interviewer. She and Elizabeth had been told they would be able to get back in the water to warm down once they had finished their TV bits and before they had to go to the interview room. But as soon as the BBC finished, an IOC official appeared and announced they were being taken to drug-testing.

"But," Susan Carol said, "we were told we'd get to warm down first."

"You can warm down after the medal ceremony," said the official, whose name tag said JEAN RENAUD.

"That will be almost an hour after we finished swim-ming," Elizabeth said. "You've got to give us five minutes or something."

"No, we don't," Renaud said. "You both have to be drug-tested, or you will be considered to have tested positive for refusing the test."

They looked at each other. It wasn't as if either one of them had never skipped a warm-down; it was just that you didn't want to get out of routine in the middle of the Olympics.

"Okay," Susan Carol said, "of course." But she was really annoyed.

She was looking around for Ed Brennan, but he was nowhere to be seen since they were in an area where only swimmers, TV personnel, and IOC officials were allowed. They followed Renaud under the stands to the drug-testing room.

Happily they'd been drinking enough water that giving samples didn't take very long. They had just walked out of the room with an IOC official who was escorting them to the interview room when there was another brief snag. Trevor James, the USA Swimming official who had so thoroughly explained the rules to them that he'd become a joke, stopped short when he crossed their path. He was dressed not in a USA Swimming outfit but in a FINA uniform—specifically that of a meet official.

James was looking unpleasant as always. He didn't bother to congratulate either swimmer.

Elizabeth, polite as always, said, "Can we help you, Mr. James?"

"No. But you can both help yourselves by watching your turns."

Susan Carol was confused. "Mr. James, I've never had a problem with my turns," she said.

"Me neither," said Elizabeth.

"And I keep telling you, this is the Olympics. You'll be under more scrutiny here."

He turned and walked away. Susan Carol and Elizabeth just stared after him.

"What was that?" Susan Carol said.

"Another Olympic moment to treasure with Trevor James," Elizabeth said wistfully.

Both girls dissolved in laughter.

They were both crying not long after. Susan Carol had almost felt like she was in a play when the medals were presented—it was hard to believe this was real. But with the weight of a medal around her neck, and "The Star-Spangled Banner" playing, and two American flags—one for her and one for Elizabeth—being raised to the rafters, it began to sink in. She'd actually done it.

From the podium she could clearly see her family about ten rows up in the stands. Her brothers and sister were all waving when she walked out, and she waved back, feeling chills down her spine. Her mom, the family crier, was awash in tears.

But the real surprise was her dad: He had tears streaming down his cheeks too. He was definitely *not* the family crier. He was always the calm one in good times and bad. That's why it had been so hard to see him changed in the run-up to the Olympics. But this was a change Susan Carol could feel good about. Those tears told her all she needed to know about how her father really felt. And you couldn't mistake the pride on his face.

She spotted Stevie and Bobby and Tamara in the stands, waving and blowing kisses. And then she looked over at the other American swimmers, all of them facing the flags, hands on their hearts, singing. That was when she lost it completely. She thought back to all the times she had watched athletes stand at attention for their national an-thems at the Olympics and imagined what an incredible moment that must be. Now she knew.

When the final notes died away, Elizabeth grabbed her and pulled her onto the gold medal podium. Then she reached down and pulled Sjöström up too. The three of them, arms around one another, medals around their necks, waved to everyone as the applause washed down.

Stevie had gotten back to the media seating area just as the three medalists walked back onto the deck.

"I know you've got something," Bobby said as the three women marched toward the medal podiums.

"I'll tell you when this is over," Stevie said.

But when it was over, he was in no condition to tell anyone anything. He was just about as choked up as Susan Carol.

So it wasn't until a couple of hours later that Stevie fi-nally told Bobby and Tamara his tale. They had all gone downstairs to the media room in the Aquatics Centre to write their stories after the medal ceremony. Stevie was upset because he hadn't gotten to talk to Susan Carol, but she had texted him, asking if he could have lunch the next day since she had a light workout in the morning and nothing going on after that.

When they finished writing, they headed back to the Gloucester and had a late-night snack in the hotel. Stevie filled them in on his talk with Bill Arnold and Bobby Maurice as they ate.

Bobby sat back in his seat and tossed his napkin onto his plate.

"It's this close," he said, holding his thumb and forefinger about a half an inch apart. "But I have no idea what it is we're close to."

Tamara shrugged. "It may just be that they're all waiting to see what happens before they pounce on their next star."

They were all slumped in their seats, thinking. They still had only suspicions that something wasn't right.

"So," Kelleher finally said, leaning forward. "Bobby Mo likes to get what he wants, and he wants either Krylova or Susan Carol. What can you do to guarantee gold? Go out and break Elizabeth Wentworth's leg? Have Liu Zige kidnapped?"

"We never really ruled out blackmail," Tamara said.

"How does he blackmail a Chinese swimmer? With what?" Bobby said. "For that matter, how does he blackmail an American swimmer? There's no NCAA around here to declare someone ineligible."

"There is an IOC," Stevie said. "They've certainly got lots of rules."

"The only one that would matter would be a dirty drug test. I don't think Bobby Mo or J. P. Scott can get a drug test falsified."

Stevie thought for a minute. "If I was Bobby Mo or, for that matter, the Lightning Fast people, the person I'm most scared of is Elizabeth Wentworth. I know Liu's a threat, but a lot of people think she's a product of the rocket suits. She hasn't been close to her record since they went out. Elizabeth just broke the world record in the 100 in a non-rocket suit."

"I agree on all counts," Bobby said. "What's your point?"

"I'm back to bribery."

"You were the one who said you didn't think Elizabeth would go for something like that," Tamara pointed out.

"And she clearly wasn't being paid to lose tonight's race," added Bobby.

"I know," Stevie said. "But I wonder if that changes things—she's already won gold. How bad does she want two? Maybe one gold medal and a lot of cash would seem like an okay outcome to her?"

"It's possible," Bobby said.

"I suppose," Tamara said.

"I know, I'm not convinced either," Stevie confessed. "I still don't think she'd do it."

"So let's get some sleep, then," Bobby said. "And hope for better luck tomorrow."

Stevie and Susan Carol met for lunch at a Chinese restaurant called the Good Earth, which was a few blocks from the Gloucester. She wanted to get away from the athletes' village for a while, so they planned to walk around and see some of London after they ate.

"Well, how does it feel being an Olympic medalist?" Stevie asked as soon as he'd given her a huge hug.

Susan Carol laughed, clearly still giddy and excited and glowing. "Isn't it crazy?! I can hardly believe it. I wonder when it will sink in."

"Okay, let's order and then you can give me the blow by blow," Stevie said.

The race itself had taken less than a minute, but the retelling of it took them through most of lunch. Susan Carol was about to get choked up again, talking about being on the podium and seeing the flag raised, so she turned the conversation back to Stevie.

"Okay, now your turn. You weren't in the interview room, so I know you must be on the trail of something."

He filled her in on his conversation with Bill Arnold and Bobby Maurice and all of their speculations on what it could mean.

Susan Carol didn't say anything for a few seconds when Stevie finished.

"Well, what do you think?" he said finally.

"I just don't know," she said. "Look, J.P. is slimy and Bill Arnold's mean and slimy. And I'm sure they'd drop me and represent Svetlana in a heartbeat if she wins gold. But I'm not sure how far they'd go to *make* that happen.

"Besides, J.P. has been hanging on to my father like a life raft since they got here. He knows I'm pretty much off-limits as long as I'm still swimming."

"Hanging out with your father doesn't mean he *isn't* up to something. Maybe that's why it was Arnold we saw with Krylova and with Maurice instead of J.P. And what about our boy Bobby Mo?" Stevie asked. "Don't tell me *he's* not capable of some kind of dirty trick."

"Oh, he's absolutely capable of it—or at least of wanting to do it," Susan Carol said. "I just don't see *how*."

Before Stevie could open his mouth, she jumped back in. "And don't even say it, because Elizabeth is about as likely to go for a bribe as I am."

"You mean zero chance."

"Uh-huh. Look, maybe we're not finding anything because there's nothing there," Susan Carol said. "I mean, yes, they want Krylova or me to win. But if we don't, then they can move on to other swimmers or other athletes. It's not like we're the only athletes here."

"Yeah, but you are the most beautiful. And new and not yet committed to a lot of other contracts. You're more unique than you think."

Susan Carol gave him The Smile. "What were you saying about beautiful?"

They went for a walk after lunch. It turned out they weren't far from Harrods, so they went in to see what the fuss was about over a department store. A glance at the giant store map explained—it was seven stories of . . . everything. Stevie's favorite was the food halls, and Susan Carol couldn't get over that you could order a saddle. After poking around and gawking like the tourists they were, they bought mugs with the Harrods logo and Susan Carol bought a small model of the store.

Stevie had just suggested going back to the Gloucester for afternoon tea—he had learned it was served from three to five in the lobby every afternoon and thought it would be a London-y thing to do—when his cell phone buzzed, telling him he had a text.

"Probably Bobby," he said, reaching in his pocket. "Wanting to know if I've done anything today."

"Tell him you've been getting reacquainted with your girlfriend," she said, linking her arm through his. He blushed, wished he hadn't, and pulled his phone out. The text wasn't from Kelleher. It was from Chip Graber.

It said: *Playing France at 4. Meet in mxd zone after? Important.*

Stevie looked at his watch. It was 3:30 already. He really would have preferred to continue getting reacquainted with his girlfriend.

"What is it?" Susan Carol asked.

He handed her the phone.

"Interesting," she said.

"But what about getting reacquainted?"

"We'll always have Harrods." She leaned down and gave him a kiss that made him feel much better—and also a bit worse that he had to go.

"My last important race is Wednesday," she said. "After that, all I have left is the prelims of the medley relay, which you could swim and we'd be fine. I'll have lots of time."

Since Elizabeth had the best time in the 100 fly, she would swim the fly leg on the medley relay in the finals on Friday. Susan Carol, with the second-best time, would swim in the qualifying prelims in the morning. Technically, if the US won, she would be a gold medalist—she wouldn't be on the podium, but she *would* receive a gold medal—but winning gold that way wasn't what J. P. Scott and company had in mind.

He sighed. "Okay. But if this *isn't* really important, I'm going to kill Chip."

They took the subway back to Olympic Park together. From there, Susan Carol headed to the athletes' village while Stevie went to the basketball arena.

He found the media entrance and made his way upstairs to the media section. He was used to sitting courtside for basketball games, so sitting fifteen rows up in the stands felt odd to him. Even odder, he thought, was that the building wasn't full even though it only seated about 12,000 people—considerably less than the Aquatic Centre. Apparently any Dream Team mania involving the US team was long gone.

The game was already more than half over by the time Stevie arrived. Looking around, he saw his old friend Dick Weiss from the *New York Daily News*, watching the game avidly. That was why Weiss was called "Hoops." If someone was playing basketball, Hoops was probably going to be there to watch.

"Stevie!" Hoops said as he sat down next to him. "I

heard you were here, but I thought you were spending all your time at the swimming center with Susan Carol."

"She's off today," Stevie said. "Heats and semis of the 200 fly are tomorrow."

"I'm sure you were vurry, vurry proud of her getting that silver medal last night," Hoops said, his Philadelphia accent still unmistakable. "Though it's got to be tough to come so close to gold and not get it."

"She was thrilled," Stevie said.

"Good. So what brings you over to our little corner of the world?"

"Just wanted to see Chip."

"Of course. You guys are still pals. Well, he's playing vurry, vurry well. I told Mike he's going to have to play big minutes when they get to the medal rounds."

"I'm sure Coach K was grateful for the advice," Stevie said with a smile.

"He should be, shouldn't he?" Hoops said.

The US played everyone in uniform in the second half, easing to a 97–69 win. When the game was over, Stevie followed Hoops downstairs. He was heading for the interview room but pointed out the mixed zone to Stevie.

"You aren't going to see too many of the American players there," Hoops said. "The ones who don't come in with Krzyzewski tend to dress and bolt."

"Only need one," Stevie said, heading down the hallway.

Most of the journalists waiting in the mixed zone were French, hoping to talk to their players about their chances of getting through preliminary play to the round of sixteen. A few Americans were there too, hoping someone from the US team would come through.

Stevie stood to the side and waited. A few minutes later, Chip appeared, the only American player in sight. A stampede ensued. Stevie stood back, not wanting to get hit in the head by a swinging camera. When the crowd began to dissipate, he moved a little closer so that Chip could see he was there. When Chip spotted him, he nodded and then kept talking. Finally, the last questioner, someone from the *New York Times* who was doing a story on the women's team and wanted to know if Chip had watched them play, asked his last question and left.

"Glad you could make it," Chip said, shaking hands.

He was not his usual playful self. Stevie could tell right away that something was up.

"Of course," he said. "What's going on?"

"Walk over here," Chip said, pointing to the far corner of the "zone," where they would be out of earshot of the French players and the media members who were still talking to them.

Before Chip could say anything, another camera crew approached. Chip waved them off. "Sorry," he said. "I'm done. I'm just talking to my friend here. Okay? Maybe tomorrow."

The guy with the microphone—an ESPN microphone, Stevie noticed—gave Chip a big TV smile. "Chip, you're the only American who came out here. I need one non-interview-room quote. Come on. It's ESPN."

Chip sighed. "Okay. But please make it quick."

The guy waved at his camera guy, who turned on a bright light. Stevie was starting to move when the camera guy said, "Hey, kid, get out of the shot."

Before he could say anything, Chip jumped in. "Hey, you guys interrupted a conversation I was having with this *kid*. You should be thanking him for waiting, not yelling at him."

The guy with the microphone just smiled and launched into a question about what it was like to play alongside Kobe and LeBron and Dwyane. *Exciting stuff*, Stevie thought. *Chip's never been asked* that *before*. He tuned the rest out for the most part. But he thought Chip looked really uptight considering they had just won.

At last the ESPN guys left and they found some out-of-the-way space to talk.

"So what's up?" Stevie asked.

"Plenty," Chip said. "Bobby Maurice called me last night and said we needed to talk. I was out at a team dinner but said I'd meet him at the hotel when we got back. I couldn't imagine what it was about. My contract's up right now and we've agreed to renegotiate once the Olympics are over, so it wasn't that."

"So what was it?"

"Hang on, I'm getting to it. So, I meet him at the bar. He asks me if I want a drink and I remind him I don't drink during the season and I sure as hell don't drink in the middle of the Olympics. He's doing the 'has your old pal Bobby Mo taken good care of you?' bit that he's been doing since I was in college."

"I remember that from New Orleans."

"Right. So finally he tells me that Brickley has put him in charge of 'worldwide acquisitions.' I figure he's going to tell me I have to deal with a new rep for my NBA deal, which I'd be all broken up about, of course. But he says no, that's not it. So I say, 'Well, what *is* it? It's late!'

"And he says, 'You're real tight with those two kids, the girl swimmer and her boyfriend, right?' I said what about it? and he says, 'If Anderson wins the 200-fly Wednesday night, I have *got* to sign her. And if she finishes second to the Russian girl, I have to sign them both. I need the two of them. They're *my* Dream Team.'

"So I ask what this has to do with me, exactly, and he says, 'I want you to convince Anderson she should be with Brickley. We've done right by you, haven't we? And we'd do right by her too. But she's got this matching clause in a lowball contract from Speedo. Now if she only gets silver, I'm good because Speedo won't match what I'm prepared to offer for a silver medalist. But if she wins gold, it gets tougher, see. 'Cause I *have* to have her then and Speedo's gonna be ready to pay too. But how much is what I need to know—just how high is too high for them.'

"So it finally dawns on me that what he really wants is for me to find out from Susan Carol how much Speedo will put on the table if she wins."

"What'd you tell him?" Stevie asked, amazed by the story.

"I told him there was no way I was going to do something like that. I'm not an agent and I'm not a spy. He literally grabbed my arm and said, 'Look, I *promise* you I'll get you a million-dollar bonus for each year on your new contract if you get this done for me.'"

"And?"

Chip actually smiled. "Well, I knew I was going to say no even though he was offering me an extra five million bucks," he said. "But rather than just tell him he was nuts, I decided to put on my Stevie Thomas/Susan Carol Anderson reporting hat."

"What do you mean?"

"I decided to pump him for more information first! I said, 'What if neither one of them wins the gold medal? What if the Chinese girl wins?' He waved and said, 'No way. She's done. She was a product of the rocket suit.' I didn't really know what that meant, so I just said, 'Okay, but what about the other American girl—the one who won the 100?'"

"And?" Stevie could barely stand it.

Chip looked him right in the eye. "He said, 'That's already been taken care of.'"

"That's already been taken care of?"

"Yup."

"Whoa."

"Yeah, I know. That's why I texted you. Something's going on here."

"Did you ask him what he meant?"

Chip shook his head. "No. Probably should have, but I didn't think he'd tell me anything more. So I told him I didn't want to be a part of 'taking care of' things like this no matter what kind of bogus bonus he was offering, and left."

26: THE GOOD, THE BAD, AND THE BOBBY MO . . .

Chip gave Stevie a hug before he said goodbye and said quietly: "Look, I know you guys know how to take care of yourselves, but please be careful. If Bobby Mo is throwing around money on this scale, there's *a lot* at stake."

Stevie nodded as Chip was being dragged away by a USA Basketball official who said he had to get on the bus right now. "Let me know what's going on" were his parting words.

Stevie walked back to the media center and called Kelleher on the way. He and Tamara were both there writing. Stevie told Bobby they needed to talk right away.

"Don't tell me you went to lunch with Susan Carol and got into trouble," Bobby said.

"At lunch, no, but trouble, yes," Stevie said.

When they were in their now-familiar haunt, the media dining area, Stevie filled them in.

"The question is," Kelleher said, "do we tell Susan Carol and Elizabeth?"

"They've both got to swim the 200 fly twice tomorrow and then the final on Wednesday," Tamara said. "The last thing they need is having some kind of unspoken threat on their minds."

"But maybe they need to know," Bobby said. "Maybe they should have extra protection at this point."

"From what?" Stevie asked. "What can Bobby Mo do? Security is much tighter now that the Games have started. Is he going to send someone to do a Tanya Harding on Elizabeth's kneecaps?"

Tamara smiled. "That's the kind of comment Susan Carol would normally make, with the historical reference and all."

Stevie shrugged. Almost everyone alive knew the story about the figure skater Tanya Harding and her husband sending a thug to whack her arch-rival Nancy Kerrigan on the knee a few weeks before the 1994 Olympics.

Kelleher shook his head. "Well, it does seem pretty far-fetched, but it happened once. . . . And Chip made a good point: There is obviously a lot riding on this for Bobby Mo if he's tossing around million-dollar bribes."

"So what do we think it means, Elizabeth is 'already taken care of'?" Stevie asked.

"Right now, that's the 100-million-dollar question," Bobby said.

Susan Carol was very happy when the semifinals were over on Tuesday night. Even though she hadn't been at all nervous about qualifying for the finals, the grind of swimming the 200 fly twice in the same day was enough to wear a swimmer out.

The heats and semis had gone predictably except for one thing: Liu Zige had finished eighth in the semifinals, barely squeezing into the final. Top swimmers often held back in prelims to save energy, but Liu had made the final by two-hundredths of a second. No one cut it that close on purpose.

Krylova had qualified first—again—coming within fourteen-hundredths of the world record in the semifinals. Elizabeth and Susan Carol had been second and third, meaning they would flank Krylova in lane four for the final. That was good for Susan Carol: Krylova would set the pace early in the race, so swimming right off her shoulder would work well.

She had felt bad about turning down Stevie's invitation to join him and Bobby and Tamara for lunch between races and slightly less bad about turning down her family's invitation. But all she'd wanted to do was eat and get off her feet. She also explained to Stevie that Ed had outlined a strict schedule for her to follow the next day. A brief warm-up swim and then rest, rest, rest. She was a little surprised when he said, "I know." Ed hadn't said anything about talking to Stevie, but maybe they had run into each other at the pool.

By now she and Elizabeth had become all but inseparable. There was an unspoken agreement between them to discuss everything *but* the impending race. Susan Carol felt as if Elizabeth was the best friend she'd never had. It was almost as if both being swimmers and butterflyers, they spoke their own language.

"Worst set you ever had to swim?" Susan Carol would say.

"Easy. 100-200-300-400. All fly. Then do it again in reverse order."

"Brutal."

"Sickest you've ever been?" Elizabeth would then ask.

"First time I swam the 200 fly and it was *yards*. I went out way too fast. Got to the 150 wall and I was cooked. At the 175 I almost got out of the pool. On my last length I looked so bad that Ed said to the stroke-and-turn judge, 'She's still legal!' The guy said, 'Don't worry, I'm not going to DQ her. She's already suffered enough!'"

Each story or memory would lead to another.

Now, though, as they sat in the back of the car taking them to the Aquatics Centre—Ed had insisted on meeting them at their apartment to escort them to the pool—Susan Carol could feel the tension building. The 200 fly was the toughest race in swimming. That alone would make any swimmer nervous. But there was more to it than that. Susan Carol knew a lot was at stake—the look on her dad's face the previous night had told her all she needed to know. He was desperate for her to win. For her sake or for his, she wasn't sure.

One more warm-up. One more trip to the ready room. One more march to the blocks. And then, a little more than two minutes after she heard the starter's horn, it would finally be over. One way or the other. That moment couldn't come soon enough.

Stevie and Kelleher and Mearns had eventually agreed on a plan Monday night: Susan Carol and Elizabeth would be told nothing on the grounds that it wasn't fair to have them jumping at shadows before the race. Instead, they would talk to Ed Brennan and to Chuck Wielgus from USA Swimming. Ed, who knew a lot already, would hear the whole story. Wielgus would just be told—by Kelleher since they knew one another well—that the two American butterflyers needed extra security, but the kind that wouldn't be noticed. Chuck readily agreed.

Ed Brennan's first instinct was to find Bobby Mo and punch him. He had been quickly talked off that ledge. "I already have a schedule for Susan Carol for the next two days that's pretty tight," he said. "I'll talk to the other coaches to make sure Elizabeth has someone with her all the time too."

Even still, Stevie felt a huge sense of relief when they walked into the pool for the finals and saw Ed on the deck talking to both girls, who were about to get in the water to warm up. They were both safely at the pool, the race was only a couple of hours away, and no one had made any attempt to get to either one of them.

At least as far as they knew.

There were six events before the 200-fly final: four semifinals and two finals. None of the events were longer than a 200, so they didn't take all that long. Even so, Stevie was squirming by the time the women's 200-breaststroke semifinals—the race before the 200 fly—was called to the blocks.

Phil Knight was in the building again, easy to pick out in a white Nike shirt sitting in the Nike section of the corporate boxes. Bobby Maurice was also there—according to Chip Graber, who had texted Stevie to let him know he had an NBC pass and was sitting in the NBC VIP section.

"Saw him when I walked in," Chip said. "Acted like he didn't see me and walked the other way. I don't like it."

J. P. Scott had lost his access to the deck—another favor from Chuck Wielgus, who seemed surprised he'd gotten access in the first place. As consolation, unfortunately, J.P. had a media pass, so he was sitting a few rows up from Stevie, Bobby, and Tamara. When the first of the breaststroke semis was in the water, Scott appeared at their seats with a smirk on his face.

"I just thought the three of you should know since you consider yourself Susan Carol's personal reporters that we have a press conference at The Savoy at nine o'clock tomorrow morning to announce a major deal for her," he said. "You might want to be there."

"What if she doesn't win tonight?" Kelleher asked.

"She'll win," Scott said. "But either way, the deal is done."

"Does *she* know about this deal?" Stevie said.

"It's a surprise. We didn't want to tell her anything about it until after her race."

"Let me guess," Stevie said. "Her dad signed off on it."

"Of course," Scott said. "She's going to be making a lot of money."

"If she wins," Bobby said.

Scott shrugged. "She'll make *more* if she wins. But second, in this case, will be extremely lucrative."

"As long as it's second to Krylova, right?" Stevie said, causing Bobby to give him a sharp look.

"Now why would you think that," Scott said, but the smirk on his face had disappeared.

On that cheery note, he was gone.

Kelleher shook his head. "Stevie, how many times have I told you *not* to let the bad guys know what you know?" he said.

"I'm sorry," Stevie said—which he was. He should have kept his big mouth shut. "But what do you make of that?"

"It sounds like Maurice has the deal he wanted in place. . . ."

"But what about Elizabeth?" Stevie said. "If she beats them both, what happens then?"

"I guess we'll find out soon," Kelleher said. "Let's be ready to get moving as soon as this race is over. I think we'll learn a lot based on the reactions of all the different players—and I don't mean the three swimmers."

The second breaststroke semifinal had just concluded. Stevie took a deep breath, the kind he imagined Susan Carol was now taking in the ready room. She had described to him what it was like in there and how her nerves started clanging when the swimmers were asked to line up to walk on the deck.

A few seconds after the breaststrokers had cleared the pool, he heard the Olympic theme music that announced the entrance of the swimmers prior to a final. He looked up and saw them coming in—some still wearing their headphones—all in different-colored sweat suits.

Susan Carol, swimming in lane three, walked directly in front of Krylova with Elizabeth trailing her. Liu, who would be swimming in lane eight, was the last swimmer to enter. Once all the swimmers were behind their blocks, the PA announcer began their introductions. "In lane three from the United States . . . Susan Carol Anderson!"

That was it. A quick wave and then, as was her habit, the flip-flops came off and the bathing cap and goggles went on. Stevie had now been to enough meets to notice that almost all the swimmers were creatures of habit. Some didn't start removing their sweats until they were introduced. Others had their cap and goggles in place almost as soon as they got to the blocks. He saw Susan Carol and Elizabeth quickly nod at each other and smile. Krylova was standing a step in front of them, closer to the blocks, so at that moment the two Americans could see one another.

The double whistle blew and the swimmers stepped to the blocks.

"I'm having trouble breathing," Stevie said.

"It's hot in here," Tamara said.

"Nice try," Stevie said. "I'm not sure I can take this much longer."

"You won't have to," Bobby said. "Just think how Susan Carol must be feeling right now."

"Better than me, I hope," Stevie answered.

The single whistle blew. The swimmers stepped onto their blocks.

Susan Carol felt fine as she positioned her feet for the start. She had absolute confidence in her ability to swim the 200 fly and swim it well. It had taken her a long time to get to the point where she didn't dread the event, but she knew she was in the best shape of her life, and her memories of Shanghai and the trials convinced her she was going to swim a good race.

The fact that Krylova was almost certain to jump out front was also good: Having someone be a pacesetter helped her. All she wanted to do was stay about a body length behind until the 150 and then start to make her move. If Krylova went really crazy the first 100, she would let her go. You couldn't win the 200 fly by trying to outsprint the field.

She knew how much her father and J.P. and his people wanted her to win because of the money involved. She didn't really care. She had decided she would worry about all of that when this race was over. The night before, she had looked at her silver medal and thought: *If someone had told you eighteen months ago you'd be holding one of these, you would have laughed. You're an Olympian and a medalist. There's no way to lose.*

That didn't mean she didn't want to win. This was *her* race, the one that Ed had told her long ago was going to be her ticket to college—long before she had blossomed into a star. She figured Elizabeth was the person to beat, and she had done that in the trials. No reason she couldn't do it again.

The horn went. Susan Carol eased herself into the water. All she wanted was a smooth start because you weren't going to come up sprinting. As always, she counted her strokes to remind herself to stretch out. Her twenty-first stroke got her easily to the first turn. As she pushed off the wall, she saw Krylova already kicking out from her turn. Perfect.

Nothing changed over the next 100 meters. Every third breath—or sixth stroke—Susan Carol allowed her vision to wander just a little bit to the side to make sure Krylova wasn't pulling away. She could see the splash of her stroke just in front of her, which told her she was within a body length. She was almost certain that Elizabeth was in the exact same spot over in lane five.

The noise began to grow during the third length. This was the most important fifty of the race mentally. The first 100 was almost like a warm-up: stretching out, feeling comfortable, allowing your natural speed to carry you. Now, as your stroke inevitably shortened, it was important to focus on getting your arms all the way around and maintaining your kick—without picking it up *too* much. Do that too soon and you were bound to die on the final fifty.

One of the last things Ed had said before she went to the ready room was in her head as she hit the 150: *Hold that last turn as long as you can—it may save you a stroke at the finish.*

She reached for the wall, pulled her head up, and felt as if she looked Elizabeth right in the eye. They had reached the wall together. Krylova was still out front. Susan Carol pushed off as hard as she possibly could, consciously pushing herself down into the water so she would stay under a tad longer. She remembered a turn Phelps had made in 2008 in the 400 IM when he had somehow stayed underwater for an extra second and had come up a half body length ahead of Lochte after trailing him into the turn.

She came up and took one stroke before breathing—not two because she knew she needed the air—and began driving for home. *Rest later, work now*, she reminded herself as she picked up her kick. She was feeling it in her arms, but she knew she had the strength to finish *if* she remembered to finish each stroke. One short-armed stroke here could be the difference.

She didn't even bother to check Krylova until they were halfway back. When she did, she didn't see her splash—which meant she had caught her already. *It's you and Elizabeth*, she thought, then in a brief moment of panic she wondered where Liu—way outside in lane eight—might be.

She pushed that thought away and focused on the flags. In a sense, her race would be over once she got there because her head was going to go down and she was going to drive to the wall from there. Four strokes to the flags. Two. She knew that Krylova had faded; her swimmer's senses told her that.

As she reached the flags, she put her head down and stretched her arms out for each stroke as far as she possibly could. They felt as if they were going to explode. *KICK*, she reminded herself one last time, and with one last kick and swing of the arms she reached out and her hands hit the wall. She pulled her head up, gasping for air just in time to see Krylova touch.

There was yelling all around her—above her on the deck—and from the American team section. She looked at the board and the first thing she saw was a 2 next to her name. Elizabeth had beaten her again. Sure enough, she saw a 1, next to Elizabeth's name with a time of 1:59.97. Elizabeth had just become the first woman to break two minutes in the 200 fly. Susan Carol had gone 2:00.59, and Krylova had barely hung on for third at 2:01.14. Liu had finished fourth—nine-hundredths behind Krylova.

But something was wrong. Elizabeth's time was blinking on the scoreboard. Susan Carol could see an official leaning down to talk to her. Baffled, Susan Carol turned to Krylova, but she still had her head down trying to get her breath back. Susan Carol heard Ed's voice and looked up.

She still hadn't recovered enough to talk, so all that came out of her mouth was "Whaa?"

Ed leaned down so she could hear him above the din.

"They DQ'd Elizabeth," he said. "I think it was the third turn. You won. Krylova's second."

There wasn't any joy in his voice. Ed wouldn't want anyone DQ'd in an Olympic final. And neither did she.

Without a word, Susan Carol went under the two lane lines to get to Elizabeth, who was shaking with tears when Susan Carol got to her.

"They're saying . . . my hand slipped . . . on the third wall. . . ." She had to pause because she was still breathless from the swim and the shock. "I didn't. . . . I know I didn't. . . ."

Susan Carol wrapped her arms around her, and Elizabeth cried on her shoulder. Suddenly, Susan Carol flashed back to Sunday night and Trevor James's warning that there'd be higher scrutiny on turns in the Olympics.

She heard Elizabeth saying she'd never been DQ'd in her life.

Now she had been. After the greatest 200-butterfly swim in history. At that moment, Susan Carol was an Olympic gold medalist.

And all she could think was: *This is not right.*

27: PLAY THAT SONG AGAIN

It was Stevie who first noticed the official with his hand in the air.

Like everyone else, Stevie was on his feet as the swimmers approached the third turn. Krylova had been leading the entire race, but you could sense she was beginning to tire. Susan Carol and Elizabeth seemed to hit the wall at the exact same moment, and Stevie watched their push-offs carefully because he remembered Susan Carol talking about how important the last turn could be in a race where exhaustion at the finish was always critical.

Elizabeth had come up first, and Stevie was watching her and waiting for Susan Carol to surface when he saw the official standing behind lane five with his right arm up in the air, which meant he had called some kind of foul on the swimmer in that lane.

As soon as he saw the arm go up, Stevie grabbed

Kelleher's shoulder—because it was too loud to talk—and pointed.

"Oh my God" was Kelleher's only reaction.

They watched the rest in stunned shock. Halfway back, it was clear Krylova was out of gas. Not only were Elizabeth and Susan Carol going past her, the other swimmers were closing in too. At the flags it looked as if Elizabeth and Susan Carol were dead even, but in the final strokes Elizabeth seemed to have an extra gear. She covered the last five meters with two huge, powerful strokes. Susan Carol took three. That was the difference.

They looked at the board and instantly noticed two things: Elizabeth had broken two minutes and her time was not official. They could see an official bending over to talk to her and watched her burst into tears.

"They've DQ'd her for sure," Bobby said. "Come on, we've got to get moving."

Everyone else in the media section seemed to be frozen by what was happening below. Bobby, Tamara, and Stevie scrambled to the ramps leading downstairs, which were still empty. There was one more race to go before the evening was over, and there were medal ceremonies still ahead too.

Once they had cleared security and were in the hallway that led to the interview room and the mixed zone, Kelleher called a halt.

"We need a strategy," he said. "I'm going to go find Chuck Wielgus and see if USA Swimming is planning any sort of protest."

"Can you protest a DQ?" Stevie asked.

"You can protest, but it's hard to overturn. A lot will depend on what country the judge who DQ'd her is from. There has to be confirmation from a second official for it to stand. If either one is a Russian so there's even a suggestion he was trying to help Krylova, you've got a better shot."

"What if it's not a Russian?" Tamara asked.

"Then it's tougher," Kelleher said. "First thing we have to do is find out who the judge was and where he was from. They all look the same in those hats they wear."

"I'll find that out," Tamara said.

"Good," Bobby said. "I'll look for Wielgus. Stevie, that leaves you with the easy job. You gotta figure a way to get to Susan Carol and Elizabeth."

Stevie gasped. "So is this what Bobby Mo meant by Elizabeth being 'taken care of'?"

Kelleher nodded. "You're right. Forget the girls for now. Find Bobby Mo."

"And do what?"

"I have no idea," Kelleher said. "You'll think of something."

There were a lot of people running in different directions when Stevie set off down the hallway. His first thought was to head back in the direction of the corporate hospitality rooms, but then he thought Bobby Mo might be on the prowl down here somewhere—he'd want to see it unfolding.

As Stevie walked through the mixed zone—which was virtually empty except for a couple of breaststrokers talking to two or three journalists—he could hear a PA announcement coming from the pool level: "The results of the women's 200 butterfly remain unofficial due to a protest being lodged. The women's 4 × 200 relay final will begin in five minutes' time."

He reached the locker room area, which was, of course, off-limits to everyone except swimmers and coaches. He considered texting Ed Brennan but realized he wasn't trying to get to Susan Carol and Elizabeth. He was about to keep walking when he spotted Mike Unger from USA Swimming talking to someone dressed in an official's uniform. The official looked familiar. Then he realized who it was: Trevor James, the officious USA Swimming guy who had been such a pain back in Charlotte. He wandered over. Maybe Unger and James could give him some idea of what had happened.

"Chuck's filing a protest, Trevor. That's all there is to it," Unger said as Stevie came up behind the two of them. They were almost nose to nose and apparently oblivious that anyone was near them.

"He's wasting his time," James said. "To begin with, the girl clearly dropped her hand on the turn. I had confirmation. Even if it's close, there's no way the committee is going to overturn a call made on an American swimmer by an American official. He's wasting his time."

"He doesn't think so. We've looked at the replay. The turn was legal. I don't know what the hell you were thinking when you called it."

Stevie almost gasped out loud. *Trevor James* had DQ'd Elizabeth?

Whatever sound he had made got Unger's attention. He turned and saw Stevie standing there. An awkward smile crossed his face. "Um, Steve, hi. Sorry. This isn't a good time. Can you give me a minute? We're going to fill everyone in very soon."

Stevie decided this wasn't the moment to play games. "I'm really sorry, Mike, but I was walking up and heard just a little. Mr. James, *you* were the official who DQ'd Elizabeth Wentworth?"

"I don't speak to the media," James said. "I don't even know how you got here. I have work to do."

He turned and walked away. Stevie was tempted to follow.

"Mike, what happens now?" he asked.

Unger was still eyeing James as he hustled down the hallway.

"Chuck and the USOC will submit a formal protest of the DQ," he said. "There's a three-person committee that reviews the tape. There are two problems: the first is that since a call was made, the burden of proof is on the swimmer, basically. Plus, like Trevor said, an American calling an illegal turn on an American, it's unlikely they'll overturn it. They have to see evidence she did *not* make an illegal turn."

"But you said the tape—"

"On tape the turn looks fine. But remember their hands

are on the wall for little more than a split second. Trevor's angle is much closer than the cameras' are unless we somehow have a close-up that clearly shows both hands."

"What did he mean about confirmation?"

Unger sighed. "If a lane judge sees an illegal turn, he's supposed to confirm it with the walking stroke-and-turn judge. But it's rubber stamp stuff. No one is going to overturn something like that on the spot."

"What's the second problem?"

"One of the three people on the committee is always the official who made the call. He's not going to reverse himself no matter what the tape shows. That means the other two officials have to reverse the call, and one of them is Russian and one of them is Chinese."

"Oh God. Not only does Krylova benefit if Elizabeth's DQ'd, but Liu gets a bronze medal."

"Exactly."

"How exactly did James end up on Elizabeth's lane?" Stevie asked.

Unger shrugged. "You got me there. It's supposed to be a blind draw. Instead, poor Elizabeth got blindsided."

Stevie's phone was buzzing. He pulled it out and saw a text from Susan Carol. *Meet in mixed zone*, it said. *HURRY!*

Stevie thanked Unger. He turned and began sprinting back in the direction of the mixed zone.

Susan Carol was standing in a far corner of the mixed zone when Stevie rounded the corner. Ed Brennan was up at the fence talking to the media and, apparently, holding them off at the same time. When Stevie came into sight, Susan Carol waved him over and spoke to a security guard. The guard nodded and pointed at Stevie. "You there, come on ahead. Others, sorry, chaps, you need to wait a moment."

"This isn't right," Susan Carol said as soon as Stevie walked up, dispensing with any niceties. "We looked at the tape in the locker room. Her turn was legal."

"Yeah, and guess who called it," Stevie said. "Our old friend Trevor James."

Susan Carol put her hand to her mouth. "No one told us that. That little *rodent* . . . But if it was an American official, there's no way they're going to uphold the protest."

"That's what Mike Unger just told me."

She was silent for a moment, trying to think. "Ed told me that J.P. told him right after the race that I'm signing with Brickley tomorrow. There's a joint press conference— Krylova and me together. I told him I didn't want anything to do with it. He said J.P. told him my dad was going to sign the contract."

"J.P. pretty much told us he already had. Do you know where your dad is right now?"

"No idea. He can't get down here."

Stevie was trying to think of what to do next when they heard another PA announcement. "Ladies and gentlemen, the results of the women's 200 butterfly are now official. Ms. Wentworth, United States, swimming in lane five, has been disqualified for an illegal turn."

"NO, NO, NO!" Susan Carol shrieked, causing all the reporters to turn in her direction. Several TV cameras were pointed right at her.

"Stevie, get in front of me," she said.

He complied, which caused some angry arm-waving but little more. There wasn't much they could do with Ed and, he noticed, several security people holding them off.

"What now?" he said.

"I'm not accepting the medal," she said. "I just won't do it."

"Look," he said. "Clearly Bobby Mo got to James. He had to. Why else would he have told Chip he wasn't worried about Elizabeth?"

"What? He told Chip what?"

"No time to explain." He snapped his fingers. "I have an idea. Do me a favor—text Chip and ask him to send me Bobby Mo's cell phone number."

"What? Why?"

He looked at her. "You usually have the ideas," he said. "You've been swimming, so your mind has been on other things. Trust me to have the idea this time."

"Is it crazy?" she said.

"Completely crazy."

She smiled. "Okay, then, I like it."

Stevie had to push his way out of there. The TV guys and reporters wanted to know who the hell he was and what Susan Carol had said to him.

"I'm her boyfriend," he said. "It's private. Sorry."

He had to find Kelleher and Chuck Wielgus and con-vince Wielgus to let him talk to Trevor James. He figured by now there would be officials being taken to the interview room to explain what had happened. The swimmers wouldn't come in until after the medal ceremony, which was still at least twenty minutes away.

Sure enough, Kelleher was with Wielgus outside the in-terview room. That was the good news. The bad news was that half the world's media had Wielgus backed up against a wall. Mike Unger was lingering outside the circle, trying to explain to people that Wielgus would be in the interview room in a few minutes to answer all questions, but no one was listening to him.

Stevie grabbed Unger by the arm to get his attention amidst the chaos.

"I need a big favor," he said.

"Now?" Unger said.

"I gotta talk to Trevor James." Unger starting shaking his head, but Stevie pressed on. "Just for one minute. He's a big part of this story."

"We know that," Unger said. "But he's not going to speak to the media. The Russian guy who chaired the pro-test committee is going to talk."

"I understand," Stevie said. "But this isn't about some statement for the press; I'm trying to get the real story so maybe we can fix this. Please trust me. I know you don't like the guy any more than I do. And I think I can nail him. *Please* tell him to meet you right outside the cordoned-off drug-testing area. Tell him Chuck Wielgus wants to put out a statement supporting him, but you need his input and you need one minute with him someplace that's quiet."

"But that's a lie," Unger said.

"I know," Stevie answered.

Unger looked at him for a second. "I shouldn't do this. I know I shouldn't do this." He took out his phone and began dialing.

Stevie pushed through a couple of people around Wielgus to get to Kelleher.

"I need you to come with me," he said.

"Now?" Kelleher said.

"Right now. Tamara can handle this. I need you."

Kelleher didn't ask why, he just followed Stevie out of the scrum.

"Where are we going?" he asked.

"Just follow me," he said.

They headed in the direction of the drug-testing area. About twenty yards short of the door that said DRUG-TESTING AREA. AUTHORIZED PERSONNEL ONLY there was a gate and two security guards. Stevie stopped just short of the guards and began looking around.

"Stevie, whatever you're up to, we haven't got time—"

"Here he comes," Stevie said as Trevor James, coming from the other direction, still in his FINA officials' uniform, came into view. "Follow my lead."

"I *know* that's a bad idea," Kelleher said. "But what the hell."

James had his cell phone pressed to his ear as he approached them. When he saw Stevie, he stopped short.

"Looking for someone, Mr. James?" Stevie said.

"What? None of your business. What are you doing here? This area is off-limits to media."

"No, it's not," Kelleher said. "Inside that gate is off-limits. We're fine here."

"Whatever," James said. He walked past them and peered down the hallway.

"He's not coming," Stevie said.

"Who?"

"Mike Unger," Stevie said. "Bobby Maurice will be here soon, though, if you're patient."

Stevie could tell he'd hit a nerve by the look on James's face. He recovered quickly, though. "Bobby who? What are you talking about?"

Stevie felt his cell phone ping in his pocket, and he hoped it was a text from Chip Graber.

"I'm talking about the guy who bribed you for, I'm guessing, a *lot* of money to DQ Elizabeth Wentworth tonight. You know just who he is."

"You are completely out of your mind. And if you write anything like that, I will sue you for—"

"No, you won't," Stevie said. "Because I'm willing to bet that when your cell phone records are subpoenaed, there will be dozens of calls and texts between you and Mr. Maurice."

Stevie took his phone out and glanced at the text on his screen. There it was: Bobby Mo, 310-555-4289.

He walked over to stand directly in front of James. He held out his phone so James could see the number. "See that?" he said. "I've got the number in my phone and so do you."

"I would *love* to see you prove that," James said.

Stevie shrugged and started to turn away as if the conversation was over. "I guess we'll see you in court," he said.

James opened his mouth to reply, but Stevie wasn't listening. He turned back and pounced at James, catching him off balance and wrestling him to the floor. James had been holding his phone in his hand and now it went skittering across the floor.

"Bobby, quick, the phone!" he screamed.

Stevie's one concern when he had come up with this idea a few minutes earlier had been the two security guards standing outside the drug-testing area. If they were bothered by what was going on, they didn't show it. Apparently wrestling matches outside the testing area were not their problem.

"Flip me your phone, Stevie," Bobby said as Stevie held on to James, who was smaller, older, and a good deal weaker than he was.

Bobby hit a couple of buttons on James's phone, glanced at the number on Stevie's phone, and smiled. "Four phone calls from that number and three to that number in the last hour," he said. "Stevie, you got him."

"You're both going to jail!" James screamed.

"Don't think so, Trevor," Bobby said. "Come on. Let's go see Chuck Wielgus. He's going to need to get this phone into the correct hands right away."

* * *

The medal ceremony for the women's 200 butterfly was delayed. In fact, it was held after the ceremony for the 4 × 200 freestyle relay because there was a good deal of explaining to do.

Once Stevie and Bobby had delivered James—still screaming he had been assaulted, which, in fairness, he had been—and his phone to Chuck Wielgus, Wielgus instantly let FINA and the IOC know he had new evidence they needed to consider in the matter of the women's 200-butterfly final.

As it turned out, Bobby Maurice got nervous when the protest had been filed and called James. And left messages. Urgent messages. And then more urgent messages asking him to delete the first urgent messages. Unfortunately for James—and Bobby Mo—he hadn't had time to do that.

Bobby Maurice was arrested by members of Scotland Yard on charges of bribery and race-fixing while he was having a drink and eating some shrimp with Bill Arnold in the NBC corporate area. Maurice instantly fingered Arnold—somehow thinking *he* had brought about his downfall. Apparently Arnold had once been one of Trevor James's business partners and had introduced Maurice to him.

Stevie's only disappointment was that Arnold insisted J. P. Scott wasn't involved. All Scott knew was what he had told them before the race: that if Krylova and Susan Carol finished one-two—regardless of order—Brickley was going to give each of them a five-year contract worth ten million dollars with the winner getting a two-million bonus. They would have rolled out the new line of Brickley Gold swimwear together in a hands-across-the-sea marketing campaign.

Krylova knew nothing, just as Susan Carol had known nothing. Krylova's father had been negotiating, it turned out, for her as well.

When Wielgus presented the cell phone evidence to FINA and the IOC, a brand-new three-member protest committee consisting of FINA officials from Brazil, France, and Australia was instantly formed. They looked at the tape for less than five minutes and ruled Elizabeth Wentworth's turn legal. She was restored to first place, Susan Carol to second, Krylova to third.

Because of the unique circumstances, the two American swimmers had been taken into one of the ready rooms along with several people they had asked to see before the medal ceremony finally began.

Stevie, Bobby, and Tamara were there along with Ed Brennan and Peter Ward, the US assistant coach who had been working with Elizabeth. Mike Unger was there so that Stevie and Bobby could tell him what they'd done to get the phone.

"He's telling Scotland Yard you assaulted him," Unger said. "Unfortunately, witnesses say he just slipped."

"Witnesses?"

"Well, one witness," Unger said. "Me. I was just turning the corner when I saw him slip and drop his phone. Nice of you to pick it up for him."

"The security guards?" Stevie asked.

"I don't think they saw anything," Unger said. "Shame."

Susan Carol and Elizabeth had both greeted Stevie with lengthy hugs. Elizabeth had squeezed him so tight he thought he might explode.

Don Anderson was clearly stunned and horrified by everything that had happened. "Honey, I am so sorry. You've been trying to tell me not to trust these guys. But I never imagined . . . I mean, I wanted . . . But not . . ."

"I know," said Susan Carol—and somehow, she did.

"I don't care what contracts we have to break, but we are through with these people. From now on you just swim, and we'll figure it out together."

"Daddy, I'm retiring from swimming," Susan Carol said quietly. "At least for a while." He started to say something, but she put up her hand. "Nothing I do will ever match the two races I swam here this week. I'll swim the relay, but then I need a break. I think we both do."

Stevie looked at Reverend Anderson, waiting for a protest. None was forthcoming.

"I'll support whatever you want to do, 100 percent," he said, nodding. He turned to Stevie. "And, you, I owe you a big apology and a thank-you. Bobby and Tamara too. You and Ed were Susan Carol's true friends through all of this."

Susan Carol put her arm around Stevie. "He's my *best* friend," she said, kissing him on the cheek. "In so many ways."

She gave him The Smile. "Ready to be partners again?" she said.

"Oh yes, Scarlett," he said. "Definitely, yes."

* * *

Ten minutes later, with their friends and family allowed to watch from the deck, the three 200-butterfly medalists marched back into the pool area for the medal ceremony. Amazingly, the place was still almost packed, and Susan Carol couldn't help but notice that the entire American team had stayed. Michael Phelps and Ryan Lochte were holding an American flag over their heads.

Svetlana Krylova had graciously hugged Susan Carol and Elizabeth just before they walked onto the deck and said, "I hope we race many more times."

The cheers were long and loud as each of them was given her medal. Then Susan Carol again heard: "Ladies and gentlemen. Please rise for the playing of the United States' national anthem."

As the first notes began to play and the three flags started up to the rafters, Susan Carol felt a hand on her shoulder.

It was Elizabeth.

"Hey," she whispered. "They're playing our song. Get up here."

She grabbed Susan Carol's hand and pulled her up onto the gold medal stand.

So they stood there together, arms around one another, tears streaming down their faces, singing at the top of their lungs.